Signed, Sealed, Delivered

T0345455

Also by Sandy James

Ladies Who Lunch series

The Bottom Line (book 1)

Signed, Sealed, Delivered

SANDY JAMES

FOREVER
YOURS

New York Boston

Copyright © 2014 by Sandy James
Excerpt from *Sealing the Deal* copyright © 2014 by Sandy James
Cover design by Elizabeth Turner
Cover photo © Yuri/iStockphoto
Cover copyright © 2014 by Hachette Book Group, Inc.

Forever Yours
Hachette Book Group
237 Park Avenue
New York, NY 10017
www.hachettebookgroup.com
www.twitter.com/foreverromance

First published as an ebook and as a print on demand edition: July 2014

Forever Yours is an imprint of Grand Central Publishing.
The Forever Yours name and logo are trademarks of Hachette Book Group, Inc.

The publisher is not responsible for websites (or their content) that are not owned by the publisher.

The Hachette Speakers Bureau provides a wide range of authors for speaking events. To find out more, go to www.hachettespeakersbureau.com or call (866) 376-6591.

ISBN: 978-1-4555-7400-1 (ebook edition)
ISBN: 978-1-4555-8535-9 (print on demand edition)

Serendipity put my agents in my path one summer evening, and we shared a cab. That ride changed my life. Their guidance has helped me in more ways than they will ever know.

This one's for Joanna MacKenzie, Danielle Egan-Miller, and Abby Saul, with much love.

Acknowledgments

As always, I have to thank my husband, Jeff, for allowing me to ignore him for hours on end to write and edit.

Without Cheryl Brooks, Nan Reinhardt, Sandy Owens, and Leanna Kay as critique partners, I would never have made a name for myself as an author. Thank you, ladies!

My editor, Latoya Smith, has always pushed me to become a better writer—even back before she took me on as an author. I'll always be grateful for that!

Signed, Sealed, Delivered

Chapter One

One more thing. I dare you, universe. Just throw one more thing at me and...

Juliana Kelley growled as she paced down the brown terrazzo hallway of her school, tossing faux smiles at any students she passed, subtly checking their hands for hall passes. Her destination? The mailroom, situated about as far from her special education classroom as physically possible. As angry as she was, steam had to be pouring from her ears. The click of her heels echoed like a metronome, marking the time she'd spent marching these stark corridors.

I mean it this time. One more thing gets fucked up today, and I'm walking out the door.

If only it weren't an idle threat she'd tossed around far too often. She could no sooner leave her teaching job than stroll on the moon. But after fourteen years of teaching, she no longer found joy in spending time with her students.

She was exhausted. Plain and simple. She'd been hired at Stephen Douglas High School right out of college, a wide-eyed twenty-one-year-old with a sparkling-new bachelor's degree and ideas of changing the world of special education. She'd been at the school ever since.

Even though she was only thirty-five, she was the senior-most teacher in her department. No matter how much she loved teaching, fourteen years of working with special needs children was a lifetime, and the burnout of her chosen discipline weighed on her more and more each day.

Unfortunately, she had nowhere else to go and no skills beyond her teaching abilities. Who wanted to hire a smart-ass redhead and the volatility she brought in tow? It wasn't as though switching to a new school would help. Besides, with her years of experience, no other school would touch her. Why hire an exhausted teacher when a fresh-faced kid right out of college could be had for half the price?

One idea plagued her thoughts, put there long ago by her uncle Francis. He'd made a nice life for himself selling real estate. Whenever he cornered her at any family function, he tried to persuade her to move to Virginia, join his firm, and peddle houses. She always listened then politely told him, yet again, that she loved teaching.

Today, she'd give him an entirely different answer.

From time to time—usually after a particularly rough group of students—she'd looked into real estate sales as a new career. An online class here. A seminar there. Her overwhelming obsession with HGTV. She'd fantasized more times than she could count of seeing her name proudly pronouncing a house for sale, or better yet, sold. But could she really leave the teaching profession, especially for something as risky as real estate, where the salary was never guaranteed?

"Hey, baby," a familiar masculine voice called. "How you doin'?"

Juliana heaved a sigh, thinking there should be some law about ex-spouses not being allowed to work together. Ever. "I'm fine, Jimmy." She winced the moment the old nickname slipped out, knowing how he'd react.

"Jim!" He fisted his hands at his sides instead of hitting the wall. At least he was finally learning to control his temper. If he weren't one of the best wrestling coaches in the state, the administrators probably would've fired him years ago. "It's Jim now. Only boys are called Jimmy."

Then grow up and I'll stop calling you that. "Sorry. Old habits. Blah, blah, blah." She dismissed her slip with a wave of her hand. Plucking the pieces of mail from her tiny box, she tried to get the hell out of there before her ex could start a real conversation. She'd had little enough to say to him when they'd been married a good ten years ago. Now he grated on her already-frayed nerves like a loud dentist's drill.

"Hey, wait." Jim hurried over and grabbed her elbow. "I wanted to ask you somethin'."

She glared down at his restraining hand, refusing to respond until he took the less-than-subtle hint and let go.

As always, he was slow on the uptake and pressed on. "Heard you were going to the mixers at Bayside Church."

"And that's your business because…?"

He ran his hand over his balding head, a trait that had only developed in the last year but was rapidly overtaking him. "I just… you know… figured if you needed some male companionship—"

She snorted a laugh. "Oh, Jim. I'm not even letting you finish that sentence because you know damn well I'll slap your face if you say what I think you're gonna say."

It wasn't the first time he offered to service her like some male escort, but in the mood she was in he was going to be the lightning rod she unloaded all her anger on. She needed to get away from him before he became her "one more thing."

Robert Ashford stopped at the door, his gaze shifting between the couple.

The cavalry!

"Looks like I'm interrupting something," he said with a note of laughter in his voice.

"Not at all," Juliana replied. She tossed him a grateful glance.

Jim left the workroom, huffing and puffing as he mumbled under his breath.

"Thank God," she muttered, flipping through the mail and tossing almost all of it into the trash. Most were flyers trying to sell teachers overpriced products they didn't need.

A waste of trees.

"He still hovers, doesn't he?" Robert fished his own mail out of his cubby.

"My fault for working where he works. After the divorce, I should have left, but..." She shrugged. "I liked it here."

"Liked?"

Robert was astute. Always had been. He knew people, something that had helped him earn a huge following for the custom homes he built as a second job. Why he still worked as a shop teacher was beyond her. He had to earn a hell of a lot more money moonlighting.

"Yeah, *liked*. Feeling the burnout bad lately," she said.

"Kinda early in the year, isn't it? I mean, we've got a while before summer break."

"I'm not sure I'll survive that long."

He leaned back against the worktable. "I've been meaning to ask you something."

"Um, ask me something?" The day had held nothing good in store for her, and Robert's tone made her wary.

Then his smile helped her quickly relax. "Easy there, Jules. You're thinking too hard."

"Probably because Jim just tried to proposition me."

Robert chuckled but shook his head. "I'm not thinking of asking for a date or anything. I mean...you're a mighty pretty lady, but I go for blondes who don't have quite as much fire as you do."

"Well, then. Ask away."

He stepped over to the door and glanced up and down the hall as though he wanted to make sure they had privacy. That action put her right back on edge. What was so shocking he couldn't ask in front of other teachers or any boss who'd actually taken a moment to come out of his office?

"I'm going to a real estate seminar Friday. Thought you might want to come along. You're thinking about getting outta here, right?" Robert asked.

"How'd you know that?"

"C'mon, Jules. You've got 'runaway' written all over you. I've been here every bit as long as you have. I'm sick and tired of it, too."

She leaned back against the table next to him, sagging to the side so her shoulder pressed against his. She allowed herself the comfort of his touch, the assurance of a friend. What she really wanted was someone tall, handsome, and warm so she could lay her head against his shoulder and let him take a little of the weight of the world away. Not that she wanted another husband. But she missed masculine attention, hence the singles' mixers that had yielded nothing. Not even an interesting date.

Her fault for living in Cloverleaf, Illinois—translated "Nowhere, USA."

"At least you have something to fall back on if you leave," Juliana couldn't help but point out. "What do I have?"

"You're selling yourself short. You've got one really big asset. You're a born salesman."

Exactly what her uncle Francis always said. "Did I hear you right?"

"If you heard me say you're a born salesman, you did," Robert replied. "I've seen the way you get all those kids and their parents excited about the European trips. They aren't even your students."

"Yeah," she admitted, knowing how difficult it would be to take special needs kids to Europe. The biennial overseas adventures gave her a chance to get to know more of the school's student body. "Most of the kids on the trips are from the honors department."

"Those tours cost a pretty penny, but you always take at least a dozen kids with you."

"I never thought about it that way."

Sure, the trips were expensive, but the benefits to the kids—the historical sites, the visits to museums, experiencing other cultures—were well worth the cost.

Robert was right. She had to sell people on the idea to get them to pony up the dough. "I sold women's clothing in college," she said.

"See?"

"My uncle is a Realtor. He's always trying to recruit me."

"Serendipity?"

"Maybe. So you really think I could sell houses?"

"Absolutely. I'm taking control of my own life. I'm building these great houses—"

"They're gorgeous, Robert. Absolutely gorgeous. If I were rich, you'd be building one for me."

"I do believe that's the nicest thing you ever said to me." His smile made her smile in return. "I've been thinking for a long time, why shouldn't I profit by *selling* those houses, too? As it is, some Realtors pocket seven percent of the profit that should be mine."

"Makes sense," she said.

Real estate.

Suddenly it felt as though the universe had sent her a sign: her restlessness and her feeling that her life at the school was coming to an end; Robert echoing Uncle Francis, both pushing her toward something she thought she might enjoy doing; the timing of the seminar to learn even more about selling homes as a career. All of it had to be more than mere coincidence. "When did you say the class was?"

"Friday. Six o'clock. I could swing by and pick you up."

"Who's teaching this 'class'?"

"Max Schumm."

"Oh, the guy from Schumm Homes. They pretty much sell every house in Cloverleaf."

"Then he should know what he's talking about. And look at it this way—if we sign up for the class online, they're buying dinner for up to fifteen people. Last I checked, only eight slots were filled. The class is at Byran's Steakhouse."

"Isn't that the restaurant at the Ramada?"

"That's the one. A steak dinner is worth the twenty-buck fee and an hour or so of your time, don't you think?"

Pushing away from the table, Juliana gave Robert a smile. "Pick me up at five forty-five."

* * *

"I'm thinking about trying something new," Juliana announced when she sat down at the lunch table.

Her three friends, the women she'd shared her lunch and life with for so many years, all turned curious eyes in her direction.

Mallory Carpenter was the first to speak. "Something new?"

She stirred her microwaved soup as she eyed the sack Juliana had dropped on the table. A year younger than Juliana, Mallory was a beautiful woman with brown hair that barely brushed her shoulders and brown eyes that held both intelligence and warmth. "No more yogurt and salad?" she asked.

Juliana fished out her lunch, setting the mentioned items in front of her. Strawberry cheesecake yogurt and a tossed salad. "Nope. Guess again."

Bethany Rogers took her turn, her big brown eyes bright and her typical smile lighting her round face, a face framed by a mop of brown curly hair that reached her jawline. "Um...not going to the mixer on Saturday this week?"

"Strike two." Juliana glanced to Danielle Bradshaw, arching an eyebrow. "Care to take a turn?"

Danielle blew a raspberry and then grinned. Blonde and blue-eyed, the woman was a no-nonsense realist whose disposition kept her feet firmly on the ground. "I suck at guessing games. Besides, we've only got twenty minutes left to eat. I'd rather you tell us, 'cause you seem pretty excited, which means it must be something good."

Now that she'd decided to explore this new path in her life, she was anxious to share it with her friends. Learning to sell real estate might seem like a pipe dream, but the more she thought about it, the more Juliana began to believe she might have found her bolt hole, her escape route from the hell that the school had become.

Yet she suddenly realized what she could lose.

The Ladies Who Lunch.

The four friends had given their ragtag group that name. Even other teachers called them that now, the way they used the name always seeming a bit envious of the closeness the women shared. It was no wonder they were close. They discussed everything from horrible love lives to Mallory's heartrending battle with breast cancer. They were survivors, every single one of them.

And that was what forced Juliana's honesty. If she was thinking of jumping ship, her friends deserved to know. "I'm thinking about getting the hell out of this place."

Mallory stared at her, blinking several times as her gaze searched Juliana's. "This isn't just blowing off steam because of a bad day." A statement not a question. Mallory knew her far too well.

"No, it's not. I'm just so ... *tired.*"

"You're a special ed teacher," Danielle said. "It's no wonder. I mean, we all deal with kids, which takes a toll. But the kids you see? Shit, Jules, I think you're a candidate for sainthood."

"She's right," Bethany insisted. "I might get some bad things tossed my way, but I've never had to change a student's diaper or help one into a padded area while he flipped out."

Juliana shrugged. "It goes with the job. I could have chosen something else, but I wanted to work with special needs kids. I always figured they needed me."

Mallory was still staring holes through her. "So what's the plan?"

"Robert's taking me to a real estate seminar."

"Real estate? Interesting." Bethany took a sip of her soda. "You know, that might just work for you. You're a born salesperson."

"That's exactly what Robert said." *And Uncle Francis.*

The universe was definitely sending her a message.

"Well, think about it," Bethany continued. "You're gorgeous. That red hair, those green eyes. When you put on a business suit, you look like you could take on corporate America and win. You show someone a house, you'll have them buying before they see every room."

Bethany's eternal optimism was a blessing. While that trait

sometimes bordered on naïveté, this time it helped Juliana feel stronger about risking a change. "Thanks, Beth."

Beth saluted her with a mock toast of her Diet Coke.

"You haven't mentioned this to the principal yet, have you, Jules?" Mallory asked.

"I'm not that stupid," Juliana replied. "Besides, it's just a seminar. Who knows if I'll even decide I want to give it a whirl?"

"You can use summer break to get a good start," Danielle said.

Juliana nodded. "That's what I thought, too. I'll just head to the seminar with Robert, see what Max Schumm has to say, and—"

Mallory choked on her Diet Cherry Coke. "Did you say Max Schumm?" The anger in her voice came as a surprise.

"Yeah, why?"

"Ben hates that guy."

Ben. Mallory's husband. The two of them had a bit of whirlwind romance that started when he renovated her house, which turned into true love when they connected at the Bayside mixers.

If only Juliana could be so lucky to land a hunk like Ben Carpenter. "What happened that made Ben hate him?"

"Schumm screwed up the paperwork on the house he sold when he got divorced. Cost Ben a pretty penny to get things straightened out. The lawyer told him Schumm doesn't know his ass from a hole in the ground."

"Then why is he head of the biggest real estate firm in Cloverleaf?" Juliana asked.

"Because there's not much competition," Mallory replied. "The other firms are national chains, and you know how tight-knit this town is."

"Always use a local," Danielle said, stating the town's informal motto.

"Look," Juliana said. "I'll go to the seminar, find out what I need to do to get licensed, and see if I can stomach Max Schumm. Then I can make some hard choices."

But did she have the stomach to walk away from her career and risk starting over?

Chapter Two

Connor Wilson leaned back in his chair and waited for the presentation to start. Not that the seminar was going to change his mind about facing this new real estate market solo. He was there strictly for research, learning everything he could about the competition.

He'd made this move to such a small market for all the right reasons, and there was profit to be had here. He could smell it as easily as a pig sniffing for truffles.

Max Schumm. Cloverleaf's number one Realtor. He held court near the front of the conference room, close to the table his assistants had piled with swag—calendars, pens, refrigerator magnets. Not a surprise that his office staff, his minions, were all women while his Realtors were mostly men. He counted only two ladies in the bright blue Schumm blazers, and every advertisement he'd checked contained listings by males.

The town and the surrounding counties were ripe for the picking.

Time for the king to get knocked off his throne.

Glancing around the three big, round tables set with six places each, Connor sized up the people who thought they might have the chops to sell homes. A pitiful lot it was. He'd dismissed each and every one, noticing Max doing the same thing as he appraised the newbies. The only person Max kept staring at was Connor, probably because he knew a true salesman when he spotted one.

Perhaps he even recognized him from his past. Indianapolis wasn't a huge market, but it was somewhat close and Connor had been well known there. Two years away wasn't all that long to distance himself from making sales or getting new listings. Their paths might have crossed on a long-distance move, although he was sure he'd have remembered a man like Max. Damn if the guy didn't look like an eighties game show host, from his oversprayed hair to his fake tan to his far-too-white teeth.

What Max didn't know was that Connor had no intention of becoming part of Schumm Homes. While Max would undoubtedly make him an offer of employment, there was only one firm Connor intended to work for—the newest agency in town.

Wilson Realty.

The time for the program to begin came and went, causing him to make a mental note, matching the information he'd already gathered. Tardiness was one of Max's sins. He had others, but the most mentioned was his disregard for other people's time.

Just as Max stepped closer to the podium, talking in low tones with the Ramada's technical advisor, a kid who had to be right out of college, a couple appeared at the double-door entrance.

Connor caught and held his breath when he saw the woman.

Hair the color of a setting sun—the most gorgeous shade of natural red he'd ever seen. It was long and down, bouncing around her shoulders in wavy cascades. She wore a perfect black dress. Not a slutty "little black dress" but one that would work fine for business *and* pleasure, with a square neck that showed a hint of generous cleavage. She was curvy without being too curvy. Her legs seemed to go on forever, and the black stilettos were enough to finish him off.

He was no longer thinking about Max Schumm or real estate or the Cloverleaf market. Connor wasn't going to be paying an ounce of attention to anything anyone had to say tonight. Not with the redheaded vision heading right for his table. Too bad she was with another guy, because there was nothing he wanted more than to take her home.

It had been a long time since he'd felt such a swift and severe attraction. The closer she drew, the harder his heart pounded. Since the last empty seats were at his table, it was a given she and her escort were going to sit next to him.

"Mind if we sit here?" she asked, her husky voice hitting him right in the groin.

"Um, no. Go ahead." Then the blood started flowing back to Connor's brain long enough for him to remember his manners. He stood up and pulled out the chair for her, drawing a lopsided smile from her escort, who hadn't made a move to help.

She dropped a rather large black purse on the floor, sat down, and smiled sweetly over her shoulder as Connor pushed her up to the table. "Thanks."

"You're welcome."

Her perfume drifted his way. Something light yet sensual. Hell, everything about her was sensual. She moved like a feline, all sleek lines and confidence. He wanted to sweep the gorgeous creature into his arms, carry her up to his third-floor room, and make love to her until they both collapsed in sated exhaustion. He let a light chuckle slip as he wondered what she'd say if he up and told her exactly what he was thinking.

She tossed him a charming smile, but he couldn't enjoy it

because he was too busy looking to see if she or the guy who'd escorted her to the table wore a wedding ring.

Neither did, and Connor did a mental jig. He wasn't leaving without this beautiful creature's phone number.

Maybe his fresh start in this new place was truly going to be his salvation. Maybe he could really leave his past behind and forge a new life here after all. Maybe a leopard could finally change his spots.

For the first time in as long as he could remember, he felt the confidence and purpose that had been missing for far too long. He would make a life for himself here, earn a decent profit, and maybe get back to the world of the living.

Only time would tell.

* * *

Juliana's hopes fell with each word out of Max Schumm's mouth. What he was proposing was a sales position where she'd slave away for him, selling real estate yet giving back far more in commission than she thought necessary. All for the privilege of being able to use his logo and wear a tacky blue blazer. The way he parceled out office space was ridiculous, and although he was the number one Realtor for miles around, she couldn't help but think there had to be someone with more warmth and personality than the rather cardboard Max Schumm.

Dinner had been a steak that was about the size and consistency of a hockey puck, a baked potato, and a bowl of tossed lettuce. The only drink provided was water. Twenty bucks didn't buy much anymore.

Then Max had proceeded to tell them how lucky they all were to even be *considered* as one of his representatives. Once he finished putting himself and his business on parade, he settled in with one-on-one conferences.

Juliana held back, wondering if whatever he could say was worth waiting for if she got a turn with him.

Robert scooted his chair back and stood. "I'm done, Jules. This guy's a jerk."

She nodded, still unsure of her next move.

"You staying or going?"

"I'm gonna stick around for a little while. Okay?"

"How will you get home?"

"I'll call a cab."

His frown was a bit fierce coming from such an easygoing guy. "Are you sure? I don't want to leave you stranded."

"I won't be stranded. Just going to grab a drink then call a cab. Stop worrying about me."

He glanced back to Max. "If I spent more than five minutes alone with that guy, I'd probably shove my fist right down his throat."

She let a chuckle slip out. "I can understand that inclination."

"See you Monday." Robert gave her a goofy little wave and headed for the exit.

Juliana fished her cell phone out of her purse and texted Mallory.

Seminar was a bust.

It didn't take long for Mallory to reply.

Sorry. Want to come over?

As if she'd interrupt the Carpenters' peace and quiet.

Nope. Heading to the bar.

Mallory texted right back.

That bad?

There was only one word needed in reply.

Absolutely.

Juliana turned the phone's ringer off, shoved it in her purse, and started to push back from the table. Then she realized the man who'd pulled out her chair was helping her again. "Thank you," she said as she stood. Whatever else she'd planned to say evaporated as she took a good look at him.

How preoccupied had she been with planning a new career to have missed *him*?

He had to be around six foot. Black hair, trimmed short. Not quite a military cut, but definitely no-nonsense. The darkest brown eyes she'd ever seen. He wore a light gray suit that fit him perfectly. His tie was a mixture of black, silver, and purple, the perfect complement to complete the outfit.

No matter how hard she tried to imagine it, Juliana just couldn't see him in one of the Schumm blazers. It would be an abomination.

His smile washed over her, making her blood heat to the point that her face flushed hot all the way to her ears.

"So what did you think?" he asked in an appealing baritone.

Since she had no idea who this man was or what his connection was to Max Schumm, she shrugged.

"Are you going to talk to him?"

"I think I'll pass tonight." She slung her heavy purse over her shoulder as she cast one last look at the queue to talk to Max.

As though he knew she watched, Max turned toward her. His dark brown hair seemed a little too perfect, and his smile made a shiver run the length of her spine. She had a passing thought that he looked a little bit too much like Ted Bundy to allow her to be comfortable being alone with him. He gave her a practiced smile that she responded to by shifting her gaze to the dark man who still stood with his hands on the back of her chair.

Disappointment weighed heavily, making her frown despite the welcoming smile he gave her. Right now, she wanted a drink. She *needed* a drink. "Thanks again. I'm getting out of here."

Had she been her normal outgoing self, she would have invited him to accompany her. Since he didn't reply to her farewell, she left the room, heading for the bar on the other side of the hotel. She'd been there with the Ladies before. Kicks was small, had loads of televisions to keep people from trying to start conversations, and the booze wasn't overpriced.

A hand on her shoulder dragged her to a stop in the lobby. "Um...hey."

She whirled to find the raven-haired man. Knowing he followed her left her as tongue-tied as a girl with her first crush. "Hey."

"Were you leaving?" he asked.

"Not yet."

A quick look down the hall and his eyes fixed on the overhead sign pointing to Kicks. "Heading to the bar?"

"Yeah. I am."

There was reluctance in his eyes and another glance down the hallway as though he was making up his mind. "Care if I tag along? I'd love to buy you a drink."

How long had it been since some man, especially one as good-looking as this guy, had tried to pick her up? At all the mixers she'd attended, only twice had she accepted a date. Both guys were nice, but there simply wasn't any chemistry. One kiss with each was more than enough to convince her of the sad lack of attraction.

"I suppose I should introduce myself." He held out his hand. "Connor Wilson."

Juliana put her hand in his. Heat shot through her body so

swiftly she gasped. What a cliché—a touch being akin to a light-ning strike. Yet she was affected anyway.

He didn't let go of her hand, and she wouldn't even consider pulling it away. They just stared at each other. He was only a few inches taller, which kept their eyes locked. People moved around the lobby, coming and going as though the world was still spinning.

Yet her universe had been reduced to the touch of this man.

Max Schumm broke the magic spell. "Connor Wilson? I knew it! I *knew* it was you!" He stuck his hand right above where Connor still held Juliana's.

Feeling ridiculous, she drew her hand back while Connor shook Max's hand.

"Wasn't sure you'd recognize me," Connor said.

"One of the leading salesmen in Indiana?" Max snorted a laugh. "I always know the competition." He gave Connor a head-to-toe appraisal. "You're thinking about getting back in the biz?"

Back? She filed that bit of info away, figuring it might be a conversation starter as well as a way to get to know more about Connor.

Max turned to her, giving her such a fake salesman smile she almost rolled her eyes. "Sure didn't know you'd married such a looker, Wilson. What's your name, doll?"

Doll? Oh, Max. You're an asshole.

"I'm Juliana Kelley, but we're not married."

"Well, then." Max rubbed his hands together. "What would it take to get you to come sit and talk? You came for the seminar, which means you're interested."

Was interested. "I—I'm not sure about anything yet, Mr. Schumm," she said, hating the hesitation in her voice. For some reason, she couldn't just come out and tell him to buzz off. Perhaps that reason was Connor. She was dying to hear what he had to say to Max.

"Oh, sorry," Max said. "I meant Connor."

How the hell would she have known that? The guy had been staring right at her. Now he was summarily dismissing her.

Her pride shattered. Not only had she been rudely dismissed, it had happened in front of the first man she'd been attracted to in just about forever.

With a shake of her head, she walked away. Somewhere in that bar was a shot of Patrón with her name on it.

Chapter Three

How about I call you Monday, Max?" Connor said.

He'd never make the call, but all he could think was that the woman of his dreams was getting away and there was no way he'd let that happen.

Connor inclined his head toward the conference room. "You've still got people waiting to talk to you."

"Sure, sure," Max replied. His eyes had narrowed enough to show his anger at being dismissed. "Give me a ring." On that, he left.

Connor kept his gaze on Max until he disappeared down the hall toward the conference room. Then he turned to face the other long corridor, the one that led to the bar.

Should he go after her?

Juliana Kelley. Temptation on two very long legs.

If he had any brains, he'd go back to his room. The closing on his new house was Tuesday. The place was a wreck, so he'd have more than enough to keep him busy. That, and he was going to start his own agency. He'd sworn he was going to simplify his life, to keep the demons from eating him alive. No unnecessary stress. Nothing to throw him off track. He didn't need any…complications.

Juliana Kelley was most definitely a complication.

His gaze fell on the small kiosk in the hotel lobby. As though drawn there, he went inside, found the display of toiletries, and plucked up a box of condoms. The saleslady gave him a sly smile as he made his purchase, and the giggle was there in her voice when she thanked him, told him to have a nice evening, and handed over his change. He shoved the coins and the box in his jacket pocket and headed to Kicks, excusing his action as being presumptuous, born of an attraction he simply couldn't fight.

There were no guarantees, but a guy needed to be ready for anything that popped up.

He chuckled at his double entendre.

The place was next to empty, but it wouldn't have mattered even if it had been packed. That red hair was a beacon, as was her innate sensuality. She sat at the bar, shoulders lowered as she played with an empty shot glass.

Connor approached slowly, trying to let common sense and intellect argue to stop him. He had no business getting involved with her. Not now. His life was being held together by a frayed shoestring. Yes, things were looking up after far too long, but the control he held came to him day by day, sometimes hour by hour. He was tempting fate by going to her, introducing a complication that was risky at best.

Yet he couldn't stop himself.

"Another shot and a lime, please," she said, setting the empty glass upside down on the wooden surface.

The fiftysomething bartender put a fresh shot glass on the bar, filled it with Patrón, and plucked a lime wedge from his store of condiments. He plopped it on a small plate and set it next to the tequila. "Anything else?"

"Give me ten minutes," she replied with a wink. "Then I'll let you know."

The bartender chuckled as he headed back down the long bar to chat with a pair of guys closer to his age.

She jumped when Connor pulled out the barstool next to hers. Her eyes fixed on his face, then her mouth bowed into a frown. She might as well have held up a stop sign.

He wouldn't let that chilly reception discourage him. Sitting himself down, he gave the bartender a dismissive wave of his hand when the man held up an empty mug, clearly asking if Connor wanted a drink.

Sure, he wanted one. But he wasn't going to indulge.

Juliana picked up her shot glass and neatly downed the contents. Grabbing the lime, she grasped it with her teeth, sucked hard enough to make Connor's groin tighten, and then grimaced. Her body gave a little shudder before she dropped the lime wedge on the plate, leaned back, and sighed.

"So where's the tacky blue blazer?" she asked, her voice low and irritated.

"Don't have one," Connor replied. "My clothes are all very fashionable."

Her lips twitched as if she might grin. When she finally turned to face him, her eyes made his ability to think logically evaporate. Green as clover, they were as hypnotic as a metronome, drawing him into their depths until she was the only thing in his mind.

"There's obviously one in your future," she said. "One with an equally tacky logo. You and Max got pretty chummy in the lobby."

Seeing no need to mince words, he spoke his mind. "Max Schumm is a douche bag."

She snorted as a small smile bloomed.

"I mean it. I have no intention of being a part of his egomaniacal agency."

"Then why were you there?"

"Keeping an eye on the competition."

"Competition?" Juliana cocked her head. "Do you work for Carl Barton, then?"

"Nope."

"Those are the only two decent real estate agencies in Cloverleaf."

He loved that she was interested enough to keep pressing the point. "As of now."

"Meaning…?"

"Give it a little time."

Those lovely eyes shot fire. "I'm not drunk." A glance to the empty shot glasses. "At least not yet. But you're not making any sense."

The bartender put himself in front of them. "Another?" he asked Juliana.

"Why not?" she replied.

"For you?" he asked Connor as he set up another shot of tequila and lime wedge.

"I don't suppose you've got any Squirt back there?" Connor asked.

"Matter of fact, I do." The bartender reached under the bar, fished out a two-liter bottle, and set it next to Juliana's empty glasses. "Use it for mixing." He retrieved a large glass, tossed some ice into it, and filled it before sliding the soft drink closer to Connor. "Anything else?"

"Could you shoot those pretzels down here?" Connor gestured to the full bowl on the far side of Juliana.

After complying, the bartender returned to his other customers, leaving Connor and Juliana to sit in silence.

She didn't immediately down her shot. Instead, she fiddled with the fresh lime wedge, turning it in circles on the plate.

Connor picked up a few of the pretzels and munched on them as he slid the bowl closer to her. She was right. She wasn't drunk. But he'd watched how she'd picked at the pathetic dinner Max had provided, and if she kept drinking tequila without eating something, it would catch up with her. "Pretzels?"

"Why are you here?"

Tossing a couple more of the tiny pretzels into his mouth, he chewed them slowly as he tried to think up a brilliant answer to that question.

None came to mind.

Since his past relationships had been nothing but disasters, often falling apart because of lies told to spare feelings or avoid discussions, he decided honesty was going to be the only way to approach her.

"I followed you," he finally replied.

"Why?"

"Because I think you're beautiful and I want to—"...*make love to you.* He nervously cleared his throat. *That* honesty would have cost him. Dearly. "I want to get to know you better."

Juliana picked up the shot, quickly drank it, and pressed the lime wedge between her lips. After tossing the rind aside, she hopped off the bar stool, slung her purse over her shoulder, and walked away so quickly she might have been running from a threat.

Fishing a few bills out of his wallet, Connor tossed them on the counter and hurried after her.

He caught her in the middle of the long, empty hallway. Wrapping his fingers around her upper arm, he dragged her to a stop. "Wait. Please."

Although she stopped, she glared at him with an anger he didn't deserve, not for stating a simple fact. "Why?" she asked.

"Why what?"

"Why do you want me to wait? Trying to think up another brilliant pickup line?" She gave her head a shake, sending her red hair bouncing around her shoulders. "Don't bother. That last one has to be one of the worst I've ever heard."

"Worst? You mean because I told you you're beautiful?"

"No."

When she didn't elaborate, his frustration grew. Nothing about this was going to be simple.

Simple had gotten him absolutely nowhere so perhaps complicated might be a better tack. "Then why?"

"It was what you *didn't* say."

He loved verbally fencing with her, not realizing how much he'd missed feminine company.

No, that wasn't quite right. This woman was different from other women he'd known, and the attraction was making it hard to use any intellect. The blood just wasn't getting to his brain. "And what exactly was that?"

"That you're trying to seduce me."

Seduce. Simply hearing the word spill from her lips had him groaning. Quaint and so much sexier than he'd expected. Most women might have just said *fuck*. Not this lady, and that's what she was.

A lady.

From the top of her shimmering red hair to the toes she had tucked in those shiny black pumps that were incredibly sexy.

"I suppose I am," Connor admitted. "Can you blame me?"

When she turned to face him, giving him her undivided attention, his cock swelled even farther, and he questioned whether his zipper would pop. How could any man resist Juliana Kelley?

"What if I'm married?" she asked.

"You're not."

"And you know that because…?"

Since she hadn't thrown a drink in his face and marched away, his hopes began to grow as much as his erection. Braving a brazen approach, he took her left hand in his, holding it up as though he were a courtier preparing to brush a reverent kiss over her knuckles. "No wedding ring."

She didn't pull away, giving him the courage to gently rub his thumb over her fingers. "Doesn't mean I'm not married. Lots of people don't wear rings."

"Mostly married men who want to cheat on their wives."

Juliana picked up his left hand, gave it a deliberate stare, then turned it over to look at the palm. "You're not married, either. And you do some work with your hands. Not a lot, but…" She pulled her left hand from his and traced the small calluses on his palm with her fingertips.

Did she have any idea what she was doing to him? Never had such innocent touches filled his body with need. Had the place been empty, he'd have picked her up, laid her on the ebony table with the enormous vase of flowers, and buried himself inside her. As it was, his heart was pounding rough and fast enough she had to be able to hear it above the canned music.

He couldn't wait a moment longer to taste her. Connor grabbed her shoulders and walked her backward until he had her pressed against the wall. His eyes searched hers, waiting for a denial. He wasn't hurting her. He'd never hurt her. But he was drowning in the need to know she shared the desire that held him so tightly in its talons he felt as though he'd explode if she didn't let him make love to her.

* * *

Connor Wilson was going to be the death of her.

Everything about him affected her, made her blood run so hot she couldn't keep from squirming. The dark hair. The dark eyes. The way he exuded masculinity had her entranced. When he'd pushed her against the wall, his touch insistent and arousing, she'd had to bite her bottom lip to keep from moaning.

His face was so close to hers, his eyes looking for ... something, left her breathless with anticipation.

She met him halfway.

The first touch of their lips and she dropped her purse, looped her arms around his neck, and fit her body to his. His hard planes pressing against her sent her soaring. She couldn't even blame the tequila. It might have warmed and relaxed her, but she wasn't drunk. Not on Patrón.

On Connor Wilson.

His tongue thrust past her lips, claiming her mouth with bold strokes before coaxing her tongue to follow his retreat. Then he grasped it with his teeth and tugged at the same time he ground his hips against her. Her core throbbed with want, needing this man to fill her.

Juliana wanted to wrap her legs around his slim hips. Preferably while they were both naked.

This wasn't like her. Not at all. Sure she was boisterous, leaned toward bossy, and was far too extroverted for her own good. But making out with a guy right after she met him? Entertaining the notion of taking him home with her?

What would the Ladies Who Lunch say?

She honestly didn't give a shit. Tonight was for her. Tonight was something incredible, something too special to let pass her by. Tonight, this was going to happen—she *needed* it to happen.

Tearing her mouth away, she panted for breath, grateful to see Connor doing the same.

"We're in public," she had to point out.

"We are," he replied.

"I'm a teacher. If anyone sees us..."

"No one's here. We're alone."

When he didn't add to that comment, she figured he'd made a move and now wanted to see if she was ready to accept his invitation. "We should find someplace more private," she suggested.

"We should?" He arched an eyebrow. His eyes were so dark, so appealing. Everything about him was appealing.

Too appealing to ignore.

"We should. I live pretty close to here and—"

"I have a room upstairs." He stepped back and took her hand. "We can go there and see what happens."

She knew damn well what was going to happen, and judging from his smile, so did he. What she didn't know was why he would be staying at the Ramada. "Why do you have a room?"

"Waiting for my house to close next week." On that flimsy explanation he headed back toward the lobby as she hurried to keep up with his long strides.

By the time they reached the elevator, Juliana's common sense kicked in.

What in the hell am I doing?

She didn't even know this guy. Shit, for all she knew, his name wasn't even Connor Wilson. The sane part of her brain almost blurted out a demand that he show her his driver's license.

They were alone in the elevator, making her feel vulnerable when the doors closed. If he crowded her, pushing her against the wall again like in the hall—

"I'm not a serial killer," he said, the humor clear in his voice.

"I never thought you were."

He snorted. "Sure you didn't. Look, Juliana…we don't have to do this. I just"—he raked his fingers through his short hair—"there's something about you, something that makes me want you beyond reason. I've never wanted a woman as much as I want you right now."

A tone alerted that they'd reached the third floor. He stepped out of the elevator, his hand on the door to hold it open. "It's your choice."

All she could do was stare at him as thoughts tumbled through her mind.

She should leave. She should push the button to close the doors and get the hell out of the Ramada. She had no business going anywhere with a strange man.

But she wanted him, plain and simple. She wanted to reach out and grab what she needed for the first time in her life and to hell with the consequences.

The evening had dashed all her hopes and dreams of starting a new career, a new life. They lay in ashes at her feet. Her job was becoming impossible despite her passion for working with children. What did she have to look forward to? Twenty-plus more years of unhappiness?

Connor extended his other hand. "Come with me, Juliana. Please. Let me show you how much I want you."

His voice was a caress, making her close her eyes to allow the words to cascade over her mind and body.

"Let me show you how much I want you."

Juliana opened her eyes and took his hand.

Chapter Four

The electronic lock was giving him a hard time. Juliana didn't care. She wasn't in any hurry. Once she'd made up her mind to go with him, to see if he could follow through on the sensuous promises he'd made with that incredible kiss, she found herself remarkably calm. Still more turned on than she'd ever been, she had no fear. No worry of regrets to come when the stark light of morning dawned. Only anticipation and a hunger that gnawed at her insides.

After his fifth attempt, she put her hand over his and plucked the key card from his fingers. "Let me."

The lock opened on her first try.

She went inside, letting him hold the door for her. His sexy smile, pure alpha-male, reminded her of the Connor who'd taken charge in that empty hallway, the one who'd backed her up to a wall and practically screwed her brains out right there in the open. And God help her, she would've cast aside all modesty and common sense and let him.

While she'd never shied away from sex, this was new to her. The desire he created was so overwhelming she might have feared it had she been younger. Thirty-five was no longer a child, and Juliana basked in the glory of feeling so free, in taking what she wanted for once in her life. *Damn the consequences, full speed ahead.*

Why should she feel any shame for accepting the invitation of a man she desired more than any she'd met before? Especially when she'd be much more likely to regret letting him slip right through her fingers. Life had taught her a hard lesson—that regrets over what could've been were stronger and more damaging than regrets over what happened.

Dropping her purse on the chair, she took a deep breath, preparing herself to face him. Before she could turn, he was behind her, arms snaking around her waist as he pressed his body to hers. Heat seeped inside her, creeping through her veins and stirring her desire. Connor was like Patrón, warming her from the inside out. When he brushed his lips over the tender spot where her neck met shoulder, she shivered and tilted her head, letting him have access and encouraging him with a purr to continue.

She put her hands over his, interlacing their fingers and loving how he stroked her stomach. Wiggling her backside, she smiled at the hard length that greeted her. Her smile grew when he groaned, his hot breath against her skin.

"I want you." His hoarse whisper sent heat shooting straight to her core.

Juliana turned in his arms. Sliding her hands up his chest, she helped him shrug out of his suit jacket. He tossed it over her abandoned purse. It was then she saw part of a white bag hanging out of the front pocket. "What's that?"

"What's what?" He leaned in and kissed her neck again. A delicate nibble of her sensitive skin made her giggle.

"That sack. What's in it?"

Not that she didn't already have a good idea. Connor's pockets had been empty at the dinner, something she'd noticed when she'd given him a good once-over. They'd been flat, showing the excellent tailoring of his suit. She was fairly certain that somewhere between dinner and talking her into coming up to his room, he'd bought condoms.

Smug bastard.

Although that cockiness was one of the things that drew Juliana to him, watching the emotions on his face was amusing as he struggled to explain.

"Um...I figured...er...I thought...hell."

"You thought *what*, Connor?" She tried to bend down to pluck the sack from his coat.

He beat her to the punch, coming close to knocking heads with her. After he fished out the box of Trojans, he held them out to her. "Condoms. I got condoms."

"You bought condoms. Before or after we kissed?" Asking was a formality. If he was thinking at all, he'd realize they'd been pawing at each other since they'd shared the kiss. But would he admit that he'd planned on taking her to bed before he'd come to the bar?

"Before. I got them before." His voice was that of a naughty child.

"Good thinking." She took the box and dropped it back on top of his coat.

His shocked expression made her grin. "You're not mad?"

Juliana wrapped her arms around his waist and pulled him close. Then she nuzzled the base of his throat. "Not one bit." She nipped at his skin, soothing the sting with a long lick. "You were being careful. That's not a reason to get angry."

"I was afraid you'd think I was too cocky." The last word

ended on a squeak when she rubbed the heel of her hand over the fly of his pants, tracing the length of his erection.

"Oh, you're *cocky* all right."

"Sweetheart, you crack me up." He drew her back into his arms.

His hands caressed her back, nimble fingers finding her zipper and dragging it down. As he helped her pull her arms out of the garment, he kissed her with an infectious hunger before he pushed the dress over her hips. It fell into a puddle of black silk at her feet. Breaking away, he took a step back and gave her a very deliberate visual appraisal that brought heat to her cheeks.

When his gaze settled on her legs, he sucked in a breath, nearly choking. As he regained his control, Juliana tossed him what she prayed was a seductive smile as she fought the urge to cover herself. Instead, she stood her ground. If he didn't like what he saw, now was the time to know.

* * *

Thigh-high black stockings.

Sweet Lord, the woman was a temptation Connor could never resist. As she stood there in her lacy black panties and bra, she didn't try to cover herself with her hands. Not Juliana.

No, she boldly faced him, letting him stare from the top of her head to her full breasts to those sexy stockings that led to a pair of shiny black pumps. He finally had to close his eyes, fearing he was losing every ounce of the self-control he'd always prided himself on having.

His eyes flew open when Juliana unbuckled his belt. Instead of whipping it off, she left it hanging from the belt loops and popped open the button at the waist. After she dragged down the zipper, she mimicked his actions, smoothing her hands over his hips to push the pants and briefs down his legs. The garments dropped to the floor.

"I love what you're wearing," he said. The notion that she dressed so seductively all the time made him worry she might have captured a lot of men the same way she'd so easily captured him.

He just couldn't believe that of her. Not with the blush that bloomed on her cheeks when he'd drunk his fill of her beautiful body.

"Thanks," she said with an enchanting grin. "After my divorce, I started buying beautiful lingerie. No one ever sees it but me, but *I* know it's there. Gives me confidence."

Extending a finger, he traced a small pink ribbon tattooed on the swell of her left breast. "Who's Mallory?" he asked about the name etched on the ribbon.

"My best friend."

Since Juliana didn't elaborate, he didn't ask any more questions. Before he could move, she knelt down to help him step out of his clothes and shed his shoes and socks. Then she plucked the box from where it rested on his jacket and fished out the string of condoms. She ripped one off, opened it, and before he knew it, she had him sheathed.

The way she slid her palms up his legs had him so full of need, he was afraid he'd embarrass himself when he finally got inside her. And damn, if that wasn't soon, he was going to lose him mind.

Instead of touching his erect cock again as it jutted out at her, she skirted around it and began unbuttoning his dress shirt from the bottom up. As the shirt opened, she pressed her lips to his abdomen, stopping every now and then to rake her bloodred nails over his skin. When she got to his tie, she undid the knot, leaving it in his shirt just as she'd left his belt in his pants. Then the shirt was on the floor.

Looping her arms around his neck, she molded her body to his, the contact of her hot skin making him groan against her lips before she kissed him.

Connor fumbled with the back of her bra until he growled in frustration when he couldn't find the clasp.

Juliana stepped back. "It's in front." Her fingers found the fastener in the valley between her breasts. She deftly popped it and cast her bra aside. Before he could ask her to get rid of that bit of black lace serving as panties, she did so almost in obedience of his unspoken command.

He stepped forward to grab her wrists when her hands went to her stockings. "Leave them on. Please."

Her smile was like a punch to the chest, stealing his breath away. "Like them, huh?"

"Oh yeah." Lifting her arms, he put his hands on her hips. Again, she seemed to know exactly what he wanted and slipped her arms around his neck.

Their kiss was as consuming as a raging fire. Waiting any longer to make her his was unbearable. Since she'd rolled the condom on, Connor had to assume she felt the same. Lifting her, he headed straight for the wall, not even wanting to wait long enough to toss her on the bed. Once he had her back against the wall, he slipped his hand under her knee and dragged it up the side of his body. Rubbing his erection over her core, he whispered in her ear, "Now, Juliana?"

"Yes. Yes." She gasped and clutched at his back.

He plunged inside her, letting her heat envelop him and squeeze his cock as though her body were made for him. The pleasure was so intense he had to grit his teeth and hold tight to his self-control.

She felt so damn good.

Juliana wrapped her legs around his waist and gently bit his shoulder. "Move," she said, her voice full of the same need that held him enslaved. "Now."

So he obeyed, pulling almost out and then thrusting back inside her, finding a rhythm that had her whimpering and arching her back. Although her weight wasn't a burden, he couldn't move as he wanted to. "Hold on to me, Red."

Her legs squeezed tighter as he backed away from the wall and carried her to the bed. As he leaned down, she grabbed the duvet and tossed it aside, leaving behind pristine sheets.

He laid her down, still joined intimately with her as he dragged her farther up the mattress so he could find better leverage. Holding himself up, he gazed into her eyes. Then he eased back, nearly withdrawing from her body before pushing inside her again. Buried to the hilt, he sighed in pleasure.

"You feel *wonderful*," she said, her voice a caress.

"So do you."

Her fingers tangled in his hair. "Shut up and kiss me."

Connor ravaged her mouth as he thrust into her again and again. Her hips rose to meet him as her heels drummed against his thighs. A climax was building deep inside him, but he wouldn't leave her behind.

Juliana surprised him when she put her palms against his chest and pushed. "Stop."

Instantly obeying, he searched her eyes. "What's wrong?"

"Nothing. Roll over on your back."

Women had always let him take the lead in bed. Having her order him around was an exciting change. "Yes, ma'am." He rolled to his back, holding her tight to take her with him.

Still joined with him, she straddled his hips. "Now I've got you where I want you."

"Think so? Maybe I've got *you* right where I want you."

Her hands dropped to either side of his face as she brushed the tips of her breasts against his face. Connor seized the opportunity to capture one of her hardened nipples with his lips and suck it deep into his mouth.

She drew in a breath, letting it out in a low moan. After he released her, she pushed herself back up and smiled down at him. Picking up his hand, she slid it to where their bodies were joined.

To have Juliana showing him exactly what she wanted was beyond exciting. He used his fingers to find her sensitive nub. As soon as he did, she reared her head back, letting her hair spill over her shoulders and back. He gave her the attention she'd asked for, loving how whimpers spilled from her lips.

Knowing he was pleasing her, Connor found himself well past waiting. He moved, thrusting up into her with a cadence that increased in speed and force as she matched his movements. The first tremors of her orgasm made her body clench around his cock, setting off his own climax. He pushed into her. Once. Twice. Then she cried out, arching her back as she surrendered.

He was a heartbeat behind, coming in a blaze of heat that seemed never-ending. Spots dotted the darkness behind his closed eyelids.

A peace like he'd never known settled on his heart and his mind. After a quick trip to the bathroom, he found Juliana settled between the sheets. He slid in beside her, drew her into his arms, and let sleep claim him.

Chapter Five

Connor's rumbling baritone cut through Juliana's sleep-hazed thoughts. "Two orders. That's right." There were pauses between each item he requested. "Scrambled. Wheat and bacon. Coffee and juice. Be sure and send lots of cream. Thirty minutes? Sounds great."

Ordering breakfast was a sweet thing to do, but everything inside her was screaming to get away from him as fast as she could. The night had been magical. Sometime in the wee hours, she'd awakened to his hot mouth on her breast, his hand between her thighs. They'd made love again, taking their time to tease and savor in a way she'd never known before. Foreplay for her ex-husband had been rolling over and asking, "Wanna fuck?"

She felt free with Connor, able to tell him exactly what she wanted. There was no shyness, as though being mere strangers masked by the darkness of the night lent her courage beyond her wildest dreams. The sex had been so consuming, she'd lost herself to it, giving herself completely to her lover.

A first.

But in the stark light of day, she had regrets. Not for sleeping together.

For letting him in.

Her life was a mess, would continue to be a mess for a long time to come. No boyfriend. A career she'd grown to hate. Nothing to look forward to, especially since the Max Schumm thing had blown up in her face. She didn't need to have something new to worry about.

A relationship was out of the question. Long term never worked for her. Ever. The minute commitment became a possibility, she found herself alone again. If she stayed too much longer, she'd be begging Connor to take her on a real date so they could get to know each other better—somewhere outside of bed, although she wanted nothing more than to drag him back between the rumpled sheets. But she needed to run away from him. Not only was she unable to open up emotionally the way she had physically, the overwhelming way she craved him terrified her.

Of course, she was jumping to conclusions. For all she knew, he merely wanted a one-night stand. Sure, he'd given her tons of flattery and subtle promises for sharing time together in the future, but guys didn't keep their promises. At least not the guys she'd known.

There was no way she was staying around to eat breakfast in awkward silence while waiting for him to find a gentle way to let her down by telling her how great last night was but he wasn't ready for a relationship.

It's me, not you.

Blah. Blah. Blah.

Feigning sleep might be immature and a bit irrational, but she couldn't face him. No way. She listened closely as he shuffled through drawers, praying he was heading into the bathroom to take a shower. Then a door closed, followed closely by the sound of running water.

Juliana practically leapt from the bed, throwing the covers aside and scrambling to her feet. The room looked cheaper than it had last night, although she hadn't been paying too much attention. She searched around for her clothes, picking up the pieces as she found them. She quickly donned her panties and bra. Then she wiggled into her wrinkled dress. She found only one of her stockings and gave up the search for the other, fearing she was wasting precious time. After stuffing it in her purse, she jammed her feet into the pumps.

When Juliana reached the door, she paused, casting a glance to the closed bathroom door. Connor was humming as he showered, an endearing trait that made tears sting her eyes. She could almost imagine sharing a home with him, listening to him hum every morning as they got ready to go to work. She swallowed hard, pictured him rubbing his soapy hands over his body. That incredible chest. Flat, sculpted abs. And lower…

If she didn't get the hell out of there, she was going to strip and join him in the shower. Then she'd never let him go.

No.

She was leaving before he told her to go, before he left her behind. No matter how much she wanted to pretend, even for a little while, that she mattered to him, she didn't. They'd had sex. Twice. That was all. There was no commitment, no emotional entanglement. No true feelings. At least not on his part. She refused to let her mind wander any farther down that path, preferring to cut and run, although the thought that she might never see Connor again choked her up.

Opening the door, she slipped into the hall. The quiet click of the latch hit her like a blow to the gut. Sniffing back the threatening tears, she hurried down the hall to the elevator. Thankfully, no one else was out and about. When she reached the lobby, she walked with her head held high, moving quickly—just short of running—to reach the exit.

Outside, Juliana fished her phone out of her purse as she made her way across the street to the small shopping center. She hadn't dared call a cab and wait for it at the Ramada. No doubt Connor knew she was gone by now. If he tried to chase her down, there would be a confrontation, a very public confrontation. That, she wouldn't allow.

Mallory answered on the second ring as Juliana slipped inside Starbucks. "Jules? What's up?"

"I need a ride. Please."

* * *

Connor stepped out of the bathroom, tucking in the towel he'd wrapped around his hips. One look around the room made him frown. "Shit."

Juliana was gone.

"Shit. Shit. Shit."

Before he could even process that, there was a knock at the door. Breakfast, no doubt. Not that he had an appetite now. He checked the peephole, hoping she'd gone for ice or a soda and had locked herself out. A glance back showed her clothes were gone, except for one black stocking resting underneath the desk.

No such luck in the peephole. A uniformed employee was reaching up to knock again.

Connor opened the door, let the lady wheel the cart into the room, and had to dig his pants out from under the duvet to tip her. After she left, he picked up Juliana's stocking and sat on the bed, feeling dejected as he rubbed the silky sheer fabric between his fingers.

She'd run away.

But why?

The first time they'd made love had convinced him that their connection was going to be anything but a one-night stand. Not that he was on the lookout for a relationship. Not now. Not yet. But Juliana Kelley wasn't the kind of woman a man could walk away from. At least not *this* man.

She was a part of him now, filling his thoughts, his body. He'd rarely spent a full night with a woman. Yet curling himself around her lush shape had allowed him to sleep so deeply the bad dreams had stayed at bay for the first time in a long time. Sometime in the dead of night he'd awakened, his cock hardening as her sweet scent filled his senses, capturing him as neatly as a snare.

He'd made love to her again, waking her from a sound sleep by stroking her, touching and kissing every part of her until he was nearly crazed with desire. Just like the first time they came together, the connection was something so special he couldn't even find the proper words to describe how she made him feel. His orgasm had damn near killed him.

But what a way to go.

Connor considered jerking on his pants and trying to catch her. She couldn't have gotten too far. He might have taken a while to enjoy his shower, but even then she had to be close enough to find if he hurried.

With an angry grunt, he tossed her stocking on top of his crumpled clothes. He wouldn't go chasing after her, begging her to explain why she'd run. Part of that was because of his wounded pride. She'd left him. Just like that. Not even a good-bye. What did that say about how she felt about him?

Nothing flattering, that's for sure.

The smell of coffee and bacon set his stomach to growling. He grabbed one of the plates, lifted the thermal lid, and set it aside. The breakfasts had cost a pretty penny. Someone should at least eat them. He picked up a fork and dug into the scrambled eggs, chewing while he tried to figure out exactly what he should do about Juliana Kelley.

Since he knew next to nothing about her, finding her wouldn't be easy. At least Cloverleaf was a small city, but what if she wasn't from Cloverleaf? All he knew was that she was looking to Max Schumm for a job selling real estate. Did that mean she was investigating the other Realtors in Cloverleaf as well? Would any of them know how to locate her? She'd told him she was a teacher. At least that could help in a search. In this day and age, it wasn't as though a person could truly disappear. There were too many ways to track someone down. The six degrees of separation had narrowed considerably in the cyber age.

He should've taken more time to learn something, *anything*, about her. Of course, it wasn't as if she'd devoted a lot of effort to making conversation, either. They'd both been caught in some fever that held them hostage. Even now, he was getting hard just thinking about her.

But was that all he wanted from her? Sex?

No. Of that he was sure.

There was so much more he wanted to learn about her, and he was even ready to take a step back and play those little games lovers played as they opened up to each other instead of simply hopping back into bed. After last night, their sexual compatibility wasn't in question. If two people could connect so intimately, sharing themselves with no reservation, surely they'd have a lot of other things in common as well.

Now all he had to do was find her.

Chapter Six

Juliana put down the brush and picked up one of the discarded elastic hair ties. She gathered her hair into a ponytail, tying it neatly so she could put it out of her mind. Since she was using the spare bathroom, not the master, the tie probably belonged to Amber, Mallory's stepdaughter. The yoga pants and T-shirt had to be hers as well since Amber was about the same height and weight as Juliana. The girl wasn't around, so perhaps it was her mother's day for visitation.

"Coming?" Mallory called up the stairs. "Breakfast's ready!"

"Be right down."

Mallory hadn't asked many questions when she'd picked up Juliana, but she would. Her husband, Ben, was most likely cooking, and he'd surely have a few questions of his own. Embarrassing though it would be, Juliana was still grateful Mallory had come to her rescue. They'd invited her to breakfast, so Juliana had agreed rather than heading straight back home.

After spending most of her life as a loner, she'd never understood the power of friendship until she met Mallory. They were both teachers at Douglas High, albeit Mallory taught social studies while Juliana devoted her time to special needs kids. Their paths had barely crossed until six years ago when they'd been assigned the same lunch period. They'd connected not only with each other but also with the two other teachers who'd shared that lunch assignment—Bethany Rogers and Danielle Bradshaw. The four of them formed a friendship that had helped Juliana see what had been missing in her life.

Now they shared everything. These women were her support system, and she hoped her three friends considered her every bit as loyal. They went on excursions to shop, see plays, or simply unwind with a day at a spa. After one such trip to Chicago to take in the show *Company*, they'd dubbed themselves the "Ladies Who Lunch" after one of the songs, joking over a pitcher of margaritas that the title suited their motley crew perfectly.

Trotting down the stairs, she headed to the kitchen, padding across the walnut floor in her bare feet.

Ben stood at the stove, flipping heavenly smelling pancakes as Mallory poured three mugs of coffee. She carried two over to the table and took a seat as Juliana joined her and took one of the mugs from her hand with a murmured thanks.

"Are you ready to explain why you were at Starbucks so early on a Saturday morning, still wearing the dress you wore to the seminar?" Mallory poured some half-and-half into her coffee and handed the carton to Juliana.

Since Amber was nowhere around to hear her confession, Juliana laid it on the line as she added the half-and-half to her own coffee. "I left the guy I seduced last night in his room at the Ramada. He was taking a shower when I snuck out. Starbucks was the closest place to hide."

Mallory's eyes flew wide. "Seriously?"

"Seriously."

Ben snorted a laugh. "How was the walk of shame through the lobby? Sufficiently embarrassing?" He put a few more pancakes on the plate before setting the pan aside, picking up the plate, and bringing it to the table. After fetching his cup of coffee he waited by the vacant chair.

Juliana ignored his teasing and speared a couple of chocolate-chip pancakes with her fork, moving them to her plate, ready to chow down.

Ben still stood by his seat, tapping his foot against the floor.

She glanced up to catch his glare. "What?"

Then she saw the problem. With a lopsided smile, Juliana picked up her heavy purse from where it rested on the chair and let it fall to the floor next to her with a thud. She really needed to clean the thing out before she got back problems from hefting it around.

She beat Ben to the syrup, pouring a generous amount over her pancakes. One bite had her humming in pleasure. The man was a hell of a cook.

A fleeting moment of jealousy passed. Mallory had obviously found the last decent available man in the world, and damn it all, he could cook like a gourmet chef. In fact, he loved cooking. A good thing since Mallory hated it with a passion.

Why can't I be lucky enough to find a full-service guy?

On the other hand, could Ben make a woman feel the way Connor made Juliana feel last night? Twice?

Connor might have been Juliana's perfect man. And how had she dealt with discovering him? She'd lost any chance of getting to know him better by slinking away like a thief in the early morning light.

"What's got you frowning?" Mallory knew her far too well or was simply too damned observant.

"I was thinking it wasn't fair you got Ben." Juliana added a little more syrup to her breakfast. "I had to twist your arm to get you to go to that mixer. Remember?"

"I remember."

"I should have him at my place, cooking for *me* while he remodels *my* house."

"Tough turkey," Mallory said, a note of humor in her voice. "He's mine. You can't have him."

Ben set down his coffee. "Sounds like you found a Mr. Wonderful of your own last night."

"Yeah, well, I spoiled that right away, didn't I?" What good man would want a woman who got tipsy on Patrón and slept with him on what had to seem like a whim?

Her luck with men had been wretched since boyfriend one, a loser who dropped out of high school during his second attempt at finishing his senior year. She'd followed that fiasco by marrying a guy who was as wrong for her as bib overalls or short hair. They'd divorced after only three years of marriage that had seemed to last an eternity. Nothing but a litany of shouting matches, slammed doors, and hurt feelings.

What did it say about her that she only attracted guys like that instead of guys like Ben?

Was Connor Wilson a loser hiding under a cloak of anonymity? If she got to know him better would he end up being as big a disappointment as every other man who'd wandered in and out of her life?

She'd never know because she'd botched her one chance to find out. Sure, finding him probably wouldn't be all that hard, not thanks to social media. But there was no way she'd hunt him down only to relive her embarrassment.

When Ben snorted again, Juliana had to resist the urge to

throw her fork at him. "If you slept with him," he said, "I doubt you spoiled anything. I'd guess he'll easily agree to another date, especially one with a happy ending."

Mallory swatted his arm. "Stop making her feel bad."

"Oh, I don't feel bad," Juliana insisted. "I had a great time. I wish..." She sighed. "No. No wishing. I'm not looking for a relationship. I just needed someone last night."

"You could've called me," Mallory insisted. "I'm always here."

Juliana shrugged. "It was late and I was kinda devastated."

"Devastated? Why? What happened at that seminar after you texted me?"

"Max Schumm showed me he's an asshole. That's what happened."

Weaving the tale of that flag-waving male chauvinist and the way he'd frozen her out helped ease the lingering anger. Unfortunately, all that did was bring Connor right back to the front of Juliana's mind.

She brushed over their connection, but there was no remorse. If she was honest with herself, she'd have to admit she'd hop right into bed with him again if he so much as crooked his finger.

Another good reason to stay the hell away from him.

Schumm Realty seemed no better a fit for him than it did her, so she probably wouldn't find him there. He might not even live in Cloverleaf. Their paths might never cross again unless she went on the offensive to start searching.

"You're frowning again." Mallory studied her over the top of her coffee cup.

"Just thinking that Schumm was definitely a dead end, so my budding career in real estate died before it even took its first breath."

"Not necessarily," Ben said. "There are other firms."

Juliana gave her head a shake. "I can't see myself at one of those any more than I could wear one of Schumm's stupid blue blazers."

"Then why not start your own firm?" he asked.

"What?"

"Start your own firm. You're smart. You've got that garage that I could convert into a great office space. Everyone in Cloverleaf knows you. You'd be all set in no time."

Mallory's brows knit. "Are you really thinking of leaving teaching? You're not just venting?"

"Yeah, I'm ready to bail. I'm just so, so burned out."

"But you love teaching!"

With a shake of her head, Juliana said, "I used to. But now? Now I have to drag my ass out of bed every single day and force myself go to work. I can't imagine having to do that for another twenty years."

Putting her hand over Juliana's, Mallory offered a weak smile. "I don't know how I'd get through a day without you being there."

"I'm not going anywhere, Mal. We're friends, practically sisters. I'll always be in your life."

"Promise?"

"I swear it."

"Then Ben's giving you a great solution. I can guarantee he'll do the contracting work for the cost of supplies only."

"Is that so? You think he'll listen to you?" Juliana scoffed, knowing Ben loved Mallory enough to do anything for her.

"I have *special* ways of persuading him." Mallory winked.

The heated gaze he tossed Mallory made Juliana's heart hurt.

Then she considered what he'd said about starting her own business. A spark fired inside her even as her gut tied into nervous knots at the notion of venturing out that far on a shaky financial limb. Could she really start selling houses without aligning herself with one of Cloverleaf's existing firms?

"I wouldn't require much," Ben went on. "Just a phone and a computer and a lot of your time."

"And next month is final exams," Mallory added. "You'll have a good ten weeks of summer vacation to start hustling for listings and to take buyers out on showings. Knowing you, you'll be outselling Schumm by the end of June."

Their confidence in her was infectious. "I could take more time if I borrow from my retirement savings. I could even take the entire next school year off." A terrifying thought, but the more Juliana considered it, the more she liked it.

It was a risky venture. She'd saved up a nice nest egg, and taking money from those accounts could end up being a major setback. She had no mortgage, and her car was paid for. There were no real expenses, and if she lived frugally she could get by.

But if she lost her retirement fund, she might be teaching until she was eighty.

"Robert might even join you," Ben added. "Or at the very least, he'll give you the listings on his custom houses. I know he hates Schumm, too."

"Maybe." The more she pondered their words, the more the idea bloomed. She could talk to Robert. If he listed his houses, she might be able to talk to those buyers to see if they were selling their old homes. Schumm's reputation might be more tenuous than she'd originally thought, judging from the way everyone responded to him last night. Perhaps they only listed with him because he was one of the limited choices in Cloverleaf.

Could she really do this? Risk her savings to take a year's leave of absence and try to start a new career, a new life?

She let her worries take the lead. "I don't know. It wouldn't be easy. I mean, Schumm practically corners the market here. Between him and Re/Max, they must list more than ninety percent of the houses."

"Not that many," Ben replied. Since he was fiddling with his cell, studying the screen intently, she had no idea if he was searching for information about Schumm or only checking his e-mail. "Did you ever notice how many fizbos there are around here?"

"Fizbos?" Understanding quickly dawned. "You mean for sale by owners, right?" She smiled. "Fizbo. I like that. Sounds cute."

He nodded, still working on his cell with his right hand as he ate with his left. Mallory had always bragged her hubby was ambidextrous.

Guess she was right.

"You already know almost everyone in Cloverleaf," Mallory said. "You've taken most of their kids to Europe. If we get the word out that you're selling houses, they'll be beating a path to your door."

"You think so?" Their faith in her was heartwarming, yet right below that sat a terror that threatened to bring all of this to a screeching halt.

Teaching was a secure job. Sure, those in charge heaped more paperwork on her every year, made exponentially worse because she was a special education teacher. But overall, Juliana could count on always having a job. As long as she'd working been at Douglas High, she'd pretty much have to be caught doing something obscene with a farm animal to get fired.

"Maybe I *can* do it."

"Think about it," Mallory suggested. "With your name, you can make a shamrock logo. Kelley Realty. Has a nice ring to it, doesn't it?"

Juliana nodded, letting them talk her into the idea more with every word.

"Amber is great with putting together stuff like logos." Ben pulled his wallet from his back pocket and fished out a business card, which he set in front of Juliana. "She made these for me."

The card for Carpenter Contracting looked as if it had been professionally designed and printed. Had he not told her his daughter designed it, she would've thought they were done at a professional print shop. "Nice. Think she'd do something like that for me? Shamrocks are a good idea."

"Maybe you can do green blazers instead of blue," he added.

"Nah," Juliana replied. "Tacky blazers aren't my style."

* * *

Connor balked at the estimate. At least Indianapolis had a lot of competition, so prices there had tended to be more competitive. This place wanted to charge him an arm and a leg for a couple of sturdy yard signs.

"Let me think about it," he finally said.

"Suit yourself." The clerk shrugged and turned back to his workstation.

The bell above the door jingled as Connor walked out of the store, a quaint symbol of just how small Cloverleaf was. One of the reasons he'd come here. He needed to simplify his life. What he didn't need was overinflated prices for the swag required to get Wilson Realty off the ground. Until he actually achieved a decent cash flow, things were going to be tight. He better learn to accept that.

For what seemed like the millionth time that day, Juliana Kelley crossed his mind. He'd decided to search for her as soon as he had enough listings that he was confident his new firm was off and running sufficiently to make him a decent choice of a date. Or a boyfriend.

Or a husband.

Funny, but that thought didn't frighten him as it always had in the past. Considering how he'd avoided any kind of permanent attachment, even having the idea came as a surprise. Of course, he'd never been husband material before, not with his checkered past. Had he tried to commit to a woman, he would've destroyed that relationship the way he'd flushed the rest of his life down the crapper.

When he was finally ready to hunt her down, would she reject him? For all he knew she believed he was nothing more than a one-night stand and didn't want anything serious. He'd just have to convince her otherwise, no matter what it took. While his budget might limit the number of roses he could send, he'd find other ways to win her over.

After crawling into the driver's seat of his car, Connor picked up the folded newspaper. He'd used a red pen to make a pecking order for the fizbos he wanted to visit. He just wasn't ready quite yet.

The closing on his house was tomorrow. Then he needed to get his furniture out of storage and move in. The place was barely livable, but he wasn't choosy. The short sale was cheap, had plenty of room, and could be renovated and flipped for a nice profit. All he had to do was live and work through those renovations—and sell enough other houses to pay for it.

Cloverleaf was a fresh start, a chance to make something good of himself. It might be too soon to think of a relationship, but there was something about Juliana. She called to him on too many levels to ignore. He was clearheaded enough to know that was rare. Unique. Special.

When they'd made love, he'd tried "sweetheart" on for size. It didn't fit. Since her hair was the first thing he'd noticed, he'd wanted to call her "Red," and when it slipped from his lips it felt right. Now it was the name that popped up every time he saw her face in his mind's eye.

Red.

Chapter Seven

"Are you sure you want to do this, Jules?" Bethany asked as she fiddled with her salad, shifting it more than eating it.

Since Juliana had dropped her bombshell, it seemed Bethany couldn't do anything but repeat the same question until Juliana wanted to scream her frustration.

She'd expected some reticence, but not outright catatonia. It wasn't like she was moving to Siberia or something that drastic. She was simply changing jobs.

"Absolutely," she replied. "I'm *absolutely* sure this is the best thing for me. It's time. It's been time for longer than you know. I have to do this."

"It's just so fast," Danielle retorted. "You were only going to a seminar to check things out. Now you're leaving?"

"Not all that fast." Juliana tried again to explain it to her best friends. At least Mallory was still firmly on her side. "You know I've been unhappy here."

"We all feel that way from time to time. But we're not running away."

"I'm not running away, Dani. I'm making a change. Yes, it's a big change, but this is more than being unhappy. It's me having to force myself to get out of bed every morning. It's about how I spend every single minute here feeling as if I'd give anything to be somewhere else. It's just time to go."

Bethany gave up the pretense and put down her fork. "Look at this from our point of view. You've been a fantastic special education teacher for almost fifteen years, and now you want to quit and—"

"I don't want to quit. Not yet. Not entirely. I'm only taking a year's leave of absence. That's all. We're allowed to do that, you know. Lots of people have." Although she could only remember two. One took a year off for medical reasons—a heart attack. Then she retired. The other left to follow her husband to a new job and never came back.

Bethany tossed her a worried frown. "And you suddenly want to sell real estate. Where is all of this coming from?"

Since they probably wouldn't want to hear about her uncle Francis or how awfully long she'd been exploring the possibility, Juliana kept things simple. "I've been thinking about a change for a while, but it was Robert who helped me make the leap."

"Wait'll I get my hands on him." Beth twirled a few more leaves of lettuce, scowling at her plastic bowl.

"All Robert did was give me a nudge. I'm the one who ran with it. A good agent can make a lot of money. I worked in sales in college."

"That was women's clothing," Danielle said.

"But selling is selling, and I was damned good at it."

"You're leaving a job that's steady and safe," Bethany insisted. "Why would you want to take this kind of risk?"

"C'mon, Beth. You eat lunch with me every day. You know how unhappy I am, how frustrated I'm getting."

"We're frustrated, too," Beth countered. "It happens in this job. We all have good kids, but the bad ones are a drain. Parents aren't supportive a lot of the time."

"*Most* of the time," Mallory said with a smirk.

Beth pressed on despite the interruption. "Administrators don't back us up. Yada, yada, yada. But this is who we are—it's *what* we are. We're teachers. How can you walk away from your vocation?"

"Because it's not my vocation anymore. It's nothing but a regular old job. Clock in, struggle through the day as time drags, then clock out. It's time for me to get off this merry-go-round."

Danielle leaned back in her chair—as always, waiting to hear all the arguments and then serving as the Ladies' voice of reason, their self-appointed moderator. "I know you've got some challenging kids this year, but they promised to look at getting you a new aide next year. Won't that take some of the pressure off you?"

"It's not that…" Juliana took a deep breath and tried to find the words to make Bethany and Danielle understand.

Since she and Mallory were so close, Mallory "got" her. Always had, always would. But Beth and Dani? They were younger, not all that much, but enough that they still looked at the world with less experienced eyes. Neither had been through bad marriages like she and Mallory had, so they weren't jaded. Mallory was also a cancer survivor, well grounded in reality and living life to the fullest.

Juliana dug deep down to try to express the turmoil that was forcing this choice. "Look at it through my eyes for a minute. I work with kids whose abilities range from semi-independent to wheelchair-bound and unable to even speak. I have to feed some with tubes, even tolerate it as they unload verbal assaults or spit and punch at me. It's getting to be too much to bear anymore. I'm burned out. The kids deserve someone who's still passionate about helping them."

Mallory put her hand over Juliana's. "We understand. Burnout goes with the territory."

"But we'll hate it," Danielle added. "No more Ladies Who Lunch."

"This won't affect our friendships." At least Juliana hoped not. "I'll be able to come and have lunch with you from time to time. And we still have weekends and our getaways. Why should any of that end just because I'm out trying to sell houses instead of being in a classroom?"

"It might be different," Mallory offered. "But we're friends. Always will be. We're the Ladies Who Lunch, right?"

Beth and Dani nodded.

"Then why should our friendship change simply because Jules wants something besides teaching?"

"You're right," Bethany said. "We're friends. We'll always be friends. You're going to knock their socks off, Jules!"

There was the eternally optimistic Beth that Juliana needed.

"So what can we do to help?" Danielle asked. "If you're gonna do this, you're gonna need all the help you can get. Are you sure you want to go it alone? I mean, couldn't you go with Max Schumm or—"

Juliana shook her head. "No. No way. That man would make the worst principal seem like the best boss in the world. I need to do this on my own. Kelley Realty. It's time for someone to give Max Schumm a challenge."

"What about the other guy, that Connor, who you...um..." Mallory was evidently having a hard time saying the obvious.

"The guy I slept with?"

Bethany and Danielle appeared properly startled, both staring at her with wide-open mouths.

Knowing they'd want an explanation, she kept it succinct. "I met a guy at the seminar, and we hit it off. I went back to his room with him, and no, I don't want to talk about it."

"What are you going to do about him?" Mallory asked again.

Juliana shrugged. "I have no idea. He wasn't any more enthralled with Max than I was, so I don't know what he did after I left him."

"After you ran away."

Mallory—blunt as always. Which was probably why they got along so well.

"Yeah, Mal. After I ran away." No matter how close she was to them, Juliana had a hard time letting her friends know exactly how much Connor affected her. "Can we stop this topic now?"

He was constantly in her thoughts, and although she wasn't one to obsess over mistakes she'd made, she couldn't help but wonder what might have happened. What if she'd stayed long enough to discover if he wanted more from her than a one-night stand? If she was totally honest with herself, she'd have to admit she *had* run away like some frightened child from her own feelings.

It wasn't often she let men reach inside her deeply enough to stir her tender emotions. Sure, she might feel compassion for her students and love for her friends, but to let a man touch her heart?

Unthinkable.

Her ex-husband had been an exception, and she'd paid a high price for that error in judgment. She'd fallen in love with a selfish, immature man whom she'd thought was everything she'd ever wanted.

Then she'd grown up.

He hadn't.

Seeing him at least once a week—in the teachers' lounge, at the copy machine, at staff meetings—had become more bearable. But she still hated the constant reminder of her stupid choice to marry someone because he was good looking and made her body sing. She never should've allowed those good traits to conceal his less desirable ones. His excessive drinking. His putting himself before anyone else, especially her. His verbal abuse. A handsome face and fantastic sex hadn't been enough to make a good marriage. Not even close. At least she'd had the smarts to walk away pretty damned fast.

Perhaps that was what scared her the most about Connor Wilson. He was a man she could easily make another mistake with by taking him into her heart. He'd be an even worse error because he was better looking than her ex and had made her experience a depth of passion she hadn't known existed. With him she'd felt free with her body in a way she could easily learn to crave.

Hell, she already did. Her dreams were filled with him. Her fantasies were of no one else. He was as bad as any addiction, and she intended to fight it. She wasn't tumbling into another relationship with the wrong guy. Changing careers was risky enough. She wasn't about to fuck up her personal life as well.

Besides, she had no idea where he was or how to find him.

"Have you seen him since then?" Bethany asked in that intuitive way of hers.

Juliana shook her head. "Let's talk about Kelley Realty."

"Not a very subtle segue there, Jules," Mallory said with a grin. "In other words, you don't want to talk about him."

"Exactly."

"Then how about we talk about money?" Danielle suggested. "You think you can go a whole year off without a paycheck?"

"Oh, I intend to earn lots of paychecks," Juliana replied. "One at each house I close."

"I hope you make a million bucks, but..." Bethany took a moment of thoughtful reflection before continuing, "what happens if you can't make a sale? Don't you have a mortgage? Car payments?"

"Where did all the eternal optimism go, Beth?" Juliana teased.

"Even I have to face reality sometimes," she tossed back.

"Here's what I've got planned. The car's paid off. The mortgage, too. I refinanced several years ago and finished off the principal last winter. Everything else is manageable."

"Manageable when you're getting paid," Danielle pointed out. "But you won't be."

"I have my retirement savings."

"You're risking your retirement on this?" Bethany furrowed her brow. "That would scare the heck out of me."

Mallory let out a chuckle. "You know our Jules. Loves free-falling."

"Yeah, but this is free-falling without a parachute." Bethany shook her head. "Too scary."

"Relax," Juliana said. "I have a nice little savings account, too. I'll use it first. I've saved quite a bit over the years. I like shoes as much as the next girl, but I always buy clearance."

The Ladies laughed, so at least the mood was lightening. If she was going to do this, she needed them in her corner.

"I really don't have that many expenses. Food, electric. Shit, I don't even have cable or satellite TV."

"Seriously?" Danielle gave a little shudder. "How can you stand it?"

Juliana shrugged. "I'd rather listen to music and read. And e-books are mucho cheap. I can get by on very little for a while, at least long enough to see if I can make Kelley Realty work. If it doesn't"—she shrugged—"well, then I guess I can always come back here. Might have to tuck my tail between my legs and admit defeat, but I have that safety net."

When her three friends all nodded, Juliana smiled, not surprised to feel relief sweep over her. If she was going to get this plane off the ground, she'd need their full help and support.

"We're with you," Mallory said. "Let's make this work."

* * *

The weeks had flown faster than any she'd ever known. For the last month, she'd taken every online real estate course she could to get the rest of the instruction hours she needed to get her license. The final exam had ended and the ink on the new license was barely dried, but she was making her move.

Juliana stood at the doorway of what had been her classroom, getting ready to walk away for what might be the last time.

She'd been granted her year's leave of absence for personal reasons by the school board, but somehow she knew she'd never be back. This part of her life was ending.

For good.

After making a couple of trips to her car with boxes of her things she couldn't leave behind, she came back to grab one last box and bid Douglas High School a fond farewell.

The room was a lot different from when she'd arrived. It had been so stark, walls painted in the typical "school beige." An empty teacher's desk and a few traditional student desks but not much else. She'd had to fight for a padded area that had been necessary for some of her out-of-control students. The attached bathroom had been an even harder battle, but it was another she'd won. The walls now held murals of letters and numbers painted by art students. There was even a row of older computers her students could use whenever they wanted.

The place was finally a proper special education area. The cabinets were filled with tactile activities, many of which she'd paid for herself but was leaving behind. What would she need them for? Real estate agents didn't play with wooden puzzles or foam shapes or coloring books.

A real estate agent. Was that what she was now?

So much of her identity had been tied to being a teacher. Each time she'd introduced herself to someone, that was how she defined who she was.

I'm Juliana Kelley. I teach special ed.

Would she be able to find the strength to do this? She'd always been the strong one, especially among the Ladies Who Lunch. Mallory was the wise one. Bethany the enthusiastic one. Danielle the grounded one. But Juliana had been the backbone—the one who held them all together.

She'd planned their trips. Encouraged them in their goals. Destroyed their enemies.

A laugh slipped out at that notion. How many loser guys had she rebuffed on their nights out? How often had she been the one to tell Beth or Dani that the man she had her eye on wasn't as perfect as her young brain might have believed?

How could she handle not seeing them every day?

Tears blurred her vision, but she refused to let a single one fall. This choice was the right one. She knew it, deep in her heart. She had to do this. Now was the moment.

A hand settled on her shoulder. "Hey, Jules." Mallory had come to help her through this.

"Hey."

"Sad?"

"A little. I did good work here."

"Damn right, you did." Mallory's hand fell away. "Need any help carrying stuff outside?"

Juliana nodded at the small box in her hands. "Last of it's in here. Hard to believe I'm really going." She sniffed hard, willing herself not to cry.

This change was for the best, for her and for her students. These kids deserved a teacher who could give them every bit of her time and energy.

"I'm doing the right thing."

If only saying the words could make them true.

"I sure think so." Mallory's authoritarian tone helped soothe Juliana's rapidly fraying nerves.

"Then it's time to go."

"The Ladies are taking you out tonight. We've got a table reserved at Santiago's."

"You don't have to do that."

"Didn't say we had to, did I?" Mallory took the box from Juliana's hands. "Let's go."

One last look, and Juliana walked away from her old life.

Chapter Eight

Juliana knocked on the door before smoothing down her skirt, nervously trying to remove any wrinkles. She wanted to look her best, hoping to convince the owners of the home to list with her instead of selling the home themselves.

The Ladies and Ben had helped her search through for-sale-by-owner listings to select a few promising ones for her to call. Three calls yielded three appointments, which came as a big surprise. As she spoke to each owner, her hopes rose.

Mallory and Ben were right—people in this town really didn't like Max Schumm. They'd chosen to fizbo instead of listing with him or another firm. Each was willing to listen to her pitch, so she'd set up times to meet with them that afternoon.

House one belonged to George and Sheila Ryan, an older couple ready to sell their Illinois home and become residents of a Florida retirement community.

The door opened, revealing a man with gray hair, enough wrinkles to be wise, and a friendly face.

Giving him her most confident smile, Juliana held out her hand. "Hi. I'm Juliana Kelley. You must be Mr. Ryan."

He shook her hand then held the door open wider. "Come on in, young lady. Call me George. Please."

The place was an antiquer's dream. Most of the furniture had to be older than she was. A lot older. If they agreed to list with her, she'd offer them a ton of suggestions on staging the place, the first being to sell or store some of the rather overcrowded furnishings. But other than having too much clutter—little wonder because they'd owned the place since they'd built it when Kennedy was in office—it had loads of potential. Gorgeous hardwood floors. Newer replacement windows. A nice, large corner lot. The walls even appeared freshly painted in neutral tones—a good choice to please potential buyers.

"Thanks so much for agreeing to speak with me." She opened her planner and pulled out one of her business cards Ben had made for her using Amber's template for Carpenter Contracting. He'd switched out the hammer-and-screwdriver logo for a simple green shamrock and changed all the personal info to fit her. While it might have been a hasty job, it was good enough for her to use for now. Soon she'd have enough cash flow to order some from a print shop and could perhaps take the time to design something more flashy.

George took the card and squinted at it.

His wife came in from the kitchen, holding a pair of reading glasses. She passed them to her husband and smiled at Juliana. "Hi. I'm Sheila."

"Hi, Sheila. A pleasure to meet you."

"Can I get you some tea?"

"No, thank you."

After donning the glasses and perusing Juliana's card, he passed it to his wife. "So you think you can sell our house better than we can?"

Taking a deep breath, Juliana launched into the pitch she'd worked up and then practiced repeatedly with the Ladies. She outlined all the things a good Realtor could do to help them, from finding the right list price to staging to screening the people she'd allow into their home. Judging from the way Sheila kept nodding along with every point Juliana made, she was already on her side. George merely stared at her, stroking his chin with his thumb and index finger as though giving all she proposed great consideration.

It was a good start.

A knock at the door interrupted a question he'd only begun to ask.

"Excuse me." He went to the front door and peeked out one of the three small oval windows near eye level. Then he opened the door.

"Mr. Ryan? Hi. I believe we had an appointment."

Juliana froze, the familiar baritone washing over her in relentless waves. Her heart leapt in her chest, pounding a rough rhythm that made her light-headed.

No. No way.

She turned to find Connor Wilson standing on the front porch.

Her mind split, heading two directions. On one hand she was thrilled to see him again. On the other, she wished he'd never shown up. There was no question why he was here—he'd also decided to try getting his own customers among the fizbos. She'd never dreamed she'd be competing with him for listings. Naïve on her part considering she'd met him at Max's seminar.

Where had he been the last few weeks? She'd found herself searching each male face she passed at the grocery or the mall for his handsome visage. It was as though he'd dropped off the face of the planet after their night together, or at least from Cloverleaf. Not that she knew what she'd do if she had found him. Explain, she supposed.

She'd been the one to run away from her own passion and the feelings he'd inspired. With a note of self-disgust, she realized that had she found him she'd probably have dragged him right back into bed.

She was thirty-five, for shit's sake! She shouldn't be drowning in some adolescent hormonal surge, but that was exactly how Connor affected her. Desire ensnared her in talons as sharp as a raptor's, and she couldn't seem to break free.

His interruption was ill-timed. After what they'd shared, she simply couldn't see herself fighting him for the Ryans' business. Even if she could gird her loins and tangle with him, she had no idea who would win. Did he have experience selling real estate? Could he offer them some proof that he knew exactly what he was doing and had been successful at it?

She'd judged him to be close to her age, which meant he'd been doing *something* to earn a living. It was hard to imagine someone else taking a plunge into a brand-new career in his thirties. Sure, she was contemplating doing a one-eighty-degree turn. But was he considering taking the same kind of bold move? And if he was, what had prompted the change? A stalled-out career? A divorce?

God, she knew next to nothing about this man, a man she'd slept with, and she was clueless as to his job, motivation, or plans for the future.

"You must be Connor Wilson. Come in, come in." George shut the door behind Connor, who obviously still hadn't noticed her, probably because he was so focused on George.

"I'm so happy you agreed to meet with me. I hope I can convince you that trying to sell your home yourself can be risky."

"I already explained those risks to them." Juliana folded her arms under her breasts and leveled a hard stare at him while she drummed her fingers on her on her elbow.

Connor whirled to face her, mouth open and eyes wide. "Red?"

"Red? What a cute nickname," Sheila said, clasping her hands. "Especially because she has such pretty hair."

It took all of Juliana's self-control not to roll her eyes. Sheila was right—it was a cute nickname. Except it wasn't hers. Despite her hair, no one had ever called her Red. Not even her best friends. Only Jules. Since she didn't want to offend potential new clients, she held her tongue. The last thing she wanted to do was get into a squabble with Connor over something that petty. There were bigger things to worry about. Besides, she rather liked the name. He was the only one to use it, which somehow made it special. Endearing.

Still, she went for the kill. This was, after all, business. Her whole life was at stake, and she needed this listing. "I was just explaining to George and Sheila how dangerous it could be to let strangers into their home."

Connor nodded, his face fixed on hers. "She's right. You never know when they're not really interested in buying. They might just be giving your place a good look and making plans to come back later and rob you."

She wasn't about to let him score any points with the Ryans. "Some might even steal from your jewelry box or"—she nodded at a jar full of coins near the front door—"take your money. You really need a good Realtor to watch out for you. Let me help you through the process of selling your home. This isn't something you want to do on your own."

Sheila kept shifting her gaze between Juliana and Connor, clearly torn on who to choose. George, on the other hand, kept staring at Connor. Then Sheila must have noticed where her husband directed his attention, because she sidled up closer to Connor, all but turning her back on Juliana.

She was losing them.

Don't panic!

"So, could you give me a quick tour?" Juliana asked. "I can give you some tips of things you can do to stage this place and make it more attractive to potential buyers."

"I don't know," George hedged. "Perhaps Connor here might want to see the house first."

No, she wasn't losing them.

She'd already lost them.

Damn it.

"He seems like a very professional young man," Sheila added.

It wasn't what she said as much as the confident tone in which she said it that clicked. Juliana finally understood the problem—they were going to be more comfortable with a guy working on the listing.

Small-town Illinois. Forever stuck in the 1950s.

Catching Connor's sympathetic gaze, she almost excused herself and bolted for the door. She would pause long enough to give him a whack upside the head for interfering. Why did he have to show up and ruin things?

She should go ahead and leave. The Ryans wanted Connor. He was going to get the listing for…

For whom?

Although he was trying to get this listing, she didn't know what firm he worked for. He wasn't wearing a hideous blue blazer. He hadn't mentioned representing any firm. He hadn't even given George a business card.

Could Connor be flying solo, too?

A brilliant idea quickly bubbled to the surface, although she had no idea whether it would work. A little far-fetched, but at this point what did she have to lose? The listing was already going to Connor. Why shouldn't she try to snatch back a part of it for herself?

Juliana gambled her future on him understanding what she was about to do—not only understanding but agreeing. Using her best confident tone, she launched her new plan. "Didn't I tell you? No, it appears I didn't. No wonder you're both looking so confused." She took a few steps to get nearer to Connor and then flashed the clients a confident smile. "Goodness, I should have told you when I first got here. Mr. Wilson is my partner."

"Partner?" George glanced down at the business card he still held. "He's your partner? This only has your name on it. Juliana Kelley. Kelley Realty."

"I can explain that," she insisted, scrambling for a reason that didn't sound like the lie it would be.

"Well, then." Connor cocked his head, the only sign he even heard what she'd said. The guy had a poker face that could win every pot. "Why don't you go ahead and explain away?"

Thankfully, she heard no anger in his tone. If she judged it correctly, he was amused.

She tried not to stammer, a problem she tended to develop whenever anxiety got the better of her. "Mr. Wilson and I just formed the partnership yesterday. I haven't had time to print up new business cards."

George still appeared skeptical. "He's with Kelley Realty?"

"It's *Wilson*-Kelley Realty," Connor corrected. His eyes dared her to contradict him.

So she did. "Actually, it's Kelley-Wilson Realty. We agreed on it back when we formed the partnership at the Ramada."

"Sounds a little fishy to me." George rubbed the back of his neck.

"Nothing fishy, George. Honestly," Connor reassured. "We're not accustomed to working with each other yet. Too used to being single rather than part of a duo."

Good God, he was going along with the ruse.

Or was it a ruse?

Maybe this could really work.

Only in a romance novel…

But she was willing to give it a try.

"We've never had to check with each other before visits like this before," she said.

"We got our signals crossed," he added. "That's all."

"Well, then…" George smiled at him then at her. "If he's with you…"

She gave him a decisive nod. "Oh, yes, sir. He sure is."

He thrust a hand out to Connor. "Then you two can sell our house for us."

* * *

Connor shook George Ryan's hand, although he wasn't quite sure whether he should be grateful to Juliana or pissed at her.

What in the hell was going through her mind to dream up a partnership and spring it on him like a trap? He didn't know anything about her. Sure, they'd had sex. But the rest of her life remained a complete mystery. To agree to work with her was foolhardy at best, a devastating mistake at worst.

The woman had fled his bed as if what they'd shared was tawdry. His ego would have been flattened if she hadn't been so vocal about her pleasure in what they'd shared. Something else had set her running; perhaps she'd sensed the depth of his feelings. But wasn't it usually the guy who tried to escape something before it grew too serious?

He was supposed to be launching his own enterprise, had spent the better part of a month moving and then fixing up his own house and office to get ready for the launch of Wilson Realty. Even though it was late June, the renovation was still in the nightmare stage. Now that he was entrenched and starting to search for listings, it was time to find a good contractor and make the place something more than merely functional.

This house should've been his first listing in Cloverleaf, one that would lead to another and another until he found himself challenging Max Schumm as the number one Realtor in this town and the surrounding counties.

The Ryans' place was money in the bank, a vintage home with enough restorations to make it marketable. Some staging and it would sell quickly. One short phone conversation with George had led to an appointment that seemed like a sure thing. Connor's traveling office—his laptop and portable printer—came along with him so he could produce the contracts for the couple to sign just as soon as he got their approval to list the home.

George was an old-fashioned kind of guy who clearly wanted to work with a man. Connor had figured that out from the phone conversation alone. What came as a shock was that Juliana had seen the way the wind was blowing so quickly. Not only that, but she came up with a brilliant idea to save at least some of the pie for herself, even it cost him part of his potential commission.

He'd never known another Realtor as fast on her feet.

Except me.

One of the reasons he'd made so much money back in Indianapolis was because he figured things out swiftly and adapted easily. The competition was plentiful but a bit dismal in talent. His own innate ability to read people and tailor what he offered them to fit their needs had helped him earn top sales awards year after year.

Until...

A deep breath brought his thoughts back from the brink. He wasn't going to wallow in regrets and recriminations. The past was the past and needed to stay that way. Cloverleaf was a new beginning.

It appeared as if he was going to be creating that new beginning with Juliana Kelley as his partner. But would that be for only this one listing? Or did she want more?

Do I?

Maybe having her close would bring him luck, his own personal four-leaf clover. The one night they'd shared had been nothing short of paradise. What would it be like working with her every day?

Connor took a leap of faith, figuring it would all shake out in the end. "I'll have the contracts ready for you as soon as I can print them, George."

Chapter Nine

Connor followed her to her car, a rather ancient Accord. "You're gonna need an SUV now." He waited for her to open the passenger door and toss her enormous purse inside.

"Why? This car is fine. It's paid for. That's all that really matters to me."

"Then lease one. Trust me on this, you're gonna be driving clients around and want them comfortable and thinking you're successful. Plus you'll want a mini-office with you all the time."

"A mini-office? In my car?"

"In your *SUV.* Things happen so damned fast in this business you've got to be able to respond to e-mails, look up information, and respond in only a few minutes. Not to mention scanning, printing, and sending back contracts. I even have a wireless hotspot card." He nodded at his black Escalade. "It's not that much if you lease. I actually took over a lease to get this one dirt cheap. Only way I could ever afford a Caddy."

"I'm impressed," Juliana said.

"Good. I *should* impress my new partner. Now I'm going to go and make some adjustments to my—to *our*—information and print out the contracts for the Ryans. It'll only take me a few minutes."

"So you have been a real estate agent before. I wondered about that, although the way Max Schumm was acting it was hard to tell for sure."

"I was rather hoping you'd wonder about a lot more than my employment history."

"Oh, I have. Trust me. I have."

He tried to read her expression and found wariness. "I admire you for jumping in there and saving this listing, Red, but are you thinking about really being part of a partnership? You'd planned solo. Like me. Right?"

She shrugged. "I suppose. Look, I'm sorry I sprung it on you like that. I just, George was going to go with you and—"

He held up his hand to cut her off. "He was. You're smart enough to have seen it and snatched back some of the commission for yourself. Quick thinking."

"Thanks." Lips drawn tight, she stared at him for a few moments that stretched to seem interminable.

Connor didn't understand why he was willing to change all his plans—his life—so quickly. He simply...was. He wanted her agreement, and he wanted it now.

More than that.

He wanted *her.*

This listing would be not only lucrative but enjoyable. The thrill was back, and he gave Juliana credit for that. Besides, having a partner could benefit him in a lot of ways, best of all accountability. He'd work hard because her future was going to be at stake, too.

"Do you think we could?" she asked.

"Could? Could what? Be partners for more than this listing?"

She nodded.

"You're willing to try, right?"

"I am."

"Then what have we got to lose?"

His cell phone chose that loaded moment to ring. The tune, "Lean on Me," was one he could never ignore. "Excuse me. I have to take this," he said as he popped his cell off his belt.

Turning his back and hoping Juliana wouldn't consider it too rude, he answered. "Hey, gorgeous." His pat phrase made him wince. What would Juliana think?

"Just wanted to see how that first step felt." Tracy Barrett's voice was, as always, a comfort. Nothing like hearing from your best friend and number-one cheerleader to perk a guy up.

"It felt great."

"You got the listing?"

"Yes." He chuckled. "And no."

"That was cryptic. Care to elaborate or do you love leaving me guessing? My bet's on you now representing those owners." The confidence in her voice meant more to him than she could ever know. But that was Tracy. She'd nursed him through his darkest hours, from his parents' deaths to his hitting rock bottom. Then she'd made him get right up, dust himself off, and start all over again. They couldn't be closer if she was his biological sister.

"You're right. As usual. I got the listing, but... I'm sharing it."

"Sharing? You're just playing with me now, and I don't like it. I want the whole story. Spit it out."

He chuckled. She'd never let him get away with anything but the absolute truth. "I might've acquired a partner." A quick glance over his shoulder made him wince again.

Juliana frowned so fiercely the look sent shivers up his spine, and he didn't think that was a good way to start out a new enterprise.

"Look, Tracy, I gotta go. Kinda busy. Can I call you back later?"

"It's a *she*, isn't it?"

"Jealous?"

"She's there with you right now, isn't she?"

"Yeah. It's making things a bit…awkward."

She chuckled. "Why? I thought she was your partner, not your—Oh, God. You're not dating her, are you?"

"Call you back soon?"

"You are! Bad enough you're diving into a new business, but a new relationship, too? Can you handle all that stress?"

"Trace, not now. Okay?"

"Connor, be careful. You're putting a lot of pressure on yourself."

"I know. I know," he insisted. "Tackle things one at a time and do my best. I remember. Call you later. Bye."

"Bye."

Connor clipped the cell back on his belt. "Sorry."

"Sure you are." Juliana tossed him an inelegant snort. "This was a bad idea. I'm sorry I trapped you like that. It wasn't fair. You obviously didn't want a partner. After what you just told your girlfriend, I get it. I do."

Her voice held a barely restrained fury. While the jealousy might be flattering, he didn't want her angry with him from the get-go, especially when she'd jumped to all the wrong conclusions. "That was just a friend."

She gave him a dismissive wave of her hand, but he could tell from her pinched expression she was hurting. "Whatever. This partnership thing isn't a good idea anyway."

He crossed his arms over his chest and leaned his ass against her Accord. After her bold suggestion, she was balking.

But why?

Because he'd been talking to another woman?

Back inside the Ryans' house, he'd seen the Juliana who'd ensnared him so completely that night in the bar. Confident. Daring. Downright brash. Those qualities were why he'd fallen for her immediately, more deeply than he could've imagined. She haunted his dreams and filled his thoughts, making him ache for her. No other woman had gotten to him in such an overwhelming way.

Why was he trying to get into a partnership with her? Tracy was right. It was a stupid, stupid thing to do.

First, he'd never be able to keep his hands off her. As it was, if she so much as winked at him, he'd be tossing her in his car, driving her to his desperately-in-need-of-repair home, and making love to her. How could he work with her and not lose his mind?

Second, he was risking what little was left of his nest egg to give himself this new start. So far, he'd handled that stress well, most of that strength and confidence funneled to him by Tracy. He needed to find his own strength.

And finally, if things didn't go smoothly, he'd have to bear the guilt of ruining not only his own future but Juliana's.

All that was more than enough to drive a man to drink.

But Connor wanted this partnership anyway. Despite the temptation of his redheaded Siren, he'd resist her call because she had what it took to be a good real estate agent. He'd listened to every word she'd said to the Ryans, and she'd spoken like a seasoned professional. Having trained other agents for his firm back in Indianapolis, he had a great eye for seeing potentials who "had it" and who didn't.

Juliana had it. *All* of it. She was the genuine article in an irresistible package. She'd have clients eating out of her hands. And to have two sets of eyes watching the books, keeping track of profit and outlay?

Even better.

"You suddenly think us working together is a bad idea?" he asked. "Why? What made you change your mind?" He tried to keep his voice calm and not let her know how panicked he was at losing this opportunity.

Some niggling part of his mind told him this woman would be the best thing that ever happened to him. He wanted to see exactly where this path would lead.

"I—I shouldn't have done that," she replied.

"Done what?"

"Painted you into a corner. It wasn't fair and—"

Connor wouldn't let her back out now. "First of all, I'm a salesman, have been all my life. I know every single trick you can play in this game. If I didn't want to do this, I would've put you in your place fast enough to make your head spin."

She arched an eyebrow, her green eyes easily showing her relief. "You'd do that in front of the Ryans?"

"In a heartbeat."

* * *

Juliana had to stop herself from letting out a whoosh of breath. Connor wasn't angry. Judging from what he'd said, he was every bit as ready to make this partnership work as she was.

Why was she risking everything she'd planned for him? Her new firm, her savings, her fresh start.

God help her, she wasn't sure. All she knew was that she wanted this, and she wanted it badly.

If only she could pretend she hadn't heard that phone call, the one from his girlfriend.

Don't jump to conclusions.

She scoffed at her own naïveté.

Right. He called everyone who phoned him "gorgeous." The way he'd gotten her off the phone was nothing short of "I'm with someone I slept with, and I don't want her to know about you or vice-versa."

"What's so funny?" he asked, easing his stance by dropping his arms.

"Me."

"Why?"

"Because I might've just made the best career move of my life. Or the worst." She shifted her gaze from the house to his face. Then she pushed away from the car and turned to face him. "So which was it, Connor? Is starting a partnership with you the best thing I could've done or the worst?"

When he reached for her hand, she tucked both of them under her armpits like a simpering coward. But she was afraid. Very afraid. If he touched her, she had no idea what she'd do or how she'd react. She wanted to touch him. Everywhere. The images of the night they'd spent together floated through her thoughts, making heat rush through her veins.

His face became an expressionless mask. "I can't make that decision for you, Red. Only you can figure out if you want to do this or not." He sighed. "Here's the deal…If you want to try to make this work, we might just do pretty damn well. I have lots of ideas, and I'm good at what I do. Loads of experience and a little inside information that I'd be willing to share with my partner and no one else."

That enigmatic comment got her attention. "Inside information? About what?"

"Cloverleaf."

Her curiosity rose to a fever pitch. "Profitable information?"

"Oh yeah. So are you in?" he asked.

"You really think we can work together?"

"I do. Max Schumm doesn't have the stranglehold over this town and the surrounding counties that he thinks he does. He's a guy who got lucky and had very little competition. You and me working together? We could take him down. He'll never even know what hit him."

"And the other firms?"

"Even easier pickings. They only have a few agents, most of who couldn't cut it in bigger markets and got sent out here to the boonies."

"You really have done your research, haven't you?"

"Absolutely. And I have more to share. A lot more. But only if we're doing this together." He held out his hand.

Juliana reluctantly shook it. She still wasn't entirely sure she hadn't just screwed up her life, but for now, she'd be content simply to learn from someone with so much experience. "Kelley-Wilson Realty it is."

His chuckle helped her relax. "How about we discuss the order of the names over dinner?"

"Why wait? I've got time now and—"

"I want to iron out all this someplace where we're both relaxed. Let me work on the Ryan contract, get that signed, and then I'll pick you up for dinner. My treat."

"Dutch treat. It's a business expense." She fished out a business card and handed it to him. "Guess we'll need some new cards, huh?"

"Guess so. Is this your address?"

She nodded. "Pick me up around six?"

"It's a date."

"Oh no. No dating. A business dinner. Just two partners."

His grin should have put her on edge. But it didn't. "We'll see."

Since the question was going to drive her crazy before evening got there, Juliana let it out. "You don't have a girlfriend?"

"No, Red. I don't have a girlfriend."

Chapter Ten

Hope you like Italian." Juliana waited while the maître d' pulled out her chair, then she sat as Connor took the seat across the small table.

"Not much else to choose from," he said with a shrug.

"Yeah, well, small towns only have a few good places to eat."

His grin was mysterious.

Damn, but that dimple.

"That'll be changing," he said, still grinning.

She liked the confidence almost as much as she hated the confusion. "It will? Is that part of your inside information?"

"It is."

It was a struggle to be patient as the waiter took their orders and brought their drinks. Since Connor was driving, she'd decided to go ahead and have some wine. As tightly as she was wound, she'd snap if she didn't have something to soothe her. A nice white wine was the answer to her prayer.

Sipping her drink, she stared at him over the rim of her wineglass. Connor served them each a good portion of salad from the big bowl, even taking the time to set equal amounts of every-thing from onion slices to croutons on each plate.

Onions. No good night kiss?

That would be damned disappointing.

But partners shouldn't kiss good night. Should they?

"Is that indicative of this new partnership?" she asked, hoping he knew teasing when he heard it.

"What?"

"The salad. You portioned it out almost perfectly. Each serving's equal. Is that what our partnership is going to be like?"

"I sure hope so." He handed her one of the plates and set the other in front of himself. "Although I have to be honest, I've never been in a partnership before."

"Not even a marriage?" She hadn't meant to ask. The question just fell right out of her mouth.

Liar.

"Not even a marriage." He ate his salad with enough gusto to make her wonder if it had been a while since he'd eaten.

She, on the other hand, picked at hers.

"Don't like the romaine?" he asked. "I can order an appetizer instead. Calamari? Or can't they get that here?" Connor picked up the basket of bread. "Want a roll?"

What she wanted was another glass of wine. Or two. Or Patrón. "No, thanks. The salad's fine. Just not very hungry."

Waiting patiently as he ate his salad and a couple of rolls, Juliana tried to decide which of the thousands of questions fly-ing around her mind to ask first. Despite the scary proposition of stepping into this partnership arrangement, she was more obsessed with who this Tracy was and what she was to Connor.

"Hey, gorgeous."

Instead of letting her adolescent infatuation ruin this new

venture, she fired her first business-oriented question. "Do you have an office?"

"So we're really going to do this, Red?"

She cocked her head. "Do what? Talk about our partnership?"

"No. *Have* one."

"But I thought...after the Ryans..."

Connor's expression and tone were entirely business. "It's a risk. For both of us. I can sell houses by myself. You can, too. We can just split the Ryan listing and walk away."

Juliana let her exasperation show. "I thought we talked this all out."

"We've both had a little time to think. Didn't know if you'd changed your mind."

"I seldom do that. Too stubborn."

Here was her out, her escape hatch, if she wanted one. Yet not a thought of dissent or concern appeared.

She wanted this. With all her heart.

"Have *you* changed your mind?" Juliana asked, concerned perhaps his offer of an "out" was for him rather than her.

He gave his head a shake.

Releasing a relieved sigh wouldn't be very subtle, so she asked again, "Well, then do you have an office?"

"I will."

"So you don't yet. Where will this new office be?"

He set his empty salad plate aside. "My new house. I bought a ranch in Cumberland Hills on a short sale. Needs a lot of work, but I'll have a nice office with an outside entrance one day. At least I will as soon as I find a decent contractor."

"I already have one."

"A contractor?" His eyes seemed to sparkle a little more when he teased.

"Actually, yeah, but I meant an office. Mine's ready to go. Has an outside entrance, too. We could use it for now if you'd like."

He considered her proposition for a moment before nodding. "Since mine is good enough for me but not nearly good enough for clients yet, we can see if your place works. Wanna head there after dinner so I can see it for myself?"

Connor at her place. Exactly where would that get both of them except right back in bed?

If this was going to work, she needed to set some ground rules pretty damn fast. "Look, Connor, we should talk about what happened first. I didn't propose us working together so that our...connection at the Ramada could happen again."

"Oh really." He sarcastically dragged out the second word. "Then may I ask exactly why you did it? I mean, if you don't want anything to do with me romantically, why in the hell would you tell the Ryans we were partners?"

"I panicked. Okay? I could tell George Ryan wanted to work with a guy, and I thought I'd lost the listing." She fixed a hard stare. "You could've told them I was a liar. What I should be asking is why you agreed. Sure, I might have been a bit impulsive, but you could've pulled the plug on this immediately."

"I couldn't do that."

"Why not?" she asked. "You don't owe me anything. You could've walked out of there with that listing and not anchored to me."

"You're right."

If he kept answering without actually answering, her temper was going to explode. As it was, Juliana could barely keep from screaming at him. Nothing had been decided. Not really. This dinner was going nowhere fast as neither of them seemed to have the courage to say the things that needed to be said.

She took a deep breath and then let it all out. "You scared the shit out of me."

"I beg your pardon?"

"That night when we were together…I got scared. After what happened, I had to get out of there. You were more than I could handle."

"Funny. I thought you handled me quite well. Best sex of my life."

All she could do for a moment was blink. "It was?"

With a crooked smile, he nodded.

Despite the warm fuzzy feeling she got from his praise, she still needed to make him understand. "I wasn't ready for someone like you."

"You realize you're making absolutely no sense. Right?"

Since this was going to be one of the most difficult conversations of her life, she signaled the waiter for another wine.

"Getting blotto won't make things easier, Red." His mouth had dropped to a frown.

"Two glasses of wine isn't 'getting blotto.' Look…" She took the new glass and handed the waiter back the empty. Then she waited for some privacy before opening up. "We were good together. Damn good."

At least Connor smiled again. "Like I said, best sex of my life. Both times."

"That's what scared me." Sitting back, she wrapped her arms around her middle. Sure it was the universal body language of self-comfort and protection, but that's what she needed at that moment. Some comfort and protection. And some courage— even the false kind that came in a glass. "I'm divorced."

When he tried to interrupt, she stopped him with a shake of her head. "Let me get this all out. Please?"

He leaned back, sitting rather casually with an elbow crooked over the back of his chair, which helped relax her. "Fine. I'll be a good boy and listen."

"Thanks." Juliana launched into her story. "Like I said, I'm divorced. Got married right out of college, and I picked the absolute wrong guy. He was...abusive." As Connor started to sputter in what she assumed in anger, she held up a hand. "He didn't hit me. That, I would have dealt with pretty quick. It was more of a slow whittling away at my confidence. Plus he got mean when he drank. Thankfully, I figured out before too long that he wasn't worth any more of my time and cut him loose."

"Smart woman," he said with a nod. "I thought so from the first moment we spoke."

The compliment made her cheeks flush warm. "Um, thanks. Anyway, I promised myself I wouldn't do that again. I wouldn't fall head over heels for some guy and end up right back in the place where I lost me."

"That's what you think I'll be like? Shit, Red. You don't know anything about me, and you're already judging me."

"I'm not."

His nod was as definite as his words. "You most certainly are."

"I'm not. I'm judging *me*. I have terrible taste in men and—"

This time, he was the one to halt words. "Stop. Just stop. You're talking and talking and saying nothing. I'm tired of running around in circles." He leaned in closer and then waited.

Tentatively, Juliana put her hands on the table and copied his action, giving their discussion more privacy, more intimacy.

"Let me see if I can translate everything you said, okay?" Connor asked.

"Go for it." Since she wasn't even sure what she was babbling about any longer, perhaps he could figure out what she was trying to say.

"Here goes. You had an ex who treated you like garbage. Didn't smack you around, but he was psychologically abusive. Right so far?"

She nodded.

"You decided being single's the best way to live. You've been that way since your divorce, which means you're really used to doing things alone, making your own decisions, planning everything without answering to anyone else."

"Keep going."

"Then we met. We connected in a way that frightened you."

"Wow. You're a man of many talents."

He quirked an ebony brow.

"You're a real estate salesman *and* a psychiatrist."

* * *

Connor let the sarcasm slide, mostly because he enjoyed using it as much as she seemed to. While he might not be trained in psychology, being a salesman meant he knew people very, very well. "Now you're worried if you let me in, even just a little, that I'll end up being like your ex."

"Not exactly. But…" Her shoulders rose and fell in a delicate shrug.

Since Juliana had found the guts to be honest, he gave her equal measure. "Would it help you to know I'm terrified, too?"

Her eyes widened. "You are?"

He resisted the urge to roll his eyes. "I am. You scared the shit outta me. I don't need a relationship right now. Maybe ever. I've got enough on my plate. I'm trying to set up a new business and keep from...Look, you scared me because what happened between us wasn't just sex. At least not to me. It was like we had a connection. Something pretty special."

"Very special."

"Then the question is, what do we do about it now that we're partners?"

Having given that dilemma a lot of thought from the moment the Ryans' signatures were drying on the contracts, Connor was no closer to an answer. From the way Juliana kept giving her head small shakes, she had nothing to offer, either.

The waiter delivered their dinners, and instead of addressing the weighty question, they ate in relative silence. The only true conversation was about what a great find the Ryans' house was and the things they both thought would help with staging. Things between them were light and easy until the waiter put the little black folder with the check on the table.

Connor snatched it up and tugged his wallet from his jacket pocket.

Juliana plucked her wallet from her purse, pulled out a credit card, and held it up between two fingers. "We agreed to pay for our own."

The gentleman in him didn't want to give in. He slid some bills into the folder. "How about I get it this once?"

"Nope. Rule number one for our partnership, that's exactly what we are. Partners. Each pulls his or her weight."

When the waiter came over, she handed him her card. "Please put my bill on this."

No way she'll give in. He might not know her too well yet, but the determined expression on her face said it all. She'd already admitted to a stubborn streak, and she was giving him a peek at it now.

Connor picked up one of the twenties and put it back in his wallet. "Anything the lady wants."

Twenty minutes later, Connor drove through Juliana's neighborhood, ready to take a look at what might be his new office space. The house was in a nice neighborhood, one well established enough there wouldn't be a Homeowners' Association. That would be a plus if they were going to run their office out of Juliana's house.

When he'd picked her up, Connor had given the place only a cursory inspection. He'd been much more interested in Juliana than her home. Then again, he hadn't known this would be his new office.

It was a nice redbrick ranch. Mature trees. Large lot. Her two-car garage was now the office of Wilson-Kelley—correction, Kelley-Wilson—Realty. He'd agreed to her choice of name since that was a small skirmish in what might end up being an epic war.

He was going to choose his battles carefully.

After he pulled his SUV into the driveway, he killed the engine. Although he'd intended to go around and open the door for her, she let herself out and met him at the entrance to the office, keys already in her hand.

"It's not perfect yet," she said as she opened the dead bolt. "But I think it'll work for us, especially if your place is still a mess."

"'Mess' is an understatement." He held the door after she opened it, waiting for her to step inside. Then he followed.

He only needed a quick glance around to know that despite what she'd said, the office *was* perfect. The walls were painted a pleasant, soft green, and the floors were a dark-stained laminate. The décor was limited to framed prints of the Chicago skyline and a large shamrock that had been painted on the farthest wall. Tasteful, but still a good representation of her personality.

There were two chairs and a coffee table in a waiting area. She'd even thought to leave out a few magazines. Behind a half wall that served as a formal division of the office space, two desks faced each other, although only one had a computer.

"Two desks?" Connor asked. "Were you expecting to have a partner?"

"Nah. Nothing like that. Bought them both in a used furniture sale at the school. Twenty-five bucks each. The chairs were only five. Figured it made the office look busier if people thought there were two agents."

So she was frugal, a good quality in a partner, especially when the money he had available to put into this venture was pretty skimpy. "Good thinking. I take it I get the one without the computer."

"Of course." She pulled out the chair and dropped her big purse on the seat. "I'm still waiting to hear that inside information, Connor. You made it all the way through dinner without showing me the ace you're hiding up your sleeve."

Connor went to his new desk, gave it a good look, and then took his seat. "Comfy."

"Glad you approve," she drawled as she leaned a hip against his desk. "Details now?"

He dropped his bomb. "Hudson County is about to get a new Barrett Foods factory."

"A what?"

"A new factory that produces a bunch of Barrett products—anything from Tempt Me candy bars to Skinny Minnie frozen meals. Rumor has it that it'll create a minimum of a couple thousand jobs in and around Cloverleaf."

"Holy shit." A slow smile spread over her face. "Houses will sell like hotcakes."

"See? I knew you were a smart lady."

"How did you find out about this? Isn't that like insider trading or something?" Juliana asked.

He couldn't help but smile when the tone of her question wasn't the least contrite. She was every bit as ready to make some money as he was. "It's not a stock or anything. Just land. Besides, the Barrett CEO hasn't made it a secret she's looking for someplace in the Midwest. Her main factories are on the coasts, and she's not a California or New York kind of girl. She wants to get back to her roots, which happen to be in Indiana."

"Why don't more people know about it?"

"She's had her people buying up farmland in small parcels with various names on the titles, but they all belong under the Barrett umbrella. She didn't want the media sticking their nose into things until she was sure she could get what she wants here."

She tilted her head, her ginger brows pulling closer together. "How do you know so much about all this?"

"Remember that woman who called me, the one who made you jealous? That was Tracy Barrett. CEO of Barrett Foods."

The smile she gave him could have knocked him down for the count. "God have mercy, Connor, we're gonna make a fortune."

"Bingo!"

* * *

Juliana had one nagging thought.

It's too good to be true.

She and Connor had information that put them in the driver's seat of real estate sales in all of Hudson County and the surrounding counties. Her head swam for a moment.

Then she sobered. "Once Barrett Foods makes the announcement, Max Schumm will catch up with us pretty quick."

"I forgot to tell you the best part."

His mischievous grin sent heat shooting straight to her core. If he ever figured out exactly how much he affected her, she was in a shitload of trouble. All he'd have to do is incline his head toward the house and wiggle his eyebrows, and she'd be grabbing his hand and dragging him right to the bedroom.

Swallowing hard, she kept her mind on business. "There's more?"

"Since Tracy and I are such good friends, she's going to start sending her executives directly to me to help them find homes before the factory's construction even begins. A few of them want to have custom homes built, so we need to investigate local builders."

Her heart jumped, slamming against her ribs hard enough to make her dizzy as the ramifications started to hit her, one after another. Barrett Foods would impact a whole lot more than her life. "One of my friends builds the most beautiful homes. We'll have to make sure we put him together with those customers."

"We'll have to go out tomorrow and let me look at a few, although I trust your judgment that he's good."

His faith in her only made her want him more. "How soon before buyers start coming?"

"Two weeks."

She nodded, her mind still reeling. "We've got so much to do before then. We need to get a good inventory of the available houses and check for lots. We need information from Tracy on where the factory is likely to be built." She snapped her fingers as another thought bubbled to the surface. "We should talk to Robert right away. He might have some houses already being—"

Connor's lips covered hers. She'd been so carried away with making plans, she hadn't even noticed him standing up.

Eyes wide-open, she stared at the face so close to hers. She wanted to kiss him back. But she didn't, although it took every ounce of her self-control not to.

He finally gave up, sighing against her lips and easing back. "I'm guessing we're not going to celebrate the way I want to."

"I want you," Juliana admitted.

"Then what's the problem?"

"For now, I really think we need to keep things business only."

"Why? We're good together."

"Too good."

"That's crazy. How could we be *too* good?"

She took a seat on the desk and patted the spot next to her.

Connor sighed again and sat down.

"Whenever you touch me," she said, "I kinda lose control."

"And that's a bad thing?"

"No. And yes. We're both crawling out on a shaky limb with this new firm, Connor. We need to give it a hundred percent of our attention. For now, at least. Let's get the business up and running, make sure things are going to work in this partnership, and then we can see if we want something more."

"Why can't we try being a couple *and* starting a new business?"

"Because you and I both know that would take more than either of us has to give. Besides, if we hadn't met the way we did, we wouldn't even be thinking about anything but business. At least not for a while. So for now let's make Kelley-Wilson Realty a priority."

"If I don't agree?"

"I'll be forced to pick either the relationship or the business. Right now, as much as I want you, I would choose to get my life in order first. If you don't want that, too, then we sell the Ryan house, shake hands, and part ways."

He let out a snort. "Like I'm gonna do that. Even if I hadn't shared what I knew about Barrett Foods with you, I really need this office space." He picked up her hand and wrapped his fingers around hers. "And I need you."

While she loved hearing that, she wasn't entirely sure she believed him. "You didn't even know me when you made your plans to come here. How could you possibly need me?"

"You've given me back something I lost, Juliana."

"Which is?"

"My drive. You make me want to succeed again. This partnership is exactly what I needed to help me get back to being Connor Wilson, the one who knows his job and handles his life like a grown-up." He turned his caress into a handshake. "So I'll agree to your terms. Business only. For *now*."

"Good." She punctuated the word with a curt nod.

Then why was she so disappointed?

Chapter Eleven

Connor," Juliana called across the office. She didn't look over her shoulder for fear of screwing up the form she had open on her computer. "Can you tell me again what I'm supposed to do to get the spreadsheet to total the square footage?"

"Right click, then 'update field.'" His voice came from the kitchenette.

Curious, she glanced up to see him pouring another cup of coffee, which made her smile. It was nice to work with someone as addicted to caffeine as she was. Prevented embarrassment over explaining why she was having yet more coffee. The last month, he'd matched her cup for cup. "At least make a fresh pot so I can have some when I'm done."

"Sure thing, Red." He obeyed with a wink.

She tried to ignore the flutter he set off inside her with his charming smile.

"Update field," she whispered, returning her attention to the form. "Update field." Once she got the information recorded, she could make the post active. Her first solo listing, from meeting the homeowner to getting the listing to putting the information online. If only the stupid computer would cooperate. It had a habit of messing up anything she worked on, and she'd threatened on more than one occasion to toss it in the trash. If only she could afford something better, something more up-to-date.

Not now. Not yet. But soon.

Juliana tried again, frustrated with the spreadsheet. As a teacher she'd used a bunch of different programs, but none of them were this kind of spreadsheet, not even the electronic gradebook. She'd let Connor handle all the computer work, watching and learning.

Evidently she hadn't learned enough.

A low growl rumbled in her chest when she did as he'd said—again—to try to get the square footage to calculate. "Dumb-ass computer," she muttered, fearing it was more user error than a software problem.

She knew Connor was behind her before his hand covered hers, guiding her mouse as his warm breath brushed the back of her neck. Although she couldn't swear to it, she was pretty sure he rubbed his nose in her upswept hair.

"Here. *Right* click. See that 'update field'?" His voice, so close to her ear, made her close her eyes and long for things she couldn't have as shivers raced over her skin.

The last month had been a dichotomy—paradise and torture.

The work was paradise, and she looked forward to opening the office every morning. Connor had even begun to show up before official hours with a couple of bagels or breakfast sandwiches that they'd eat at her kitchen table. He evidently hated cooking as much as she did. They'd share breakfast as they chugged coffee and talked about their appointments for the day.

He had a habit of sitting close to her, seeming to use every opportunity to touch her. A brush of his palm over her hand.

Fingers tickling her knee. Quick hugs that seemed to last a little longer each time he caught her in his arms.

Had she been a stronger woman, she might have resisted. But Juliana couldn't. She craved his touch and often had to steel her nerves to keep from taking their shared, stolen caresses to a higher level.

The morning ritual continued when they went into the office. Connor had found a great smartphone app that allowed them to synchronize their calendars as they ate breakfast, so all the data was entered before they slipped out to the office. Once there, they were totally business. No heated glances. No sexual undertones. Nothing to indicate they shared any kind of attraction.

That was the "torture."

Whenever she wasn't occupied in sales and listings, her thoughts were consumed with the night they'd shared. They'd been so good together in bed, and the sex had been...

No. It was more than sex.

Juliana had to face that revelation and deal with it. One day. Connor meant so much more to her than a great lover. One day, she would have to process what that meant for their future and the future of Kelley-Wilson Realty.

Eventually.

"It's easier if you open your eyes," he teased.

"Sorry."

He guided her through the process, helping her with only a few things before lifting his hand. Then he started rubbing her shoulders. "You're full of knots."

His magical fingers found stiff and sore places down her neck and spine before fanning out across her shoulders then slipping back up her neck. "That feels wonderful. You should be a masseur."

"Just another of my many talents."

Before she could say another word, his lips pressed against the pulse point of her neck, making her hiss in a breath. Her first inclination was to scold him. They'd agreed to keep things strictly business, but after a month of denying herself and trying to be content with simple touches, she just couldn't resist. Truth was she craved his touch, his kiss. All of him.

She tilted her head to allow him more room to play.

"Oh, Red." Connor nibbled on her earlobe, tugging gently with his teeth. "You're a temptation that's too hard to resist." He followed the shell of her ear with his tongue, sending heat pooling between her thighs.

"Connor, don't—"

"Don't?" He stuck his tongue in her ear at the same time his hand slid over her shoulder to cup her breast. "Don't what?"

Juliana was torn. Her mind screamed to keep her distance. This business was too important to risk on an office romance. Her future, and his, depended on the success of their firm.

But her body refused to listen. "Don't...stop."

He spun her chair around, fell to his knees, and cupped her face in his hands. Then he brushed his lips over hers. Once. Twice.

Unable to bear the tease an instant longer, she kissed him. Ferociously so, thrusting her tongue past his full lips to find his tongue. She stroked the inside of his mouth, starved for his taste. His groan stoked the fire raging inside her.

They were playing with a lighted stick of dynamite, one with an incredibly short fuse. She knew that. She simply couldn't make herself care. Dropping from the chair to kneel with him, she wrapped her arms around his waist, letting their bodies touch in the way she'd craved constantly since their night at the Ramada.

Connor slipped his hands down her back, skittering his fingers over her body and settling his palms on her butt. He pulled her hard against him and growled low when she rubbed against his erection.

The door abruptly opened. "Jules?" Her name was followed by a deep chuckle. "Oops."

Ben Carpenter.

Shit.

They scrambled away from each other like a pair of teenagers caught making out on the living room sofa. It seemed to take forever for both of them to stumble back onto their feet.

Juliana smoothed her hands down her skirt, wishing Ben had a better sense of timing. By the time she gathered her scattered wits and looked up to greet him, she wished she hadn't bothered. Ben's grin made heat bathe her face and neck.

"Didn't mean to interrupt." He closed the door behind him.

"Sure you did," she grumbled.

He only broadened his smile. "Anything to drive you crazy, Jules."

Their relationship was one of mutual respect and unmerciful teasing, something that had begun early in Ben and Mallory's courtship and had endured. Juliana liked Ben now. But because Mallory had seemed so fragile at the time, she'd feared he would be more than her friend could handle. Her mistake was in underestimating them both. Mallory was made of the strongest steel, and Ben's heart was bigger than the Montana sky. They were so very good to each other and for each other.

Still, the teasing was fun, and he didn't seem inclined to end their little game. Neither was she.

Ben checked his watch, probably for effect. "I had an appointment. Am I too early? If you want a few more minutes alone"—he reached for the doorknob—"or does he take longer than a few minutes?"

"Stop it, Ben. Connor, please go keep an eye on him before he pockets a calculator or something. I'm going to work on my laundry before it takes over the place." Juliana headed into her house. Since his appointment wasn't with her, she figured the guys might want to talk business without her eavesdropping.

* * *

If Connor hadn't just gotten Juliana back into his arms, even if only for a brief yet highly pleasurable moment, he might've been jealous of the way she bantered with Ben Carpenter. Their obvious caring reminded him of his relationship with Tracy.

"Hey, Ben." Connor offered his hand as he held open the swinging door on the half wall separating the desks and conference area from the clients' waiting area.

Ben shook his hand and followed him to the table.

After they sat, Connor picked up a pen and pad. "So what do you think?"

"I think I'd have a hard time living in that house the way it is. How can you stand it?"

Connor shrugged. "The shower and the toilet work."

"That's about all that does."

"I've got a bed and a place to hang my clothes."

"Not much else," Ben said with a smirk.

Connor frowned, not seeing nearly as much humor in the matter as Ben obviously did. "It's livable and you know it. It's not much, but it's got potential. Right?"

"Loads of potential, depending on what you'd like to do. Tell me exactly what you want an estimate on. Or are you wanting the whole place gutted and redone?"

"Gutted. Eventually."

As he fiddled with his pen, Connor hated hearing Ben's harsh words. Sure, the place was a disaster. The problem was he had next to nothing to pay Ben for labor let alone buy any of the fixtures he'd need. Almost every last dime of his savings, including his retirement money, had been used to buy the place, and it wasn't as though he could get credit from anyone other than a loan shark. Hell, he'd bought the place with cash since he couldn't even pass a credit check to rent an apartment.

He shook his head, banishing the burgeoning self-pity. Tracy's voice sounded in his head.

"One day at a time, one problem at a time. Don't let things overwhelm you."

"Right now," Connor said, "I need the kitchen working."

Ben set his electronic tablet on the table and brought up some thumbnail photos. "I took a few pictures while I was there."

As if Connor needed a reminder of the disaster he saw every time he walked in his front door. At least the place was his, an important first step. Someday he'd make it all it could be.

"I was thinking we'd try something different for the countertops," Ben said. "Granite is getting cliché. I suggest stained concrete. Durable and original." He flipped to the next picture, another angle of the kitchen. "As for the cabinets, I'd go for new. These are showing an awful lot of wear and tear."

A pleasant exaggeration. Several cabinet doors were barely hanging on, most sitting at odd angles. "Yeah, they are."

Ben went on as if he didn't hear the sarcasm in Connor's voice or simply chose to ignore it, probably from years of experience dealing with homeowners' reactions to bad news. "Although if you want to keep costs down we could paint them and add new hardware and new hinges. Would give you a nice retro look and would go well with the concrete."

"That all sounds great, Ben, but I really need to be frugal about this. The immediate problem is the kitchen sink. Evidently the water isn't hooked up to it right or something's blocking it, but anything that does get to the sink drips right through to the cabinet."

"Yeah, and the stuff you've got there is kinda gross." Ben skimmed to another picture as to prove his point. "That's all you wanted?" he asked, quirking a brow. "The kitchen sink?"

"After I get some more cash, we can talk about more substantial changes. Concrete for the kitchen. New cabinets. New floors. A few good commissions and I'll keep you as busy as you can handle."

"You know"—Ben stroked his chin in thought—"I can do a lot more than you think for a low price if you don't mind me getting things secondhand."

"Works for me," Connor said. "Anything to keep costs down and get me a kitchen I can use. I'm sick of fast food."

Juliana slipped back into the office, plopping herself down on her desk chair and attacking her computer.

"That reminds me," Ben said. "Mallory made me promise you two would come over for dinner tonight. I can do some shopping, and we can talk then." He folded his arms over his chest at Connor's dubious expression. "Don't even think about turning her down. Knowing my wife, she'll come over here and drag you there by the sleeve of your fancy suit. Besides, I'm making lasagna."

"You're cooking?" Juliana asked.

"Yep," Ben replied.

"We'll be there," she announced. Her back was still to them as she worked on her computer again, but Connor had no doubt she was smiling.

"Fine," he conceded. "We'll be there."

"Great." Ben held out his hand, and Connor shook it again. "I'm going to do some investigating and see what I can come up with to show you tonight."

He strode to the door, gave Juliana a cocky salute, and left.

"Ben's a great cook." She stood up, pushed her chair up to her desk, and grabbed her purse from the bottom drawer. "I'm really tired of eating out. Aren't you?"

"Yeah," he admitted. "I am." He raked his fingers through his hair. "Maybe Ben will be able to make a miracle for me—beyond dinner, I mean."

"If you'd have seen Mallory's house before he worked on it, you'd know how much of a miracle worker he is. I'm sure he'll get your kitchen done, and it'll be great." She slung the enormous purse over her shoulder. "Gotta scoot now. Busy Realtor. Things to do and all."

"You don't clean that thing out soon, you'll end up paying a chiropractor a fortune to fix your spine."

With a cock of her head, she tossed him a quizzical frown.

"Your purse, Red. It weighs more than I do."

She poked her index finger against his chest. "Word of warning, mister. Never try to come between a woman and her purse, especially when it's a Kate Spade. I need to take pictures of the Reid house for the website. You're still updating it this afternoon?"

"Yeah, right after Mike Walker comes in to sign his buy offer."

When she took a step toward the door, he wrapped his fingers around her upper arm, dragging her to a halt.

After a quick glance at his restraining hand, she frowned. "What?"

"Look, I want to ask you something."

"Ask away."

"About us."

"Oh, I'm sorry."

"Sorry?" He gaped at her. "For what?"

"For letting things get out of hand. You were just being nice, rubbing the stiffness out of my shoulders, and—"

A chuckle slipped out at her innocent description of what had happened between them. "I believe I also stuck my tongue in your ear, and I distinctly remember you shoving your tongue down my throat."

"It won't happen again." She dropped her gaze and tried to pull her arm away.

Connor wouldn't allow it. The way she'd responded to him spoke volumes. She still wanted him, maybe even as badly as he wanted her. Their business was up and running even though Tracy hadn't even made the announcement about the Barrett Foods factory yet. There was no reason to hold back anymore.

He brushed the purse from her shoulder, smiling at the loud thud when it hit the floor.

"Connor…"

He wasn't about to be denied. The interrupted kiss had left him aching for her, a feeling he knew far too well. While he loved working with her, often marveling at the way the two of them complemented each other in so many ways, he wanted, needed, more.

As he leaned in to kiss her, he waited for her to put her hand on his chest and push him away. She didn't want to jeopardize their business. He understood that. At least his mind did.

His body had other ideas.

Her resistance never came. When he touched his lips to hers, she sighed before kissing him back.

Every single time they touched, he lost control, wanting to drink her in and let her scent and warmth envelop him. He was the first to heighten the kiss, letting his tongue glide across hers and savoring the sexy whimper in the back of her throat.

He wanted to take her into her house and strip her naked. He'd look his fill of her curvy shape and then make love to her.

Fast the first time.

Slow the second.

Juliana was the one to bring some sanity back to them when she eased back. Her lips were rosy and glistening, and she had that slumberous, happy look that made him smile in masculine pride.

He'd rattled her.

"Connor, we—"

Connor pressed a finger to her lips. "Listen. Okay?"

She nodded.

He traced his finger against her bottom lip before pulling it away. "Things are going great. You and I are adults. We can handle being personally involved while also running a business together. Ask yourself this, what's the worst thing that can happen?"

She actually gave it some thought, which offered him hope she'd changed her mind. "What if we do get involved again? What happens when we break up?"

"Who said we would?"

Her snort made him roll his eyes.

"Okay, fine. We break up," he replied. "Then we keep working together and let it go."

"You think it's that simple?"

He nodded. "Just exes running their realty firm."

"Have you ever worked with an ex?"

"Well, no. But—"

"I have."

"You have?" This was a piece of the puzzle she'd never provided before.

"Yep. And trust me, it's not easy." She paused, clearly giving it more thought. "But we did okay, I suppose. For years, actually."

He picked up her purse and helped her put it back on her shoulder. "Then we can try the relationship thing?"

"I thought this was about sex, not a relationship."

"That's not what I want, Red. I want the whole package."

Her heavy sigh hung in the air. "How about this? I'll think about it."

Her first concession. It wasn't enough for Connor. "For how long?"

With a smile, she leaned in and kissed him—a no-nonsense kiss, but another concession. "We'll talk after dinner tonight."

Chapter Twelve

"Come on in." Mallory held the front door open. "Why didn't you come in through the garage?"

Juliana shrugged. "Wasn't sure if I should be more formal."

She couldn't say she wasn't sure the friendship rules applied to Connor, especially not with him standing right there. Mallory and Ben barely knew him, so punching in the code and walking right into their house seemed rude.

"Puhleeze. You're both friends." Mallory glanced to Connor, giving him a smile. "Right? I mean, Ben's about to take your house apart. How much more personal can things get?"

Connor smiled back. "You're right."

"Hey, you two." Ben gave them a wave from where he stood at the stove then he went back to putting pieces of bread into a basket. "Hope you're hungry."

"Smells wonderful," Juliana said. "Still having lasagna?"

"Oh yeah," Ben replied without turning around. "Amber and I made the mozzarella ourselves."

"Amber?" Connor asked in a low whisper.

"His daughter," Juliana replied, not bothering to soften her voice. "She's fourteen now."

"Wow. I guess I was *way* off. I mistook Ben and Mallory for newlyweds."

"We are," Mallory said. "Amber's my stepdaughter. I got lucky. She and Ben came as a package deal."

"I see. Any other munchkins?"

"Nope. Just Amber." She led them to the island, one of Juliana's favorite additions to the kitchen Ben had made when he'd renovated the house. "Wine?"

"Sure," Juliana replied. "Connor?"

He shook his head. "I'd love a soda, though. Any cola?"

How odd that she'd never seen him take a drink. "You don't like wine?"

"Not my thing."

"I've got beer," Ben offered. "Local microbrewery makes great stuff."

"Nah. Never learned to like the taste of beer."

"I'll get you a glass of soda," Mallory said.

Mallory poured them both drinks and led them to the table just as Ben brought over the scrumptious-smelling lasagna.

As he set the pan on the table, Juliana got a good look at his apron. She burst out laughing. Only Ben would have the balls to wear an apron that had been printed with a curvy woman's torso wearing a lacy pink bra and panties.

Connor cocked his head. "Red?"

She tried to stifle her reaction and pointed at Ben. "Check out his apron."

He took one look and joined in her laughter.

"I got him that for his birthday." Mallory sounded rather proud of herself. "Mostly as a joke. I figured he wouldn't ever use it. Would you believe he's got the guts to wear it on the deck when he barbeques?"

"Absolutely," Juliana replied. "Ben has no shame."

She'd never met a guy quite like him. He was so comfortable in his own skin he had no problem joking about anything, even if he ended up looking rather silly.

Connor seemed to have the same trait, although it was clear he still didn't feel relaxed enough to let his guard down. But she'd make sure he did. She wanted him to belong, and she also wanted her friends to accept him.

Ben cast aside his oven mitts. "Let's eat."

* * *

Connor enjoyed the easy conversation at dinner. With the exception of Tracy, most of his friends had all but abandoned him.

So be it.

To sit down and eat with people he liked, who seemed to like him, was one of the most relaxing things he'd done in a long time.

"Damn, Ben." He put his fork down on his empty plate and rubbed his swollen belly. "That was fantastic. Who taught you to cook?"

"Taught myself." Ben leaned back in his chair, rubbing his own stomach. "Amazing what you can learn to do on a limited budget. Amber's getting pretty good, too. Mallory's a lost cause. The woman can't boil water without starting a fire."

"Why should I bother?" she asked. "I've got you trained quite nicely."

Connor started to help collect the dirty dishes when Mallory put her hand over his. "Guys do the cooking. Ladies do the cleaning. Besides"—she smiled at her husband—"Ben had a busy day. He's got stuff to show you in the garage."

"Are you sure?" After they'd fed him, Connor wanted to at least lend a hand with the cleanup. As it was, it appeared as though a hurricane had just whipped through. Dishes were piled in the sink. Pans littered the stove. Ingredients were scattered across the counter. "I'd be glad to wash. Or dry." He took another quick look at the disaster area of the kitchen. "Or anything you need."

"Jules and I can take care of this mess," Mallory replied. "You and Ben go talk shop. He's been champing at the bit all afternoon, like a kid on Christmas morning."

"You know me far too well, Mal." Ben brushed a kiss over his wife's lips and motioned for Connor to follow him.

Seeing no reason to hide how he felt about Juliana from her friends, Connor gave her a quick kiss, savoring her rather startled expression. He'd meant what he said about wanting a personal relationship, and she needed to know that.

He followed Ben before she had a chance to say anything in response.

"Welcome to my *lah-bor-a-tory*." Ben mimicked Vincent Price. "Muhahaha…" He held open a door and swept his arm in invitation. "Come in. Come in."

Connor refrained from making a smart-ass comment, although he did smirk. Nice to know Juliana's friends were every bit as sarcastic as he was. People who were too serious gave him hives.

The garage was a well-organized craftsman's dream. Tools hung from a pegboard wall. Some were stacked in cases, sorted by size. A few sat on the concrete floor, cords wrapped neatly around them. Connor had never been much of a tool kind of guy. Home improvement and repair were best left to someone who knew what he was doing. Anytime he'd tried to fix something, whether a toilet or a piece of trim, he'd usually made the problem worse.

One of the benefits of being a Realtor was getting to know people in all lines of work. Back in Indianapolis, he had a dozen people from contractors to carpet installers he could call and get help from at a moment's notice. Here, he was starting from scratch. But now that he knew Ben, more contacts would follow, since Ben seemed like the kind of guy to help Connor network.

"Nice tools." He ran his fingers over one of the saws. "I wouldn't know what to do with any of them."

"Thanks," Ben replied. "Don't feel bad. I wouldn't have a clue how to deal with a mortgage company. Come on over here. I want to show you the stuff I got from Charlie Barker this afternoon. He always has some great salvage. Didn't disappoint me today."

"What've you got?"

"How about a practically new stainless steel kitchen sink?" He pointed to a double-sided sink lying on the floor by an antique claw-footed tub. Several other pieces, ranging from faucets to long pieces of crown molding, rested nearby. "Would work well for your place."

"Nice. How much?" Stainless steel appliances came at a premium. Surely a sink, used or not, in such good shape would be expensive, too.

"Would you believe fifteen bucks?" Ben tapped the rim of the tub. "Got this beauty for fifty. Refinish the surface and it'll be good as new. Cost me a third of one off the showroom floor."

"What about the cabinets?"

"Charlie had a shitload—far too many to make a selection. You're gonna have to go with me and take a look. That way you can pick new doors you like. He's got Shaker, colonial, modern, you name it. Pick what you want, we'll give 'em a new coat of paint, add the new hardware, pop in the sink and a faucet, and you've got a usable kitchen."

"A shame the countertops are that awful butcher block."

"Got an idea for that, too." He kicked a roll of thin metal. "We can wrap the counters in this, distress it, seal it, and it'll be better than new. A helluva lot more innovative than granite and a lot cheaper."

"Distress it?" Connor hated feeling stupid. While the idea of covering that hideous countertop was appealing, he didn't understand why Ben would want to ruin the metal.

"We'll acid-wash it. Give it some interesting color that'll contrast with the stainless steel. Mallory's got some pictures on her laptop to show you. She saw it on some home improvement show. She and Jules are addicted to HGTV."

"This all sounds great, Ben."

"How about we meet sometime next week to make final choices?"

"Sounds great." Connor offered his hand. "I can't thank you enough."

Instead of returning the shake, Ben folded his arms over his chest and leveled a hard stare. "Now we've got *that* solved, we need to talk about Jules."

Not that he hadn't expected some kind of response from Ben over the intimate clinch he'd seen in the office, but Connor didn't want to get pulled into a personal discussion. "Why would you want to talk about Juliana?"

"She and Mallory are pretty tight; like sisters. You might not know how close they are since the two of you have been working long days to get the business going. Jules means the world to Mallory. And to me. We're both looking out for her."

"Noble, but unnecessary."

Ben rubbed the back of his neck, the first sign he was as uncomfortable with the conversation as Connor was. No doubt his wife had put him up to it. "Try to see this through our eyes for a minute. You breeze into Cloverleaf and suddenly Jules leaves her job, starts a new career, and all but disappears. Mallory and I are a little worried."

"Again, noble on your part, but there's nothing to worry about. Juliana's an adult. She's also a woman who knows exactly what she wants, and she wanted this change in her life."

"We get the real estate. What we don't get, frankly, is you. Where are you from, Connor? What made you decide to come to a small town like Cloverleaf of all places?"

Since Ben wasn't going to let his concerns be brushed aside, Connor took a seat on one of the stools while Ben followed suit. "Has Juliana told you anything about Barrett Foods?"

Ben shook his head.

So his partner could be counted on to hold a confidence. Good to know, but he'd already judged Juliana as being honest and trustworthy.

Connor walked a thin line, trying to give Ben enough information about Tracy Barrett without getting too deeply into all of the whys and wherefores that had ultimately led to Kelley-Wilson Realty. The big reveal was coming up. Tracy would be in Cloverleaf soon and would make her announcement. Once that happened, everything would change and he could talk freely about his choice to come here.

At least the professional reasons.

Ben listened, nodding from time to time. The man had a poker face much like his own, and Connor learned little about his thoughts from his expression.

When Connor ended his rather bare-bones explanation about Barrett Foods and how he'd come to this fair town, Ben sat thoughtfully for a moment. "There's more to the story, isn't there?"

"Honesty, Connor. Always be honest."

Tracy's voice echoed in his thoughts. But this one time, he simply couldn't heed her advice. "Nope. Nothing more. Sorry to disappoint you. No intrigue. No crazy ex-wife. No...nothing."

"Ben!" Mallory called. "Dessert!"

Thankful for the reprieve, Connor stood and pushed the stool back under the worktable. "I know Juliana's important to you. You're gonna have to trust she's every bit as important to me. Okay?"

This time when he held out his hand, Ben shook it. "Fine. But know this—if you hurt her, I'm not responsible for the feminine fury that'll rain down on you."

"Feminine fury? You mean Mallory?"

"You haven't met the Ladies Who Lunch yet, have you?"

"The what?"

"The Ladies Who Lunch. I can't wait 'til they get a load of you."

As he led the way back into the house, Ben's knowing laughter made Connor wince.

* * *

"Who are the Ladies Who Lunch?" Connor asked on the drive home.

Juliana felt a pinch of guilt.

A pinch? More like a slap to the back of the head.

Her friends had been the most important thing in her world

for years. Yet here she was, reveling in the bustle of her new career and spending eighteen-hour days with Connor Wilson. She saw Mallory at least once a week. But Beth and Dani? They had to feel abandoned.

"They're my best friends. We all teach together."

"Taught." He gave her a crooked smile.

"Yeah, taught. You really need to meet them."

But when? Neither had any free time.

Then an idea hit. "How about we have a cookout? The Fourth is coming up and we could cook out and shoot off some fireworks."

He thought it over before nodding. "I guess we can do it."

"What did you think of their place?"

"Perfect. I could have ten buyers there tomorrow with offers in hand."

Knowing Connor, he wasn't exaggerating. "I know, right? Ben did all of it on a limited budget. Did he have some good stuff to show you?"

"A sink. A faucet. An interesting new surface for the counter-tops. We've got an appointment this week so I can pick cabinet doors. As soon as it's done, I'll invite you over."

Ever since he'd asked if she was ready to take their partnership to a more intimate level, she'd been thinking hard about what she would do. He was taking the route back to the office—her house. Did he assume he'd be staying?

Despite the numerous tangents her thoughts took, they always came back to the same place. Connor wanted to make love again, and she wasn't sure if she had the strength to fight her own desire let alone his.

What did they have to lose?

Kelley-Wilson Realty.

But was it truly in jeopardy?

"Thinking awfully hard over there, Red."

"Your fault."

"Good. I hope that means you're going to ask me to stay. God knows I want to. I dream about you every night. Just seeing you makes me hard as a rock."

Her body flushed hot, and a little whimper escaped her lips. She tried to hold back her physical response to his words. "What about the firm?"

"It's not going anywhere." He slipped his hand over her thigh and squeezed. "Even if we—"

"If we break up?" Damn if that didn't sound like they were a couple of adolescents.

He caressed her thigh, sliding from knee to lap, making her breaths come faster. "Shouldn't we get a relationship going before we worry about it ending?"

"Is that what you want, Connor? A relationship?"

"Yeah, I do. I'm not a player. I don't need a parade of women. I'm very discriminating. Only the best for Connor Wilson." He tossed her a smile. "You're exactly what I want. And I hope you feel the same about me."

This was uncharted territory. She'd never had the kind of relationship he'd described—two adults being both partners and lovers. Could that even work? Her experience with men was limited to jerks, which made her a poor judge of their motivations. So she thought of one of the few good men she knew. Ben.

He'd been wonderful with Mallory from the moment they met. While they might have encountered a few bumps in the road, the couple was a shining example of what a caring union could be.

That was what Juliana wanted with all her heart.

Connor eased his Escalade into her driveway, killed the engine, and then swallowed hard. His nervousness was touching.

"The choice is yours, Juliana. I'd love nothing more than to take you inside and make love to you tonight. I want to wake up tomorrow with you still there in my arms instead of sneaking away as though we've done something wrong."

"It wasn't wrong," she snapped. The picture he painted hurt, probably because of his honesty. She did run away, although not for the reason he believed.

Juliana had escaped the emotions he inspired that night, the same ones now forcing her to squirm in her seat, wanting nothing more than to feel his hands on her body again. Yet she knew once she let him back in her bed, he was only a few short steps away from her heart.

He framed her face in his hands and gave her a gentle kiss. Then his gaze searched hers. "What's it gonna be? Do I stay or do I go?"

Chapter Thirteen

Connor held his breath, waiting for Juliana to decide.

He'd taken a chance in pushing her after she'd set the ground rules that they not be romantically involved. If she turned him down flat, he might have screwed up any chance of ever holding her in his arms again. At least the kisses they'd shared revealed a hunger that seemed every bit as deep as his.

It took supreme effort not to slide her onto his lap and try to convince her with his mouth and his body since his words weren't effective. All she had to do was give him something resembling a nod and he'd be dragging her inside, heading straight for the bedroom.

Giving in to his desire, he leaned closer, slipping his fingers behind her neck. Slowly, steadily, he tugged her closer, pleased she didn't resist. When his lips were close to hers, close enough he could feel her heated breath brush his face, he stopped.

Their eyes locked, and he searched for something—*anything*—that could help him know what was tumbling through her mind. He was taut with need, his cock already hardened in anticipation. "I want you, Juliana. Let me come in. Let me make love to you again."

She made no sound, no motion. Just sat there still and quiet, her incredible eyes wide.

Connor touched his lips to hers, a gentle kiss he hoped would reach whatever held her back and knock it aside. "Let me in." And he didn't just mean her house. He wanted her heart, but for now he would take whatever she would offer.

With a soft cry, Juliana looped her arms around his neck and pressed her breasts against his chest. Then she kissed him, slipping her tongue past his lips and seeking his.

Fire shot through his body, a lightning strike of desire he'd felt for no other woman. A growl rumbled deep in his chest, and he scrambled to pop his seat belt. He might as well have been trying to remove a straightjacket. Never had he been so awkward, but he wouldn't be deterred. After the latch finally gave up the fight, he slid his seat all the way back and pulled her over onto his lap, her legs dangling between the two leather seats.

She fits. That was all he could think. Her body so tightly against his felt right.

Connor ravaged her mouth, not able to get enough of her taste. He tangled his fingers in her hair, pulling out and then tossing aside the clip that had been holding it up. The moonlight shone bright through the windshield, painting shimmering highlights in her hair.

She pulled her mouth away, but not her hands. Those she slid over his chest to the row of buttons. She popped open the first. "Let's go inside."

Tweaking her hard nipples through the thin material of her silk shirt and her bra, he nodded at the glove compartment. "Grab the sack."

"Sack?"

"I shoved the package of condoms in there after the last night we spent together. Glad I didn't toss 'em."

"Me, too."

Her sweet ass rubbed against his erection as she wiggled and reached for the handle, forcing a grunt through his lips.

"Got it." She dangled the white sack in front of her. "How many are left?"

"Don't know."

"Hope there's enough."

"No worries. I can always run out and get more."

Connor opened his door, grunting again when Juliana slipped over his lap and out onto the concrete. His cock was hard enough to crack a walnut. As soon as they got inside, he was opening the zipper and letting the poor thing breathe and expand a little more.

And now it wasn't only his fantasy. It was his reality.

There really is a God.

Outside the office door, she fumbled with the lock as the keys jingled in her trembling hands. This time, he took charge, taking her keys and opening the door with ease that belied his inner disarray.

They stumbled through the office, stopping every few feet to kiss and stroke and tease. He wasn't going to pause long enough to give her a chance to focus on anything that might change her mind or think about the consequences to Kelley-Wilson Realty. Not that she seemed to be reconsidering. Her tongue was wild. Her hands were everywhere.

When she reached the door to her kitchen, she stopped and tossed him a seductive smile.

Like he needed any encouragement.

He scooped her into his arms, held her so she could turn the knob, and then shoved the door open with his foot. Once inside, he kicked it shut behind him.

While he might've had breakfast with her every morning, he'd never been given the grand tour of her house. She seemed to want to keep the office and her home as separate as possible. After tonight, that line wouldn't just be blurred, it would be obliterated.

So be it.

He'd meant every word when he'd told her this partnership could work, both in the office and the bedroom.

"Down the hall," she whispered in his ear. "Second door on the right." Her teeth tugged on his earlobe, making his head swim.

Connor tried to take in as much of her home as he could, but with his blood flowing south, his brain wouldn't cooperate. The only thing that caught his attention, other than the beautiful redhead in his arms, was a wall full of framed photos. Later—*much* later—he'd have to take a look and see if he could learn anything about Juliana from those pictures.

Her bedroom suited her personality, tastefully decorated yet messy. She'd left a light on, an antique Tiffany lamp that cast a kaleidoscope of colors over the unmade bed.

Neither of them were neat freaks, tending more toward organized chaos. Probably a good thing they were compatible because he was too old to change his ways. Then he realized he *had* changed in a lot of ways. Hell, if she wanted him to start being obsessive-compulsive about his stuff, he'd do his best to accommodate her.

She jerked her shirt over her head and flung it aside while he finished unbuttoning his. They both stripped quickly, raising his hopes that her need was running as hot and deep as his. When he opened his zipper and swept down the waistband of his briefs, his erection sprang out, seemingly searching for her. As soon as she'd banished her bra and panties to the hardwood floor, she stroked his length.

"So hot. So hard," she purred. Then she dropped to her knees and licked him from tip to root and back again before taking him into her mouth.

Connor didn't care how absurd he looked, standing there with his pants and briefs around his ankles. His mind was full of Juliana and the way her hot, wet tongue swirled around his cock. He raked his fingers in her hair, gently pumping his hips and praying for the self-control to make this interlude last.

* * *

Juliana smiled as she pressed her lips against the crown of Connor's erection. Each of his groans and low growls fueled her passion. How she'd managed to work side by side with the man for so many weeks without giving in to the urge to touch him, to love him, was a miracle. Everything about him appealed to her. His startling eyes. His muscular physique. The wonderful taste of his lips and his cock.

"Red." He let out a moan. "You better stop now."

She glanced up to see a flush on his face. "Why? Don't you like this?"

"Shit, yes."

She took him as deeply into her mouth as she could and sucked hard.

"Juliana, I'm gonna..." Whatever he was going to say ended up in a strangled cry as he came.

She held tight, wringing every last drop from him and loving the power she had over him at that moment. Not until he carefully pulled his fingers out of her mussed hair did she ease back, hoping it wouldn't be too awkward to look him in the eye.

"I can't believe you did that," he said, shaking his head.

"Are you complaining?"

He scoffed at her. "Not even close. I just thought, you know, women didn't like that."

Not like that unique taste and the way she could make his body sing? It had been heaven, and she was glad she'd followed her instincts. "I suppose I do."

"You mean, you've never..."

She gave her head a shake as she got to her feet. It took all her fortitude not to start grabbing for her clothes. She suddenly felt too exposed, too vulnerable because of the disbelieving tone of his voice.

Had she disgusted him?

He wouldn't drop the topic. "Then why—"

"You know what, Connor? You have a nasty habit of looking a gift horse in the mouth." A laugh bubbled out. "Bad pun. Sorry."

His laughter followed hers before he tugged her into his arms. "That was fantastic."

What was wrong with her? She wasn't some simpering virgin. So she'd swallowed. So what? Yet she could feel herself blushing, and she tried to hide her face in the crook of his neck. "Glad you enjoyed it."

"Did you do that just to please me?" His tone had changed to scolding.

She shrugged, unable to keep up with his rapidly changing moods. "I figured you might be a little too...needy since it's been a while."

He lifted her face to his. "I don't want you to ever do anything you don't want to. Got it?"

"Oh, I wanted to." Since she saw nothing but humor, sincerity, and a lingering sexual haze in his features, she relaxed.

Juliana had never shied away from sex, always doing whatever felt good. There had been times her adventurous nature hadn't been received so heartily. Jimmy had called her a pervert when she'd suggested tying him to the bed.

Stop comparing Connor to your asshat ex!

Connor was not only unique, he was twice the man Jimmy had ever been. Although her marriage had started out passionate, that fire had quickly cooled. She'd grown bored with their vanilla, missionary, who-gives-a-shit-if-my-wife-comes sex. With Connor, she could, and would, be anything she wanted to be.

Even a sex goddess.

"You don't wear neckties very often," she mentioned. That had been one of the favorite fantasies she'd never been able to try.

"Pardon?"

She'd obviously changed topics too quickly. "I was thinking about tying you up, and neckties work best."

His cock had softened, but now it was growing right before her eyes. She wrapped her fingers around his returning erection and stroked.

"I have plenty of neckties. Feel free to borrow as many as you'd like."

"Trust me. I will." She rubbed her thumb over the cap of his erection.

"Enough." He gently pulled her hand away. "It's your turn."

A squeal escaped her lips when he picked her up and tossed her on the bed. Then he joined her, his tongue finding a sensitive nipple as he slipped his hand between her thighs.

Connor certainly knew his way around a woman's body. In short order, he had her squirming as his thumb rubbed her sweet spot and he slipped a long finger deep inside her.

Juliana's thoughts scattered as every nerve seemed to drift to her breast and her core. Heat rose to a crescendo, her muscles tightening with each stroke, each touch. She dug her heels into the mattress, meeting each thrust of his finger, which was joined by a second, stretching her and making her feel full and tight. The splendor he gave her had to be because of the way he made her feel so free in body and mind. Her orgasm consumed her, making her buck beneath him as he pulled every last spasm from her.

He held her close, nibbling at her neck and toying with her breasts as she slowly drifted back into herself.

"Wow." *Great.* Now she was inarticulate.

"You're welcome." He took her earlobe between his teeth, sending shivers racing over her. "Where did you put the condoms?"

Thinking was too tough when she was sated and content to simply lie next to him. "Don't know. Dropped 'em on the floor, I think."

He rose over her and let the length of his body rest on hers for a few tantalizing moments before rolling off the bed. A quick search produced the white bag. He fished out a condom and tossed it on her stomach.

"Ack! Cold!" She snatched it up.

"Sorry." After he crawled back on the bed, he licked the place the packet had rested. "Better?"

"Much." Juliana combed her fingers through his hair as he kissed his way up her body. As he feasted on her breasts, her body came back to greedy life. "Mmm...That feels—" She choked on the last word because he bit her nipple hard enough to sting, a kind of pain that increased her pleasure.

His lips smoothed across her collarbone before he nuzzled her neck. "I want you."

"I want you, too." She moved out from under him as he rolled to his back. She fumbled with the wrapper, finally ripping it open with her teeth while Connor stuck his tongue in her ear. She giggled as she rolled the condom over his cock.

He picked her up and tossed her back on the bed, blanketing her with his body. His tongue was in her mouth, and she sucked hard on it before reaching between them to grab his cock and guide him between her thighs. Then she wrapped her legs around his hips.

The man was smart enough to follow her directions as he rubbed against her before thrusting deep.

"Perfect," he whispered in her ear.

"Damn right."

Slowly, in an easy rhythm that teased her, excited her, he withdrew and pushed back inside her. While she enjoyed the slow, deep strokes, her body was demanding rougher, faster. She scraped her fingernails across his tight buns, which had the desired response. Connor seemed to lose control, and their bodies met in a rough ride to fulfillment.

Juliana won the race, her body exploding in a burst of heat that made a spray of bright lights dot her vision. A few more rough plunges and he let out a shout that was a blending of her name and a call to God.

He collapsed against her, but she enjoyed the weight of his lethargic body, tracing her fingers up and down his spine and cupping his butt. She nipped at his shoulder, knowing he needed to move soon to get rid of the condom.

With a sigh, he withdrew. "Uh-oh."

"Uh-oh?"

"Condom broke."

"Uh-oh."

Chapter Fourteen

Juliana handed the glass of soda to Connor and then poured one for herself. What she truly wanted was tequila, but getting drunk wouldn't solve their little problem. It would only delay the inevitable.

"So…" He fiddled with his glass.

"So…" She did the same.

They'd dressed quietly, neither commenting on the enormous elephant in the middle of the bed. Then he'd led her to the kitchen, and she'd asked if he wanted a drink, holding up a half-empty bottle of Riesling she'd grabbed from the fridge. He'd thought it over a good long while before pointing at the two-liter of Diet Sprite instead.

A good choice. They both needed clear heads to figure out what to do next.

The silence was killing her.

"You know," Juliana said, finding some courage, "it might not really matter."

"Are you on the pill?" He gave her a hopeful smile.

Unfortunately, she squelched it with her reply. "No. Sorry."

"Nothing to be sorry about." He held out his hand, palm up. "Shit happens."

At least he was being supportive. That boded well. She set her hand in his. "I guess I could go to the pharmacy and get a morning-after pill."

"No." His response was swift and filled with a touch of anger.

"It would make sure nothing...bad happens."

Connor cocked his head and slowly pulled his hand back. "Why would you say that?"

"Say what?"

"That it would be *bad* if anything happened. Who's to say it's not destiny?"

A baby. They were both tiptoeing around it, but that's what this boiled down to. Did they just create a baby?

She didn't have time to be a mom. Not now, especially not when her new career was on the launchpad. It wasn't the right time to scrub the mission.

A baby.

Her thoughts followed a familiar path back to the first year she'd spent with Jimmy. Being nothing but kids themselves, they were never as careful as they should've been. And she was honest enough to admit, if only to herself, she'd wanted to get pregnant. After all, she'd married her college sweetheart. Wouldn't having a baby lead them to that elusive happily ever after?

Instead, Jimmy had blown his top, something he'd done with alarming frequency after the wedding. He'd pressured her about having an abortion, and she'd waffled. At first she'd refused simply to be stubborn, but with each passing day she'd realized she couldn't go through with it. Then she'd miscarried, and his relief had been one of the things that made her love for him reach such a swift demise.

No one with a soul should be happy to lose a baby.

She, on the other hand, had cried more over that lost child than anything else in her life. Once she and Jimmy split, she'd thought—several times—about having a child on her own. Something always stopped her from driving to Chicago and making a withdrawal from a sperm bank. There was always a new extracurricular she had to supervise, another trip to Europe, a challenging group of special needs children. Excuse after excuse after excuse.

But now?

Now her excuse was more than valid. Kelley-Wilson Realty was getting started, and a pregnancy could kill it, at least *her* part of it.

"I was pregnant once before," Juliana admitted. "I had a miscarriage."

"That must've been terrible."

"It was, but...I got through it. Not like my ex was much help."

"I'm sorry."

Juliana gave him a curt nod. "We're getting the cart miles in front of the horse. It was only a broken condom. Despite what they taught us in high school sex ed, it usually takes more than once."

Connor watched her, his gaze steady but unreadable. "What do you want to do?"

"You're involved in this, too."

"Not really. Your body, your choice."

"I love a liberated man." The sarcasm came through clearly in every word.

His mouth twitched to a grin, forcing her to do the same. Then his lips fell back into a grim line. "It really is your choice."

"I'd like it to be *our* choice." Unable to sit still a moment longer, Juliana popped to her feet and paced the kitchen. "Isn't that the way everything is between us? Fifty-fifty? A partnership? Why should this be anything different?"

He watched her pace, sipping his soda.

His calm raised her temper. How could he stay so cool and collected when a broken piece of plastic might have ruined their lives?

Probably because it would be *her* problem. Not his.

"Can't say I like the way you're glaring at me right now." He set his now-empty glass aside. "What horrible thoughts about me are you having?"

As usual, she held nothing back. "I figured out why you're so fucking nonchalant about this. You can be. You're a guy. I get pregnant, you can walk away."

He rose, setting his hands on his hips. "That's what you think? That I'd knock you up and walk away?" He ran a hand over his face then shook his head. "That hurts."

Anger she'd expected. Wounded came as a surprise. It also made her realize exactly what she'd said. She hurried to him but stopped short. "I'm sorry, Connor."

"We're partners, Juliana. In everything. Even a baby—if there is one."

When he opened his arms, she hesitated.

This was so much more than she'd bargained for. She'd wanted a new job. That was all. A chance to do something different and make enough money to support herself.

Instead, she found herself with a real estate firm, a partner who was now her boyfriend, and maybe a baby on the way.

Too much, too soon.

"I should go to the pharmacy and then we won't have to worry." Juliana's words were a whisper, and she knew the moment she said them that heading to get a morning-after pill was the last thing in the world she wanted to do.

But what did he want?

"If you really want to go, I'll drive you." Connor had let his hands drop to his sides.

She wanted him to open his arms to her again. She needed him now.

Oh, fuck. No. Not that.

Blinking hard, she forbade herself to cry. She'd always been a realist. Always. Love was something that got in the way of everything. Although she'd avoided that trap since putting Jimmy behind her, it seemed that she was now firmly caught.

I'm falling in love with Connor.

* * *

Juliana suddenly went pale.

While Connor had never seen a woman faint before, he was positive that was exactly what she was going to do.

She might have been avoiding his embrace, but he wrapped his arms around her anyway, if only to be able to catch her when her knees buckled.

He should be mad at her. Furious, even. After all, she'd implied he would knock her up and then just disappear. Not his style. Not in the least.

Sure, he'd made some serious mistakes in his life, but the only person he'd ever let down was himself. He'd lost his parents in a traffic accident only two weeks after his father had retired. The only blessing in that tragedy was that they hadn't witnessed his abject stupidity and his downfall.

Of course, they hadn't witnessed his redemption, either. If he truly was redeemed.

The past was the past, and he intended to keep it there. Juliana didn't need to know his less-than-savory exploits, nor could he stand seeing shock, pity, or condemnation in her eyes. Tracy had helped him learn to walk the straight and narrow again, and he wouldn't stray from that path. No matter what life tossed in his lap. Even a...

Baby.

Shit, it was hard wrapping his mind around that. But when he did, his reaction was a shock.

He wanted this baby.

How odd that the notion of having a child used to seem like a death sentence, but now he wasn't frightened. Not when that child would be created with Juliana. He could almost picture the wonderful little family they could share. Pushing a stroller around the neighborhood. Watching a munchkin on the park swing. The whole package.

Connor really had changed. For the better.

"Shouldn't we take some time to think this through?" he coaxed softly.

At least she was staying in his arms and not trying to get away. He'd have to find a way to let her know he wouldn't be a deadbeat dad without pressuring her to have a kid she didn't want. A fine line to walk, for sure.

She sighed and rested her cheek against his shoulder. "If you want me to get a morning-after pill, we don't have much time. Thinking might take too long."

He knew very little about the subject of what to do when the condom broke, but he did know hesitation when he heard it. Not in her words. Her tone—a cross between sad and resigned—tugged at his heart. "Juliana, we promised each other honesty, right?"

"We did."

"I don't want you to get one of those pills."

Her arms were around his waist, and she squeezed him tightly. "Really?"

"Really."

"But what if—"

"We made a child?"

She nodded against his shoulder.

"Then we raise it together." He kissed the top of her head. "Think about that kid's future. He'll have it made."

She raised her face to his. "What are you talking about?"

"Your DNA and mine together? He'll be a born salesman."

Her laughter made him smile. "So what are we going to do, Connor?"

"Much as you hate waiting, I think that's our best choice. Wait and see what, if anything, happens."

"And if I'm pregnant?"

"We'll cross that bridge when we come to it. One day at a time. Best way to handle most anything. Okay?"

Juliana pressed a kiss to his lips. "Okay. Hey, wanna bet on whether I'm pregnant? With my usual bad luck, I'll even give you fantastic odds. Considering this is probably the worst moment in my life to consider having a baby, I'd wager I am."

"No!" Connor took a steadying breath. "No, Red. No betting. Especially not on this. It's too important for both our futures to make light of it." He rubbed the backs of his knuckles against her cheek. "For the record, I think you'd be a fantastic mom."

Her only reply to his compliment was a bright blush.

"How about breakfast in the morning?" he asked. "I need to run home and grab a shower and some clean clothes."

He sure wasn't looking forward to another freezing-cold shower. At least Ben was going to get the new water heater in soon. Then Connor could linger in a nice, hot shower when he had time. Which was probably never. "Looks like I need to head home soon. It's close to midnight."

"What time is the first closing tomorrow?"

"Ten." He thought about asking Juliana if he could just stay. Then he could shower at her place, but he didn't have any clean clothes and was loath to change back into dirty ones. He might be a slob about housekeeping, but he was meticulous about himself. "I'll be back at the office in the afternoon. We've got that meeting scheduled with Robert, too."

Juliana kept shifting her gaze from him to the hallway leading to her bedroom. "You know, I wonder..." When she took a deep breath, he braced himself, having grown accustomed to her doing that every time she was getting ready to deliver bad news. She was having second thoughts about the morning-after-pill nonsense.

"I thought we had this decided," Connor said.

"What?"

"I thought we'd agreed to wait and see about any pregnancy."

"We did."

"Then what are you so worried about now?"

Setting her hands against her hips, she tossed him a scorching glare. "Don't you dare snap at me."

About to say he hadn't, it dawned on him that he had. "Sorry. You worried me. Something's obviously bugging you, and I just figured it was our predicament."

"Not that. I was thinking you're here all the time at the office. Your house is still a mess. Now that we're involved again, you could keep some stuff here, maybe. For a while. Until Ben gets done at your place."

"Are you asking me to move in with you?"

"Well...temporarily. Like I said, 'til Ben finishes your place. Why waste money on a hotel when you're gonna be here most of the time anyway?"

"Just like that?"

"Not 'just like that.' I've actually been thinking about it since I heard how bad your house is."

The offer was tempting enough Connor almost took her up on it. Immediately. Then he allowed himself to consider the ramifications. "You realize how much time we'll be spending together, right? Literally twenty-four hours a day some days."

"Yeah. But we're bound to have a lot more mornings like this one. You have to leave just to get a shower and something clean to wear, then you come right back here. A big waste of gas, don't you think? I mean, I'm only thinking about Kelley-Wilson Realty. We're trying to keep costs down. Remember?" She grinned.

Somehow he kept himself from grinning at her teasing. Instead, he rubbed the stubble on his chin with his index finger and thumb while humming, as though carefully thinking over her offer.

"It would save a lot of time," she added.

"It might."

"And gas."

"You already mentioned that."

Juliana finally caught on to his banter and punched his upper arm. "The master closet's full, so you can have a little space in the guest room closet."

"Nope," he replied. "Half the master closet and three drawers of the dresser or no deal."

"Two drawers and a quarter of the closet. And you're lucky you're getting that much for a temporary move."

"Throw in one drawer in the master bath, and I think I can make it work."

Connor didn't give her a chance to reply. He tugged her into his arms, kissed her with far more passion than he'd intended, and then pulled back to kiss the tip of her nose. "I'll bring my stuff over this weekend."

Chapter Fifteen

He's not at all what I expected." Bethany inclined her nearly empty beer bottle at Connor.

"What's that supposed to mean?" Juliana snapped.

Why was she barking at Beth? For God's sake, the woman was adorable as a fluffy bunny. She'd only said he was different from what she'd anticipated, and Juliana was biting her head off.

Sitting on the enormous deck Ben had built in their backyard, Mallory glared at her.

Juliana beat her to the punch, not wanting to receive a scolding, even if she deserved one. "I'm sorry, Beth. It's just, I'm worried about what all of you think of him."

When Danielle opened her mouth, Juliana braced herself for her friend's usual bluntness.

"What we think," Dani said, "is that you've done a one-eighty in every aspect of your life so damn fast we're all a little concerned."

Both Beth and Mallory nodded as Dani pressed on. "We don't know Connor well enough to judge his character."

"But"—Mallory jumped into the conversation—"he seems

nice enough. Ben knows him better than any of us, and he likes him." She shrugged. "It's that you've gone from being a single teacher to living with your new real estate partner. Think about it from our perspective, Jules. What would you say to Dani or Beth in the same situation? Geesh, what did you say to me when I started dating Ben and you thought things were moving too fast? And now the two of you have moved in together into your house?" She heaved a sigh. "Of course we're worried."

"I can't believe you let him move in," Dani grumbled. "He's a stranger!"

"For heaven's sake, you're all overreacting. It's only temporary! His house is a wreck," Juliana insisted. "And he's not a stranger—he's my partner." She shrugged. "Besides, we spend a good eighteen hours in the office. It was nothing but a technicality to have him move in."

"Eighteen hours a day in the office, and the rest in the bedroom," Bethany said with a wink that was closely followed by a blush.

Danielle rolled her eyes. "Don't even try to lie to us and say you don't want this to be a permanent arrangement." Leveling a piercing stare at Juliana, she frowned. "How do you know he's not some serial killer?"

A scoff slipped from Beth. "Now who's being silly? Connor's not a serial killer."

"Fine," Dani conceded. "But he could be running from a slew of debts or a fraud investigation or a real estate swindle. You don't know him at all, Jules. None of us do."

"You're right. I know you're right." Juliana took a long pull from her soda, choosing her words carefully.

She wanted her friends to not only understand why she was going through so much change, she needed them to accept and like Connor. Not just for her, either.

For him.

Connor might not talk about himself much, but she'd quickly learned one important thing.

He was lonely.

Sure, he spent a boatload of time with clients, other agents, and people at the title company. But friends? Family? He never talked about either, nor had he introduced her to anyone from his personal life.

The Ladies had a point. What if he did have a checkered, or even criminal, past? He was running away from something, because no one ran *to* Cloverleaf—Barrett Foods plant on the horizon or not.

She couldn't believe he was dishonest, no matter how hard she tried. He was a person to whom she gave her normally cynical faith. Her friends wouldn't be as blindly trusting. They'd want to put a private investigator on the poor guy and hound him until they knew everything from his blood type to the name of his girlfriend in the first grade.

Maybe he was just an introvert. Maybe there simply wasn't anything to tell.

Maybe he was hiding his past.

She knew there was something, hopefully not someone, who'd sent him running from Indianapolis. He'd never said that, not in so many words. But she heard the envious tone in his voice when she talked about the trip to Europe she'd taken with her parents and how they lived in Arizona but still managed to Skype with her from time to time. They knew all about her change of profession and supported her wholeheartedly.

As far as they knew, Connor was her new real estate partner. If they suspected more, they hadn't said so, and Juliana wasn't about to tell them. Not yet.

Connor wasn't ready for Kevin and Sharon Kelley.

His parents were gone—lost to a car accident, according to him. No siblings, either. Juliana had never heard him mention aunts or uncles or cousins. So different from the Kelley clan. They might be scattered by the four winds, but there weren't too many days that went by that someone she was related to didn't e-mail her, even if only to pass along some ridiculous joke.

Tracy was the only person he mentioned ever spending time with, even before he moved to Cloverleaf. While the head of Barrett Foods might be a nice person, he needed more in his life, and she wanted the Ladies to like him. They filled her life with friendship. Connor deserved no less.

Right now, they acted like they were ready to ride him out of town on a rail.

"Why don't you just ask him?" Mallory drew Juliana back into the conversation.

"Ask him what?" Juliana asked.

"Whether he has a record," Danielle replied. "Why he left Indianapolis. Whether there's a warrant out for his arrest. How many women he's slept with. Whether he's been tested. Every damn thing you can think of."

"She's got a point," Mallory added. "The man is your business partner and now lives in your home. You really should know more than the fact you sell houses together."

With a weary sigh, Juliana nodded. "You're right. I know you're right…" She sounded like a stuck record.

"Then why the hesitation?" Dani had worked herself up far too much to ever back down.

If she shrugged, Juliana was likely to get an earful, but she honestly couldn't put her finger on exactly what she was afraid of. "I'll start asking questions. I promise."

Beth did a little clap. "Now on to better things. Is he any good?" She wiggled her eyebrows.

Juliana blinked at her friend, unsure if she'd heard the question correctly. Bethany was sweet and positive and everyone's cheerleader, almost painfully prim and proper. Innocent Beth was asking whether Connor was good in bed?

"He must be really good," Beth said with a nod. "You must be, too! Seems like I see Kelley-Wilson signs in almost every front yard!"

Faith in humanity restored, Juliana nodded. "Damn good."

In so very many ways.

* * *

If this was what Ben could do with his house, Connor had every hope he'd work the same miracle on his money pit. The Carpenters' house was a showplace, and the multilevel deck where Ben flipped ribs and steaks on his gas grill was not only functional but beautiful.

Odd that Connor felt so relaxed around Ben and Robert, and he could easily let himself form friendships with the men.

Friends had fallen by the wayside as his real estate career had developed. Not that he'd shunned anyone on purpose. He'd simply been too busy and too focused on building a name for himself in the real estate market to keep bonds fresh by going out or even calling. Unless, of course, someone needed his house sold or was looking for a new one.

What few friends he'd kept had left him as fast as lightning when Connor's life had hit rock bottom.

So be it. He had Tracy. He didn't need anyone else.

Except Juliana.

He had to force himself to stop thinking about her when his body physically reacted. He'd never been one to have the kind of sexual appetite that distracted him from business or made him hop from bed to bed. No woman had ever affected him so profoundly, and he hoped to hell no other woman would.

Juliana was almost more than he could handle.

She'd been right—they should have kept things between them strictly professional. He simply couldn't. Lord knew he tried, especially since Kelley-Wilson Realty was his fresh start. It needed to succeed. It had to or he was sunk. Maybe permanently this time.

What the hell's wrong with me?

Had he been a weaker man, he'd have blamed her. Connor knew better. Juliana wasn't at fault here. She'd been the one to try to put some limits on their relationship. He'd pushed for more.

Why?

Because he had to. Simple as that. Unless she pushed him away, he was never going to let her go.

Ben popped the cap off a long-neck beer. He held it out for Connor.

Connor waved it off. "Not my brand."

With a shrug, Ben took a drink.

"Can't wait for fireworks," Robert said with the glee of a child. "Went all out. Spent a buttload on illegal stuff. Should scare the shit outta all the dogs in the neighborhood."

"I love fireworks," Ben added. "Makes me feel like a naughty kid."

Connor couldn't help but smile at the banter. "I wasn't allowed to have too many when I was growing up. Sparklers, firecrackers, sure—but the big stuff?" He gave his head a shake. "My parents were afraid I'd burn the house down."

"But you set some off anyway, didn't you?" Robert asked.

"Of course," Connor replied. "Trace and I set them off at the park. Watched the pyrotechnics then ran the hell away before the cops came."

"And said park was where?" Ben asked.

"South side of Indianapolis." Since this was the first time he'd spent with Juliana's friends, Connor had expected questions. He braced himself for the answers he could give.

"Born a Hoosier or was it an unfortunate accident?"

"Unfortunate?" Connor chuckled. "It was good for me." *For a while...* "I actually moved to Indiana when I was five. Don't remember much of New Jersey, where I was born, so Hoosier is pretty much all I've ever known or been."

"Except now you're an Illini," Robert said. "What brings you to our fair town?"

"Real estate." Leaving it at that, even knowing it wouldn't suffice, Connor grabbed a plastic cup, scooped some ice out of the open cooler, and poured himself some soda.

"Bullshit." Robert set his beer down. "No one comes here for *real estate.*"

After a drink, Connor wiped the back of his sleeve over his mouth. "I did."

"Goddamn it!" Eyes full of anger, Robert slammed his bottle down. "Look, we all care about Juliana. A lot. We're not about to let some jerk—"

Ben put a restraining hand on Robert's arm. "Easy there, buddy."

After a few tense moments, Robert nodded curtly.

"Connor's not a jerk," Ben said. Then he leveled a hard stare. "What he *is*, however, is far too private. And that's just not gonna cut it with us."

Since Juliana had shown him some of Robert's houses, Connor couldn't afford to piss him off. They needed to work together. Plus, Connor genuinely liked the guy. "Can we start again?"

"What?" Robert's brows gathered.

"Can we start again? Let me explain," Connor set his glass down. "I *did* come to Cloverleaf for real estate, but I came knowing something you don't—something no one here knows yet." Tracy would have to understand that he needed to share this information with Juliana's friends. It was the only way to keep them from condemning him, and he wanted their trust. "I'm going to tell you both, and I'm trusting you to keep it under your hats."

He'd obviously piqued their curiosity, because both men leaned in as though Connor was about to reveal the elusive secret of understanding women. He contained a smile they probably wouldn't appreciate.

"I'm here because Barrett Foods is coming to build a new factory. With it comes a couple thousand new jobs. Real estate will definitely be shoved into overdrive."

Ben let out a low whistle, while Robert simply looked catatonic.

"Juliana was supposed to clue you in on this soon, Robert," Connor added. "Tracy Barrett is coming in a few weeks to make the announcement, and she wants you to build her new house."

"Tracy Barrett?" Robert's eyes were wide. "She wants me to build her a house?"

"Yep. Juliana swears up and down you're the best builder in the state. I have to say after seeing a few of the places you've built, I agree."

"Holy shit." Snatching up his beer, Robert drank it dry. "Holy shit."

"It's only her home away from home, mind you," Connor added. "She's only wanting a few acres and a nice house. She'd like to keep it under a million, if you can—"

"A *million*?" With a shake of his head, Robert pointed at the cooler. "You better get me another beer, Ben."

Ben obeyed, chuckling the whole time. He opened it and handed to Robert, whose hands trembled. "I'll give you this, Connor. You know how to rattle a guy. How do you know about all this?"

"Tracy and I are close. We've been friends since middle school."

"Is she the 'Trace' with the fireworks?" Ben asked.

"Yep. We're close friends," Connor replied.

"Friends?"

"Nothing more. Since you two were blunt with me, I'll return the favor. I care for Juliana—professionally and personally. I need our firm to be a success every bit as much as she does. I have no intention of playing her or using her. She means the world to me. Okay?"

Ben's smile was genuine as he cuffed Connor on the shoulder. "Glad to hear it. You understand, though, that your announcement about Barrett Foods and that little declaration don't change anything?"

So much for laying the inquisition to rest. "Pardon?"

"You might have just bribed Robert into thinking you're the best thing since sliced bread, but once he sobers, we'll both still be keeping a close eye on you."

"As will the Ladies Who Lunch," Robert added.

Chapter Sixteen

Juliana didn't notice her hands trembling until she shut the car door. She stared at her fingers, wondering whether anyone had seen the slight tremors or whether the shaking had developed after the terror of facing her first closing alone.

Terror?

At first. But as the closing went on, it became exhilaration.

Connor was going to be proud. He'd told her she was ready—*more* than ready. She'd met with the owners, convinced them to list, and then sold the house within a week; he'd decided she should see this through to the very end. Solo.

She'd done well. Both the sellers and buyers were thrilled with the deal, the paperwork had gone through without a glitch, and the closing had been pleasant and polite. And very profitable.

Not only was Connor going to be proud, she was damned proud of herself.

Uncle Francis was right. I am *a born salesman.*

Juliana slid behind the wheel of her white SUV, another of Connor's contributions. He'd helped her find it only ten days after they'd opened Kelley-Wilson Realty. Someone near

Chicago had an Enclave that was only three years old. The guy desperately wanted out of the lease, and she needed a bigger car at a cheap price. A match made in heaven. The interior was gray leather, and the inside still smelled new. Whenever she drove it, she felt successful. A silly notion, but her life had truly changed, probably forever, and the SUV served as a symbol of that.

She plucked her cell from her pocket and called Connor. By the third ring, she knew she'd get voice mail since he usually answered before the second.

"You've reached Connor Wilson. Please leave your name and number, and I'll return your call as soon as I can. Thanks."

"Hey. It's me. Closing went great. Wanted to brag, but you're busy. Call me." She gave her watch a quick glance. It was later than she thought. "Um...wow. It's almost four. We're supposed to meet Robert at the office in less than an hour. Figured you and Ms. Barrett would be here by now."

Where was he?

The appointment with Robert had been planned for weeks, and Connor had mentioned it before he left, which meant he hadn't forgotten.

After Connor had explained about Barrett Foods, Robert had been almost too excited to function. She and Connor had struck a nice deal with him so he could focus on building and not selling his homes. Robert paid them a lower commission than any other Realtors in return for putting the many Barrett clients they gave him at the front of his line. He was even hiring more tradesmen to increase the speed of his work schedule. The last time she'd talked to him, he'd put in his request to take a year's personal leave of absence from school with an eye on walking away for good when that time ended.

The meeting today was to bring Robert and Tracy Barrett

together to make long-term plans, everything from discussing how many executives would need custom houses to making arrangements for Tracy's personal home.

Juliana made it back to the office with time to spare, probably because she hadn't stopped to pick up Starbucks coffee. There was always a fresh pot at the office, and she was being as frugal as possible. A couple of months into the partnership, the firm was growing nicely, but her nature was never to crow too loudly over success or expect it to continue. The move by Barrett Foods was going well, but the real estate market was volatile at best, dismal at worst. She wouldn't assume she'd "made it," especially this early in the game. She had a year to prove to herself she could make this her new life. Hence her nearly crippling inability to spend money on anything that didn't benefit the firm, especially something as frivolous as overpriced foo-foo coffee.

What if a baby's on the way?

Her periods had been horribly irregular her whole life. Sure, she'd technically missed one. But that wasn't unusual in the least. Nor did she have a single symptom of being pregnant. Just to be sure, she'd grab a pregnancy test at the drug store on her way home.

Not gonna let that worry run my life.

As Connor had a habit of saying, *"Take it one day at a time."*

His Escalade wasn't in the driveway, but Robert's truck was.

"Hey," she said as Robert came over to open her door. "You're early. How you doin'?"

"Honestly? I'm nervous as hell." At least he was trying to smile.

"Nervous? No reason to be." Even though she was, too. She grabbed her briefcase from the backseat and led him inside the office.

Robert followed her to the conference table she'd bought.

That need was immediate, and she'd anticipated wanting to sit together with Connor, buyers, or sellers in one place. Thankfully, she found one in a local penny-pinchers' paper for dirt cheap. The chairs were a tad more expensive, but she'd insisted on something both attractive and comfortable.

Her one luxury.

She set her briefcase on her desk. "Let me try Connor again. He should be here any minute."

Robert plopped onto a chair and fiddled with one of the green pens she'd left on the table.

"You've reached Connor—"

She hit the button to go right to voice mail and tried to keep her words soft. "Connor, where *are* you? Robert's already here. Hurry."

"Something wrong?" Robert asked.

"No. Nothing like that. Maybe Tracy's plane was late." Although Connor surely would have called or texted her if they needed to move the meeting back.

One thing they did well as partners was communicate. Yet the more she thought about it, the more something niggled at her. In the weeks they'd worked together, there were times she'd been unable to reach him. She tried to rationalize those episodes. Maybe his cell phone battery had run down, or he'd left his phone in his car. Now as those memories filled her mind, she worried.

This meeting was the most important in the history of the firm, most likely determining whether Kelley-Wilson Realty would be a success or a here-and-gone venture.

"Where are you?" Juliana whispered to herself, letting her temper slowly rise.

"What's wrong, Jules?" Robert popped up from his chair

and went to the coffeemaker. He held up the empty pot. "Want some?"

"Absolutely. I'll start a new pot." At least making coffee would kill a few minutes of waiting.

By the time the coffee was done and they were both seated at the table, sipping from mismatched mugs, she was fighting a battle between worry and anger.

"Where's Connor?" Robert asked.

"Running late." She tried to ease his mind—and her own. "Could be a million reasons. Traffic. A late plane. Stopped to get a bite to eat." All of which he should've called to let her know. She might be able to forgive him for being rude to her, but she sure didn't think Robert deserved to wait. Then again, it was only a few minutes past the meeting time. No reason to have an anxiety attack.

"Tell me something, Jules, do you like the guy?"

Robert's question was the same one she thought about almost every hour of every day. That and whether a broken condom was going to toss her life into a tornado. "Yeah, I do."

I think I love him.

"Your name or Connor's comes up every time I talk to someone in the business," he added.

She cocked her head. "Really?"

"Really. Think about it. Cloverleaf isn't exactly a big city." A grin lit his face. "Most of the talk's about how pissed off Max Schumm is."

That thought made her smile as well. "Good. Arrogant jackass."

"Exactly."

That explained why she'd heard from a couple of other custom builders who'd worked with Schumm Realty in the past and were looking to jump ship. Max had clearly burned more than a couple of bridges, so why shouldn't Kelley-Wilson Realty take advantage of that?

The office door opened. A laughing blonde slipped through, followed by a laughing Connor.

Thank God.

I'm gonna wring his neck.

Juliana swallowed the litany of questions she wanted to fire at him. Not only would it be rude in front of Robert and Tracy, but she didn't want to seem like a needy girlfriend. If that's what she was. Or were they roommates? Or partners? All the boundaries were mixed up and so convoluted, it was no wonder she was confused.

What a fucking mess.

Which was exactly what she'd been trying to avoid.

At least this meeting would distract her, giving her a chance to figure things out before she and Connor were alone.

Then they could talk, really talk. The time had come to set down some more ground rules. Everything that happened between them hit her like a tsunami, and she was afraid of drowning.

"Spontaneous" wasn't in her vocabulary for anything other than ordering a pitcher of margaritas. But Connor made her spontaneous—from the way they worked together to the way they made love.

Connor's voice pulled her back from her thoughts. "Juliana, this is Tracy Barrett."

Juliana shook the blonde's hand and tried not to look like she was sizing her up, even if she was.

Tracy was a petite thing, several inches shorter than Juliana and almost painfully thin. The way Connor had tossed her name around as being an important player in the business world, Juliana had formed a picture of some Amazon woman—a warrior in a black business suit. What she got was Twiggy in a gauzy summer dress.

"Nice to meet you, Ms. Barrett."

"Oh, please." Her smile was genuine. "No formalities. As much as Connor's told me about you, I feel like we've known each other for years."

A moment of panic over exactly what he'd said came and left. Of course he'd talked about her. She was his business partner.

Tracy shattered that wishful thinking. "I'm going to help him move his stuff from storage here Saturday."

"Yeah," Robert said with a chuckle. "They're shacking up together."

"So I heard." Tracy shook his offered hand. "Temporarily, right?"

Robert chuckled again. "We both know better."

Connor pulled out a chair. For Tracy. "Have a seat. Let's get down to business."

At least there would be something going on that would help her think about anything except backing her man into a corner and firing question after question at him.

* * *

Connor didn't hesitate at the door, walking right into the kitchen. It was empty. "Red?"

No reply. He hoped to hell that didn't mean she was still angry. Not that she'd come out and told him she was pissed. She'd been wonderful with Tracy and Robert, but she'd answered any of his own questions with abrupt, almost rude replies. The tone of her voice in her voice mail messages was another clue. Pure irritation. Then there was the scorching glare she'd thrown him when he'd told her he was driving Tracy to her hotel.

Kicking his shoes into the small pile of hers by the door, he hung his suit jacket over one of the chairs. "Red? You home?"

He didn't hear the shower running until he stepped into the master suite.

His first instinct was to strip and join her, to soothe her with his touch. But he had only a tenuous grip on his emotions as it was. If he made love to her right now, he was liable to say something stupid.

Like *I love you.*

Juliana's panicked messages still rang in his ears. Once he'd picked up Tracy, they'd started talking, like always. Seeing her face-to-face was enough to make the words spill out as he told her everything that had happened, especially in the last few weeks. After she listened, she'd made her usual request.

He snorted. Actually, it was more like an order from a five-star general. And then they'd gone to one meeting and been late to another.

Tracy didn't think he should've moved in with Juliana. Not that she was jealous. They'd decided long ago—all the way back to their one and only date in high school—that there simply wasn't any chemistry between them.

By the time he'd stripped down to his briefs, Juliana had turned off the water. He crawled into bed.

"Don't freak out if there's a nearly naked man in your bedroom," he called.

"Connor?"

"Nope." He tried a terrible Spanish accent. "Antonio Banderas."

Her laughter touched his heart.

She came into the bedroom wearing nothing but a blue towel, and it looked damned good on her. "Funny, you don't look like Antonio Banderas."

Despite Connor's plan to only snuggle up to her and get some sleep, his cock went from soft to hard fast enough to make his head spin. He bunched the sheet up in his lap to hide his erection. "Damn."

Her gaze raked him from head to toe, the same way he'd stared at her. "I was thinking the same thing about you."

Would there ever be a time he didn't want to toss her on a bed and make love to her until she screamed? He faked an exaggerated yawn, hoping to convince her of his fatigue. The fake yawn turned into a real one. "I'm exhausted. Long day."

"Yeah. It was." After fishing a pair of panties and a red shirt out of her dresser, she retreated back into the bathroom. A few moments later, the noise of a hair dryer kicked in.

He hadn't been lying when he said he was exhausted. By the time Juliana came back into the bedroom, he could barely keep his eyes open. She was dressed in the oversized T-shirt, and while she looked delectable, he knew he was going to be able to sleep despite the temptation.

She stared down at him from the side of the bed. "Left or right?"

His mind was too foggy to understand. "Left or right what?"

"Side of the bed. You're on the right. Did you decide to switch sides again?"

"Hadn't realized I did that."

"You do. All the time," she replied with a touch of annoyance. "Pick one and stick with it, or I'm kicking you out."

"Left." He lifted the sheet in invitation.

She flicked off the light, slid between the sheets, and rolled to give him her back.

Connor turned to his side and molded himself to her, pressing his thighs against the backs of hers and draping an arm over her waist. Her hair smelled like flowers.

"Shouldn't we talk?" she whispered.

"About?"

He could almost see her roll her eyes. "The chance of rain."

Another yawn slipped out. "Can we save it for breakfast?"

Sleep claimed him before he heard a response.

* * *

Juliana would've answered his question if Connor had given her more than a few seconds before he conked out. Where had he been for so long after he'd picked up Tracy?

The wariness was difficult. She'd never felt anything as powerful or all-consuming before. Jimmy might have been a terminal flirt, but not once did she want to yank one of his target's hair right off her head.

But Tracy Barrett?

The woman meant something to Connor, something important. Exactly what remained a mystery, which made Juliana's mind wander down all sorts of paths it shouldn't. One led to an irrational jealousy she had difficulty crushing.

How weird that she could implicitly trust Connor as her business partner. But as a lover? As a boyfriend?

A stupid word. "Boyfriend." They were both in their thirties. To call him her boyfriend seemed absurd.

Then what was he? Her lover? Her roomie?

Thankfully, sleep began to drug her thoughts—a blessing since those thoughts ranged from immature to downright silly.

Juliana's last coherent thought before drifting off was that if Tracy wanted Connor she was in for a hell of a fight.

* * *

The moment of truth had finally arrived. Juliana had been avoiding it long enough.

Connor was at an early closing and had left before Juliana even wanted to think about getting out of the warm bed. But the moment she'd heard his SUV leave, she'd jumped up, fished the little sack from the bottom of her panty drawer, and headed to the bathroom.

Juliana set the white stick on the sink and sat down on the closed toilet seat, torn between wanting the little plus to appear and hoping it wouldn't. While it might be easier to just go back to being her and Connor as a couple, her heart wanted this child. A baby she'd created with Connor. It seemed almost too good to be true.

Why did the minutes click by so damned slowly? This was supposed to be the fastest and most accurate test on the market. She hadn't realized it was also powerful enough to change the perception of the passage of time.

Did all potential mothers have this kind of anxiety?

The bathroom smelled like Connor's cologne, so Juliana took a deep breath, letting his scent comfort her. He'd left his wet towel on the floor again and she made a mental note to scold him about it later before realizing the last thing in the world she wanted to be was a nag.

One more minute. Then she'd have her answer.

What would Connor say? He'd been rather nonchalant when the condom broke. Would he be every bit as nonchalant if they were going to be parents? For that matter, could she even handle the news?

Five. Four. Three. Two—

Juliana stared at the stick, blinking to be sure her eyes weren't deceiving her.

"I'm pregnant."

Chapter Seventeen

Jules!"

Juliana looked up from her desk. Concentrating on work hadn't been easy after last night. Why hadn't Connor wanted to make love?

Was he already bored with her?

I'll go crazy thinking like that.

At least she had a distraction now...

She smiled as Mallory and then Bethany and Danielle spilled into the office. The three of them were dressed in shorts, summery shirts, and sandals, making Juliana peek down at her business suit and envy their three months of freedom. The only thing she missed about school was summer break.

And her students. She'd expected that, but the intensity came as a surprise.

The Ladies Who Lunch surrounded her desk, shaking their heads and clucking like mother hens.

"This won't do," Mallory declared. "It's eighty degrees and the sun is shining. You should be out working on your tan."

"But here you are, stuck at your desk," Dani said.

Beth slapped her hand lightly against the desktop. "I think it's time for someone—"

"*Three* someones," Dani interrupted.

"—to come and rescue you."

Juliana put her pen down. "Meaning you three?"

"You got it!" Mallory slid behind Juliana's chair and pulled her away from the desk. "We're kidnapping you."

"Kidnapping?"

"Yep. Ben made us a picnic lunch. For an hour or so, we're going to be the Ladies Who Lunch again."

A quick check of the clock brought a frown. "But I have an appointment at—"

"No, you don't," Beth said.

"I don't? How would you know?"

"Connor and Ben arranged all this." Mallory took Juliana's hand and dragged her toward the door. "Connor's taking your appointment, Ben made a fantastic lunch, and all of us want a chance to sit and talk, just like we used to. We haven't seen you since the Fourth of July cookout."

Guilt hit her broadside. "I'm so sorry."

"Sorry?" Danielle asked.

"I've been so damn busy I've been ignoring all of you."

"Not ignoring," Bethany insisted. "This business is hectic. We get that."

"You've got a new firm to run," Dani added. "We totally understand."

"But," Mallory said, "we missed you something terrible."

A smile bloomed, and Juliana blinked back happy tears. "I missed all of you, too." Shedding her jacket, she tossed it on a chair and opened the door. "Where are we heading?"

"It's a surprise." Mallory exited, followed by Dani and Beth.

"Good thing I love surprises." Juliana locked the door behind them.

Less than ten minutes later, they were in the city park.

The sun on her face was heaven, and the picnic table inside the shelter gave them a nice place to eat.

Juliana smiled, loving every moment of being with her friends again. She banished the guilt at not seeing them as often as she used to, pleased that they realized how difficult it had been to get Kelley-Wilson Realty up and running and to keep it going.

She should've known that the Ladies would be understanding—theirs was the type of friendship that didn't need daily contact to thrive. The bonds were strong, even strong enough to allow Juliana the distance she needed to make this change in her life.

It was, however, a bit of a surprise that Connor recognized she needed a break, if only for a lunch away with her friends.

"You said Connor called you?" she asked Mallory.

"Actually, he called Ben," she replied. "He said you seemed a bit overwhelmed."

"I'm *not* overwhelmed."

"I didn't say you were. It was Connor's word, not mine. I figured he didn't know how to describe exactly what you were feeling, so he just picked a word."

Dani chuckled. "Men aren't all that great at explaining things, especially when emotions are involved."

"Amen to that," Beth chimed in.

Mallory gathered the last of the plastic containers from the picnic table and stowed them in the cooler. Then she sat down on the bench next to Juliana. "He meant well. Plus, you have to admit, you missed us as much as we missed you."

"I did. It's just…I hate that Connor thinks I can't do my job."

"Oh Lord." Danielle rolled her eyes. "There's the Jules I know and love—not happy unless she's got something to fret about."

Insults from friends always had less bite, but Dani was on to something. Juliana was a worrywart, always had been. She should be thanking Connor for caring enough to reach out to her friend's husband, and she should be grateful to Ben for going to the trouble of making that fantastic lunch for the Ladies. The man could cook.

Dani softened her words by sitting on Juliana's other side and giving her a hug. "Now, tell us all about this Tracy Barrett. Heard she and Connor are close."

"How did you know?" Juliana asked.

"He told Ben," Mallory replied. "The two of them are getting pretty chummy."

Maybe Ben can nudge Tracy right out of Connor's life.

"Uh-oh. Why the frown?" Bethany asked.

Juliana shrugged.

"What you need is something fun. How about a swim?" Bethany whipped her tank top over her head to reveal a yellow one-piece with blue polka dots. "Dani and I are going to work on our tans. Join us?"

Mallory opened her mouth before quickly closing it. She directed that intense gaze at Juliana, the one who seemed capable of seeing straight through to the heart of the matter. "You know what, I changed my mind. I'm not up for swimming today."

"But we promised Connor we'd drag Jules into the pool," Beth protested.

Sometimes Juliana forgot how much older she and Mallory were than Beth and Dani. Sure, it was only four or five years, but the difference was more than mathematics. Barely thirty was worlds away from thirty-five.

"I'd really rather not swim," Juliana said. "I sunburn in two minutes flat. I'm going to pay for today as it is—probably get a hundred new freckles."

"We brought sunscreen." Beth fished around in her bag and held up a bottle.

"Eighteen block?" Juliana snorted a laugh. "I need a minimum of forty-eight. I'm a ginger, remember?"

"Really, ladies. I'm not up to swimming," Mallory said. "Don't worry about us. Go on. Get a tan and let the lifeguards ogle you."

Beth looked back at the pool, nothing short of hunger in her eyes. "If you're sure..."

"We're sure." Mallory shooed them away with the back of her hand.

Both slung their bags over their shoulders.

"See you, Jules," Bethany said, kissing Juliana's cheek.

"Yeah, bye, Jules," Danielle added with a pat on the shoulder.

They headed toward the pool, one of the few civic advancements Cloverleaf had made in a very long time. Would the arrival of Barrett Foods bring an influx of money to the community? What other good things could the residents look forward to?

"I hope Beth and Dani don't think I chased them away." Juliana glanced over her shoulder.

Mallory followed her gaze to the women, who were showing plastic season passes to the teenager manning the pool's entrance. "Nah. Judging from their tans, they're right where they wanted to be."

They probably didn't want to deal with her ridiculous problems anyway.

"How's it really going?" Mallory watched her as if expecting her to be overwhelmed with emotion.

Since she'd never been able to hide anything from her best friend, Juliana didn't even try. "A while back, a condom broke."

"Oh…"

"Yeah. I feel the same way. *Oh.*"

"What are you going to do about it?" Mallory asked. "The baby, I mean. The condom's already a lost cause."

"You knew? How?"

"It was a joke. Did you take a test?"

"Yeah. I'm definitely pregnant."

"What did Connor say?"

"I'm not going to tell him. Not yet. Not until I pass the first trimester."

"Won't he be angry?" Mallory asked.

"It's what I want, Mal. After my last pregnancy, I just don't want to get my hopes up, let alone his. Okay? Not Dani or Beth, either. Just us. Please?"

Mallory thought it over a good, long while before giving Juliana a brusque nod.

A sigh of relief slipped out. "Thank you."

"Are we happy about this?"

"We're not even thinking about it. Not yet. I—I can't let myself hope until I'm past the scary part."

Mallory took her hand. "Then we won't talk about it. Tell me about Connor instead." A smile lit her face. "Considering you two are going to have a baby, I'd say your relationship is going strong."

"I only let him move in because his place is such a pit and—"

"You mean you finally got to see it?"

"Well, no, but—"

"Ben likes him."

A sardonic laugh slipped from Juliana. "That was an abrupt change of topic."

"Didn't want the conversation to turn maudlin." Mallory hopped up and fished a water bottle from the cooler. "Want one?"

"No, thanks." Juliana kept turning around Mallory's words. "You've piqued my curiosity. Why does Ben like him?"

After a long swig of water, Mallory twisted the lid back on. "He says he and Connor are a lot alike. Both have a rather odd sense of humor. Both work their asses off. Both are committed to the people they love."

"Love? *Love?* Are you saying that Connor told Ben he—he *loves* me?"

Mallory gave an exaggerated eye roll. "Puhleeze. Even when they're in love, men won't admit it right away."

"Then why would Ben say something like that?"

"Because every time they're together all Connor does is talk about you."

Juliana's first response was to scoff, at least until she realized that she'd spent the entire picnic talking about him. Sure, a lot of those comments were about Kelley-Wilson Realty, but damn it all if her entire life wasn't wrapped up in Connor Wilson.

So much for escaping school and asserting my independence.

Mallory let out a squeak and then giggled.

"What's wrong?"

She pulled her cell phone out of her pocket. "Phone vibrated. Always tickles me." A couple of taps on the screen broadened her grin. "Ben says we're going to help Connor move his stuff out of storage. Says we can have a barbeque for everyone after that. Since it's only a few days until school starts, we'll turn it into a back-to-school celebration."

"Wonder if Tracy'll be there."

"Tracy Barrett? Is she close enough to him to come to a barbeque?"

"Yes. Um, no." She shrugged. "I honestly don't know. Connor's never told me their whole story."

Cocking her head, Mallory said, "Do I detect jealousy?"

"A shitload," Juliana admitted. "Probably because I don't have any idea what she means to him."

Sitting down next to her, Mallory wrapped her arm around Juliana's shoulders. "How about you tell me what you do know?"

"That'll take all of five seconds. They grew up together. End of story."

"Perhaps you and Connor need to talk. He should tell you all about Tracy, and you should tell him all about Jimmy."

My thoughts exactly. Although she'd already told Connor she was divorced, she'd never explained about Jimmy's drinking or told him she'd lost a child. "We will. Not knowing is killing me."

Can a person die of stress?

On the other hand, this was exactly what Juliana had wanted. At least it was what she thought she wanted when she'd blurted out the invitation for him to move in. Now she was thinking about making it a permanent arrangement, especially if she didn't lose this pregnancy.

So what exactly was Connor to her? A temporary roomie? A permanent boyfriend? A potential husband?

Problem was she wasn't exactly sure what she wanted. Only one thing was certain...

She loved Connor and the possibility of this baby, which meant there was no turning back.

Chapter Eighteen

Connor looked out over the small crowd standing in the parking lot, not at all surprised to see so many people. Tracy Barrett was a woman who demanded attention—even back when she was class president—and most of the town had turned out to hear her announcement.

The entire Cloverleaf Chamber of Commerce was in the audience, front and center. No wonder. In a quick, private meeting that morning, they'd been told of what Barrett Foods had planned for their community. The three men and two women had been glued to Tracy's side ever since, as if losing sight of her would make her disappear and take her new development along with her. They'd arranged for her to make her announcement at Douglas High School, even getting the principal to set up a podium and microphone for her to use.

The new factory would bump up Cloverleaf's population by a good twenty-five percent. Those people would need houses, and Connor's goal was for Kelley-Wilson Realty to sell as many of them as they could manage. Thankfully, Juliana worked every bit as hard as he did, which was a good thing for their relationship.

He didn't have to explain or make excuses for working eighteen-hour days.

He scanned the throng again, searching for red hair. Finding Juliana was easy, but he frowned when he recognized the man chatting her ear off.

Max Schumm.

No surprise. A guy like him hadn't become successful without being informed about what was going on in and around his town, and he wasn't going to simply roll over and play dead. Connor and Juliana's instant success was surely a sore spot.

Max had to be seething at how easily they'd toppled him from his throne.

Question was—did he view Juliana as a worthy competitor, or was he trying to lure her into a trap? An image of a spider with Max's face flashed in Connor's mind, luring an innocent Juliana into the web that was Schumm Realty.

Damn if some of the anxiety running through him wasn't based on jealousy that Max wanted something more from her than business.

"You ready?" Tracy took his hand. "I hate talking to crowds."

"Bullshit." Connor gave her a squeeze. "You can't lie to me. You eat this stuff up." A nod toward the reporters who'd arrived in vans complete with satellite dishes. "Chicago even has some stations here."

"You'd think I was announcing a run for president."

"It might not be *that* major, but I imagine your announcement will stir up the piranhas."

"Yeah." She snorted. "Hope they don't eat me alive."

"I've got your back."

The mayor stepped up to the makeshift podium. His first words were lost because the microphone wasn't working. A tech guy who didn't appear old enough to shave fiddled around until he fixed the problem, then he gave the mayor a thumbs-up.

In a heartbeat, Tracy morphed from his sweet, supportive best friend into the "barracuda" who'd earned her reputation as a tough person to please and who demanded the best from everyone who worked for her. Dropping Connor's hand, she fixed a determined expression on her face and strode to the mayor's side.

The time had come to rock Cloverleaf's world.

* * *

Max Schumm was the last person Juliana wanted to see, let alone talk to. He sidled up to her and offered his hand, but his greeting wasn't at all what she'd expected.

"I've gotta admit it, I underestimated you," he said as she shook his hand.

While she bristled inside, she kept the mask of calm firmly in place, the one Connor had taught her to use with clients.

"Never let them know how bad you want their listing."

"So, Max…is that a compliment or an insult?" She kept her tone calm and even despite the urge to let disdain drip from every word.

"Never thought the two of you could take things as far as you have."

"Ah, then it was an insult."

"Not at all."

She withdrew her hand since he didn't seem at all inclined to let go. "Then what did you mean?"

"You've proven yourselves to me. It's time to welcome you and Connor into my firm."

His audacity accomplished a rare feat. It left Juliana speechless.

Max was oblivious to the fact he'd stupefied her. "I'm even

thinking about letting you and Connor have a special place at Schumm Realty, just to add a little incentive for my other agents. You know, make them try harder to be more like you two." His expression was so smug she had to clench her hands into tight fists to keep from smacking his face. "What do you think about green blazers? Something to set you two apart and go with your Irish theme?"

"Irish theme?"

"Yeah. You know, the shamrocks and stuff you use. It plays to stupid clients really well, so I might even let you keep them on your business cards. Hell, I might sweeten the pot by having some signs made special for you two." He waggled his eyebrows.

Did he think what he offered was even remotely seductive?

He had another think coming.

"So what do you say? We can make our announcement right after the barracuda's done."

"I say thanks, but no, thanks, Max."

His scoff hung in the air. "I'll give you one chance to change your answer."

"No, thanks," she repeated.

"You can't be serious."

"I'm dead serious," she replied. "We're doing fine, and we're not looking to change things." Afraid she sounded too harsh, she added, "Thanks so much for thinking of us, though. I'll be sure and tell Connor everything you said." And then they'd probably have a good, long laugh.

Max's façade of friendliness fell away, leaving behind a fierce scowl. "Do you have any idea what you're passing up? For Christ's sake, you're nothing but a—a fly-by-night firm in a pissant town. I could crush you both like bugs." He clamped his hand into a fist as if doing exactly what he'd said he could do.

Underneath the trappings of success, he was nothing but a schoolyard bully.

As if she'd ever allow a bully to get the best of her. "You could try," Juliana shot back.

"Don't worry, sweetheart. I will. Oh, I will."

As he marched away, she smiled, picturing a cartoon character with steam literally pouring from his ears.

Oh yes. She was definitely going to tell Connor all about this.

The mayor's voice screeched through the speakers, drawing winces from the crowd.

Her gaze shifted to the stage, quickly settling on Connor. The way her heart jumped at the sight of him told her she was already a goner. This man had a grip on her that she'd never be able to break.

I love Connor Wilson.

Fuck.

He was at Tracy's side. Juliana caught their joined hands, which made her stomach plummet to her feet.

The day just kept on giving.

Tracy took the mayor's place at the microphone. Juliana paid little attention, instead watching Connor. As if knowing she'd focused on him, his gaze caught hers. He smiled and motioned for her to come to the stage.

Her first and entirely immature response was to flip him the bird for holding hands with another woman. But she refrained, not wanting to end up on the front page of the *Cloverleaf Gazette*. It would be great publicity for the firm to have one partner giving the middle finger to the other at the ceremony announcing the new Barrett Foods factory.

Besides, she was angrier at herself than him. It was her own ridiculous jealousy that tainted her thoughts. What she needed to do was sit the man down and ask him what was going on between him and Tracy. Then she could brush the wariness aside and focus on all the wonderful things Tracy and her company were going to do for the town—and for Kelley-Wilson Realty.

Although the whole speech took only ten minutes, Juliana couldn't help but be impressed. Tracy gave the most influential people in Cloverleaf a passionate, stern talk, leaving Juliana in awe of the woman. Tracy reminded her of the only female principal she'd worked for, a woman who had no fear of saying exactly what needed to be said, and damn people's feelings.

Tracy had explained that the new factory would bring many current Barrett Foods employees to Cloverleaf, but then she'd smoothed over the rather shocked crowd by letting them know at least half of the employees would be new to her company, hired from the town's workforce.

"Nice speech." Juliana resisted the urge to cuff her on the shoulder like one of the Ladies. "You really got the town buzzing. They'll think you're their savior."

"Thanks." Tracy looked to Connor. "Ready to head out to the site?"

"Sure," he replied.

"Wanna come with?" Tracy asked Juliana. "We're going to see the overpriced farmland I now own."

"You're going to the factory site?"

"Yeah," he replied. "But you don't have to go, Red. You've got plenty to do, I'm sure."

It chafed that he was revoking the invitation, and she wasn't about to appear the fool by begging to go.

"It's just a field," Tracy offered, throwing Juliana a glance full of pity. "No big thing. Then we're heading out to see the house Robert's building in Buffalo Springs. I imagine you've seen it already."

"We need to get going," Connor said to Tracy before he stared at Juliana. "We won't be long. I'll catch you back at the office."

Which translated into *I want to be alone with Tracy.*

God, she needed to get a grip on this irrational jealousy. *Quickly.* Or she was going to turn into a raving shrew.

She tried to save face. "I imagine the phone's ringing off the hook now that Barrett people have the green light to start searching for homes." Just to chastise Connor, she added, "It's very nice of you to invite me to come along, Tracy." She scowled at him.

He was too oblivious to get the hint. "I'll take Tracy, then I'll be in later to help you."

"You do that." Juliana strode away before she poured a bucket of angry over his head.

* * *

"You're in the doghouse now, mister." Tracy poked Connor's chest. Hard.

"I am?" Sure, Juliana looked like something was bugging her. But why would she be mad at him? He'd just figured her encounter with Max had soured her mood. "What did I do?"

"You should have asked her to come along."

"Why? You did."

"Oh, Connor"—she shook her head—"you really aren't much of a ladies' man, are you?"

"It would help if women made a lick of sense."

Especially Juliana.

While redheads were notorious for having tempers, hers could fire as hot as the sun in a matter of moments—easily forgivable since her passion ran every bit as deep. He'd have to smooth over whatever he'd said or done when he got home tonight.

Home.

After such a short time, he probably shouldn't be thinking of his temporary residence at Juliana's as home. Yet he did, and not because that was where the office was and his clothes now hung.

Home was wherever Juliana was.

"She's mad at you and you're *smiling*?" Tracy asked. "Uh-oh. She's coming back."

Juliana fished a piece of paper out of her purse as she hurried back to them. "I forgot to give you this." She handed the paper to Tracy. "My friends are having a barbeque this weekend. They wanted to invite you. I mean, you don't know too many people here, and we figured if Connor and I were going, you might like to go, too."

"That would be great." Tracy glanced at the paper before shoving it in her pocket. "With you being Connor's partner, I can finally get to know you better."

"Good." Without a word to him, she turned on her heel and left.

"You are in *so* much trouble." Tracy snickered.

"It would help if you'd explain why."

"Oh no, Casanova. You dug the hole. You find your own way out."

He rubbed the back of his neck, straining to figure out why his girlfriend was in a huff. Nothing came to mind. "Women are too confusing."

"No, we're not. How hard is it to tell us we're pretty and smart while you give us roses and chocolates?"

Connor tweaked her nose, treating her like the sister he'd always wished he'd had. "C'mon, Trace. Let's go take a look at where you'll be spending all your time from now on."

Chapter Nineteen

Connor yawned, not even bothering to hide it behind his hand. A glance at the clock revealed why.

Midnight.

And here they were, still working.

He was exhausted—too tired to do another thing. Not fill out a single piece of paperwork or answer another e-mail. There was nothing else he could do.

Except make love to Juliana.

Despite how much he'd wanted her, they'd both been so tense the last few nights, he hadn't pushed her. Or himself, knowing there were sometimes bad repercussions to his self-control when he got too overwhelmed. That, and her mood had been...odd.

Something was bothering her. He'd waited patiently for her to tell him what was wrong, but she hadn't opened up to him, which stung until he thought about how he hadn't opened up to her about his past.

Soon.

Perhaps she would tell him what weighed on her mind if he could get her to relax, and he knew the perfect way to accomplish that feat.

"Hey, Red." He was up and moving, needing to touch her.

Easing back her chair, he slid his hands over her shoulders and nibbled on her earlobe.

Juliana let out a sigh and dropped her head to the side. Her hum signaled her surrender. "Connor...that feels wonderful."

He brushed his lips over her neck as he eased his palms down until they covered her breasts. "I want you," he whispered, teasing her ear with his tongue. "God, I want to be inside you."

"Not too tired this time?"

They should talk, especially about that acerbic comment, but he was too lost in the desire to feel her soft skin beneath his fingertips.

Her clothes were in his way, so he helped her stand and started unbuttoning her blouse. "Definitely not too tired."

After he eased the garment from her shoulder, he walked her backward toward the conference table. The idea of making love to her—right there on the table—had his cock hard as granite. That one act would forever remove any barrier between their professional and personal lives, and he imagined they could share sly, flirty glances at meetings, remembering the interlude.

Connor popped the clasp on her bra and eased her down, pressing her back against the table.

Juliana shivered. "C-cold."

"It's ninety-five out."

Her sensual smile made him grin. "It's August. Of course it's ninety-five. *Outside.* The table's cold."

"Then I'll just have to warm you up."

He drew a nipple between his lips, suckling as it hardened into a tight nub. With a rather loud moan, she tunneled her fingers through his hair and drew up her knees. Taking that as an invitation, he tugged her skirt up until he bared her blue panties, which matched the bra he'd cast aside.

Damn but the woman wore the sexiest undergarments.

Dragging them down her shapely legs, Connor inhaled, loving the mixture of her perfume and feminine arousal.

"Connor…" Juliana tried to sit up, but he pressed her shoulders back to the table.

"I'll please you. I promise. Just relax and let me have control this time."

"But…"

He kissed her to stop her protest, a bit worried at why the woman who'd always been so free sexually was suddenly hesitant. That would definitely be one of the things they'd talk about.

But not now. Right now he wanted her too much to spit out a coherent sentence.

Tearing his mouth away from hers, he reverently kissed each breast, teasing the nipples with his tongue, before licking and nipping at her stomach. Then he eased his fingers against her core, spreading the folds as he stabbed his tongue into her.

* * *

Juliana gasped, digging her fingers back into his hair since there wasn't anything else to hold on to—just a bare, slick table.

Sweet Lord, they were having sex in the office. Thankfully, it was late. She'd locked the door and the shades had been pulled down. What would a client think if he walked in on them right now to see Connor's face between her thighs?

The man was talented, quickly finding and torturing the bundle of nerves that set her on fire. Although she felt far too vulnerable lying there exposed when he was fully dressed, he'd distracted her. Now the whole episode became erotic in a way that sent her desire higher and higher and…

He thrust his finger inside her at the same time he sucked hard on her sensitive nub, sending Juliana tumbling into a strong release. She squeezed his head between her thighs and moaned as a burst of heat spread from her core to her limbs. She rode the wave until he redoubled his efforts, making her rise to the summit again before a second climax seized her. Her body bucked as spasm after spasm shook her. A squeal slipped out, and she tugged hard enough on his hair that she probably jerked out a few strands.

"Enough. Please." She whimpered before panting like a marathoner at the twenty-sixth mile. "I—I need a minute."

He granted her quarter by easing away, but with a sly look in his eye he hummed a racy tune and started to strip for her. Not wanting to miss a moment, she sat up on her elbows to watch as she tried to catch her breath.

Slowly, enticingly, he unfastened his buttons, still humming before breaking out into song—"Sexual Healing," no less. His voice was passably pleasant. As if she gave a shit. Right now, she wanted to see that rock-hard body, every single inch of it.

Connor tossed his shirt at her and then went to work on his belt, unfastening it before whipping it through the loops and spinning it in the air like a lasso.

Juliana put two fingers to her lips and whistled. "Take it off! Take it all off!"

With a wink, he kept singing, adding some hip thrusts and undulations, clearly enjoying himself. Dancing closer to the table, he slipped the belt behind her shoulders and pulled her closer. His lips were on hers, his tongue sliding between her lips to rub hers. One deeply arousing kiss before he stepped back and tossed the belt aside. Then he opened the front of his pants and freed his erection from his briefs. It bobbed at her as he swiveled his hips.

She couldn't help but laugh when his sexy dance suddenly turned comical. Evidently he hadn't thought about how difficult it would be to kick off his pants when his shoes were still on.

While he hopped around, trying to get his shoes and pants off, Juliana kicked off her own shoes and wriggled out of her skirt. The thing had to look ridiculous bunched up around her waist. By the time she was entirely naked, so was he.

They stared at each other for a long time, the sexual excitement building. She should have felt absurd. After all, the two partners of Kelley-Wilson stood arm's length from each other. Naked. Aroused. Instead, she felt sexy and powerful and more turned on than she thought possible.

Juliana couldn't wait a moment longer. Two orgasms and she still wanted him with an intensity that left her breathless. She kissed him as she wrapped her fingers around his cock, loving the feel of his heated, silky skin and the way he trembled at her touch.

Connor gently rocked his hips toward her, making her hand move from crown to root, over and over. Their kiss was openly carnal, a chase of tongues followed by gentle sucks.

"Now," he said. The word trailed off into a growl as he backed her up to the table again. He laid her against the surface, fitting himself between her thighs and rubbing his erection between her folds. His mouth claimed hers, his tongue pushing into her mouth the same time his cock filled her.

She gave up the last shred of control, letting herself go and raising her hips to meet each of his thrusts. Any concerns she'd nurtured that he didn't want her disappeared in the strength of his passion. Each stroke of his body spoke of raw desire, and she answered by raking her nails across his back and wrapping her legs around his hips.

Snatching breaths between heated kisses, Juliana let Connor

lead her straight to ecstasy, her muscles tightening almost unbearably, clenching him tightly inside her. Lights popped behind her closed eyelids, and she moaned against his mouth when the fire raced through her.

He growled, rising to hold tightly to her hips as he slammed into her a few more times, and then shuddered as he came. Unaccustomed to feeling a man spend himself inside her, she gasped at the responding aftershocks rocking her body.

She traced her fingers up and down his spine because he seemed unable to do anything except lie on top of her and try to regain his lost breath. Since she still wanted to keep the pregnancy a secret, she figured she should mention what they'd forgotten. "No condom?"

"Don't care," he said again. "It was wonderful."

"It was, wasn't it?"

Should I tell him?

Probably. But a tiny voice rose from deep inside her heart, telling her the time wasn't right. Not yet. Not until she was past the dangerous twelve-week mark. She didn't want to get his hopes up. Worse, she didn't want to get her own hopes up.

He pushed himself up. "I'm probably too heavy for you."

"Nah. You're fine."

He chuckled as he eased out of her. "Liar. I must weigh a ton." He offered a hand and helped her off the table.

That horrible vulnerable feeling captured her again. Scrambling around, she found her blouse and held it over her breasts while she picked up her skirt, bra, and panties. "I'm sweaty and… um… sticky. I'm going to take a shower."

"Me, too. We can share." Without even fetching his clothes, he strode to the door and walked into the kitchen. "You coming?" The man didn't have an ounce of modesty.

"Already came. Three times, actually."

He was still chuckling when she led him to the master bath.

* * *

Connor wiped the foggy mirror with the hand towel so he could watch Juliana dry herself while he combed his hair.

He'd never get tired of looking at her. The woman was a work of art. If he had a choice, he'd have her walk around nude all the time.

On second thought, he'd have her wear some of her lacy panties and a bra, or those thigh-high stockings that always made his cock twitch. She liked her underwear skimpy, and they enhanced her beauty rather than covered it up.

No granny panties for his woman.

Her gaze caught his in the mirror. "You're staring."

"So?"

"It's embarrassing." Her checks flamed.

"You weren't embarrassed when I stared at you back in the office."

"Yes, I was," she admitted.

"You were?"

She nodded.

"Then *that's* what was bugging you. Glad you got over it. That had to be the best sex I've ever had."

"Really?"

"Oh yeah."

After she wrapped the big blue towel around her body, she tucked the end between her breasts. She stood in front of the second sink and fished a brush out of the drawer.

They hadn't used a condom, but he honestly didn't care. An

odd reaction since this would be the worst time in the world to have a baby. The business would suffer. The stress could be enough to send him plummeting back down into the hole he'd worked so hard to crawl out of.

But he wanted a child anyway—with Juliana.

Because he loved her.

Connor could almost see them pushing a stroller through the park, showing their kid the flowers and the birds, doing all those family things he'd sworn he never wanted to do. He'd never been one for the syrupy sweet family dynamic. Never. There had been a few munchkins accompanying their parents as they searched for houses. They'd often turned into brats from hell. After any of those showings, he'd always sworn to have a vasectomy.

Maybe the change in attitude was because of his age. He'd heard guys in their late thirties were anxious to settle down. Perhaps his desire to have a child with Juliana was simply evolution having its say.

Whatever the reason, he wanted this. With her.

"Would it be so terrible?" He hadn't meant to say it aloud.

Juliana cocked her head. "Would what be terrible?"

"Having a baby."

Her hand trembled as she laid her brush on the marble vanity top. "You want us to have a baby together?"

Afraid he was coming on too strong, he shrugged. He couldn't force her into this or it might one day blow up in his face. He knew how awful it was to feel trapped, and there was no way he'd do this unless she wanted a child as badly as he did.

"Connor, I mean, we're only living together until your house is done and—"

"Never mind," he snapped. "Ben's making great progress. I'll be out of your hair in a few weeks."

Despite how he felt about her, he had to admit things were moving quickly and maybe a permanent living arrangement was happening too soon. Besides, if he admitted how much he wanted to move in and how badly he wanted them to have a family, he'd have to open up and tell her exactly how he felt about her. The only thing keeping him silent was her hesitation.

Whenever their discussions got too intense, she pulled back, like a doe scenting danger. Her ex must've been a major asshole to leave her so scared of falling in love again, and Connor was pretty sure Juliana loved him. No woman could fake the kind of passion she gave him every time he made love to her. Besides, most women didn't let go that way if their hearts weren't involved.

"Someday," Juliana announced. "Maybe." She picked up her hair dryer and flipped it on, drowning out any response he might have made.

Connor brushed his teeth, still watching her in the mirror. Now he understood why couples always wanted a double vanity in the master bath. Without that second sink and enormous mirror, the two of them would be tripping over each other to get ready for bed.

He was already between the sheets and drowsy when she finally came out of the bathroom. Lifting the sheet, he waited for her to lie down. Then he covered her and hauled her up against his side.

He needed to hold her. The afterglow of what happened in the office still lingered, and he'd missed the way she usually slept in his arms after they'd made love. How totally she'd captured him was confusing, but he stopped questioning good luck.

Luck.

A small shudder raced over him as he was again reminded of how fragile this new life he'd created for himself truly was. All it would take for the house of cards to come tumbling down was one stupid mistake.

Better give Tracy a call and hit a meeting tomorrow.

"What is Tracy to you?" Juliana whispered in the dark, as though she'd read his mind.

"What?"

"Is she truly just a friend? An ex, perhaps? A cousin?"

"Just a friend. My best friend," he replied. "We met in middle school and were inseparable ever since. She's always been there for me, no matter how rough the road got. Middle school. High school. She got me through my parents' deaths." He shrugged, not sure how to make Juliana understand. "To me she's like a twin."

"Oh. I guess I just...worry."

"Worry? Why?"

"Never mind." She tried to roll away, but Connor wouldn't let her.

"Tell me what you're worried about."

She heaved a sigh. "You're with her a lot. Sometimes I can't find you when I need you, and you always tell me you were with Tracy."

"Are you jealous, Red?" While it was flattering, he wasn't about to let her think he had any intention of being unfaithful. "There's no reason to be. Tracy and I are close because we've known each other forever. She helped me through some tough times—keeps me on the straight and narrow. When my parents died, she kept me from totally losing it. I've lost track of how many times she's saved my hide." How could he explain it so Juliana would understand without tossing his past at her feet?

He wasn't ready for that. Not yet. Not until he was positive he had her heart.

Once Juliana admitted that she loved him, he would tell her everything.

Then he'd pray she would be understanding enough not to run like the wind in the other direction.

"So you don't like her? I—I mean, she's not—"

"There's zero chemistry between Tracy and me," he said. "Zero. We're friends—*good* friends. I need her in my life, but as a *friend*."

She eased up to stare at him. "Zero chemistry?"

"Subzero."

She settled back against him. Without another word, her breathing grew deep and even, which helped relax him, too.

He was worrying for no reason. Things were going well— *great*, actually. The firm was going strong and would only grow stronger now that Tracy was here to work her magic.

His relationship with Juliana was also growing stronger, and he hoped one day soon, she'd be able to give him the three words he craved. He'd try to be patient and let her take the lead. At least he would try, unless her inability to express her feelings dragged into the winter months. Here in the heat of August, he was willing to wait.

But not forever. If he had to say *I love you* first, he would.

Chapter Twenty

One sentence from Tracy, uttered rather matter-of-factly, rocked Juliana's world to its foundation.

Juliana had arrived at the Carpenters' house first, hoping to help Mallory with last-minute chores for their back-to-school cookout while Connor went to pick up Tracy.

The memory was burned on Juliana's brain.

When they arrived, Connor made introductions before Ben had taken over as host. He'd held up a bottle of Miller Lite.

"Want a beer, Tracy? We've also got some local brewery labels, an assortment of wine coolers, and a couple of different wines."

"No, thanks." Tracy waved him off. Then she dropped the thermonuclear warhead. "I'm an alcoholic."

Juliana didn't remember much anyone said after that.

She sat down rather hard on the bench. The world spun as all the implications whirled through her mind. Everything suddenly added up—from Connor's far-too-close relationship with Tracy to why he was starting his life over in Cloverleaf.

Connor's an alcoholic.

No. No.

No!

But she couldn't ignore the truth staring her right in the face.

What was going to happen to her now? What was going to happen to Kelley-Wilson Realty?

She was too stunned to cry, not that weeping would make things any better. No crying. But screaming and running around like a crazy woman, tearing at her hair?

Maybe.

She'd sworn she would never walk that path again. No more drunks for her. One had been enough for a lifetime.

Jimmy was an alcoholic—one of those guys who turned good and mean when he tied one on. Not that he would ever admit it. After all these years, he still wouldn't acknowledge he had a problem with alcohol because he didn't have to. No one, other than Juliana, had ever confronted him or forced his feet to the fire.

His family was full of alcoholics, so they accepted Jimmy's behavior as normal. The high school swept his two DUI convictions under the rug since he'd participated in court-ordered counseling that eventually helped expunge his record. But they knew. They didn't want the school's reputation tarnished. At least the administrators watched him like hawks. One more fuckup and he was out of a job. That threat was the only thing that kept him in line.

Oh, he still got drunk. A lot. He'd just learned to hand over the car keys or call a cab.

By not telling Juliana everything about himself and his past, Connor had, in essence, lied. If he was an alcoholic, he should've confessed the day they become partners. Information like that might have forced her to make a different choice. Instead, he'd kept silent about the most important thing in his life, something that now impacted *her* life as well.

What would happen if he started drinking again? Would he start missing appointments—or worse, show up to meet clients while he was intoxicated? Would she find herself holding the bag, trying to do the work of two people?

Two people? More like four, since both of them already worked inhuman hours, tackling enough projects to keep that many people well occupied.

What it boiled down to was that she was good and stuck, not only because he was her business partner but because she loved him.

Her world was falling apart and there wasn't a damn thing she could do to stop it.

She bowed her head.

Mallory came to sit at her side. "Jules? Did you want a soda?"

Juliana lifted her face, unable to utter a single word. She was in a stupor, feeling as though someone had hit her over the head and she was too stupid to fall down.

Mallory gripped Juliana's knee. "Oh my God. What's wrong?"

Closing her eyes, Juliana shook her head. Although she wanted to talk to her best friend, she wasn't going to do it—not here, not now. Too many people, and she hated to cry in front of anyone.

Especially Connor and Tracy.

Tracy.

His best friend.

She had to be his Alcoholics Anonymous sponsor, which explained why he needed her so much. She was the one he called whenever the urge to drink struck. AA also explained his mysterious absences—he'd been attending meetings. That made perfect sense considering how each of those times he'd been missing in action had been a period of high stress. He'd felt the need to drink, so he'd gone to a meeting.

Juliana almost wished he'd had a secret girlfriend instead.

A scornful laugh slipped out. Only strength of will kept it from turning into a pathetic sob.

Mallory stood, grabbed Juliana's hand, and tugged. "C'mon. We're going for a walk."

"I—I can't leave."

"Sure you can." She pulled Juliana to her feet. "Ben?"

Ben flipped some chicken breasts on the grill before calling back to his wife. "What's up, buttercup?"

"Jules and I are taking a walk. I want to show her Joanne Fritz's flowers. Will you keep an eye out for Bethany and Danielle? They should be here any minute. I think Robert's coming, too."

"Don't be long. Stuff might burn." He went right back to tending the food.

Connor had been playing lawn darts with Tracy. He glanced up and frowned. "Red? Did you say you're leaving?"

Thankfully, Mallory replied. "We'll only be gone a few minutes." She dragged Juliana out of the fenced yard to the front sidewalk. Then she set a slow pace as they headed up the long block. "Now tell me what's wrong."

Juliana had no idea where to begin. "Mal, I can't."

Mallory could make a rather impressive growl for such a tiny woman.

"Fine." Juliana took a deep breath. "Did you happen to hear what Tracy said to Ben?"

"Tracy said a lot of things to Ben. Which one in particular?"

"She said she's an alcoholic."

"That's what turned you into a basket case? You had me scared to death it was something important."

"It *is* important," Juliana insisted.

"At least she's open about it."

A heavy sigh slipped out. "Think about it for a second. She's Connor's 'best friend.'" Juliana sarcastically punctuated the quotes with her fingers. "How many guys check in with their best friends a couple times a day? He goes missing sometimes for a couple of hours at a stretch. And he's here in Cloverleaf, trying to start a new business even though he had a super job in Indianapolis. What does all that add up to?"

"I don't know. I guess..." Mallory's jaw dropped. "No. You don't think Connor's an—"

Not wanting to hear the word, Juliana cut her off. "I do. In fact, I'm sure of it."

"Oh shit."

A tear spilled over Juliana's lashes. She scrubbed it away. "I can't believe he didn't tell me! I mean, we have a business together. For Christ's sake, we're partners!"

"That, and he's still living with you," Mallory added. "Not to mention you're carrying his baby. I think I'd be more pissed about the personal side of this mess."

"What am I gonna do?" Juliana swallowed hard, hating the frantic timbre of her voice. She tried to stay calm, even if she was on the verge of crying like a baby.

"I'd say the only place to start is Connor. Talk to him. Give him a chance to explain."

Juliana stopped, gaping at Mallory. "Explain? What's there to *explain*? The man's an alcoholic. How can he possibly have a good reason for not telling me that before we went into business together?"

"If you think the only reason you're pissed is because of the partnership, you're lying to yourself. You love him, and you feel betrayed that he wasn't honest with you. Besides, don't you think you should confirm your suspicions first? You could be wrong."

A sarcastic retort formed, but Juliana refused to let her temper have free rein, especially since it was aimed right at Mallory instead of the guy who deserved it.

Of course she felt betrayed! Everything had changed, everything that she'd gambled her new life on, and she wasn't sure there was anything she could do that would make things better.

Juliana wrapped her arms around her middle. "What am I going to do, Mal?"

"I already told you what I think you should do."

"Talk to Connor."

But that was the last thing she wanted to do. First, she'd throw all the stuff he'd moved into her house in a big box and set it on the porch. While she was at it, she'd be tempted to pour gasoline over it and toss in a lit match.

How could she love the man as much as she did and still want to punch his lights out?

"Please don't tell Beth and Dani," Juliana begged.

"I won't. I haven't said anything about the baby, either. But they're bound to know something's wrong the moment they see you. Besides, they might be able to help you through all of this."

"I don't need help. I need a huge stick to beat over Connor's head."

Mallory stopped and put a hand on Juliana's shoulder. "Connor isn't Jimmy. Don't let all the anger you have at him shift to Connor."

"Meaning?"

"Connor really hasn't done anything wrong. It kinda sounds like he's done everything right."

Juliana quirked a brow, trying to let her friend's words ease her fear and fury.

"Think about it, Jules. Whenever he feels too stressed—something that might make him want to drink—he gets his ass to a meeting."

"That's what I think he's doing, but he might not be."

"Don't start overthinking everything," Mallory said. "For once in your life, adopt Beth's optimism."

Juliana snorted.

"I know. Thinking positively isn't in your DNA." She squeezed Juliana's shoulder. "Another thing in his favor is Tracy. If you're right and she's his AA sponsor, he's in close contact with her, which means he's committed to staying sober."

Now that her temper had a chance to cool, Juliana was able to let everything Mallory was saying soak in. "He's had tons of opportunities to drink with me, but he always had soda."

"See? Optimism isn't that tough." Mallory smiled. "You should try it more often."

"Oh my God. I drank in front of him."

"So?"

"I could've made things easier on him if I hadn't."

Mallory gave her head a shake. "First of all, you didn't know. Second, aren't alcoholics supposed to be responsible for their own actions despite what other people might be doing around them?"

"All I know is what drunks like Jimmy do. I've never even talked to someone who follows AA."

"Then we're back to square one," Mallory said.

"Talking to Connor."

"Bingo."

* * *

Connor kept stepping to the gate to see if Juliana and Mallory had returned from their walk. His relief that they'd returned was short-lived the moment he got a look at Juliana's distressed expression.

Something was wrong. *Very* wrong.

Her face was flushed, and her eyes seemed a bit swollen. Had she been crying? Didn't help that Mallory kept patting her shoulder.

They'd only been gone fifteen minutes. What horrible thing could have happened in so short a time? A phone call about a relative dying? Had her parents been in a car wreck or something?

As if aware he was thinking about her, Juliana stared right at him.

Connor swallowed hard. He knew that look. They might not have been together more than a couple of months, but he knew it anyway. That stormy green her eyes turned. The way her mouth pulled into a grim line. Her hands fisting tight enough that her fingers blanched.

Juliana was good and angry.

At him.

"Uh-oh."

Tracy picked up her lawn dart and tossed him a quizzical frown. "Pardon?"

"I'm dead meat."

"What in the hell are you talking about?"

He folded his arms over his chest. "Juliana's pissed at me about something."

She scoffed at him. "You can tell that all the way across the yard? What are you, psychic?"

"Don't have to be psychic. I can tell by the way she's looking at me."

"Seriously?"

Tracy had only been around a couple of weeks. Once she got to see him interact with Juliana more, she'd understand. "Seriously."

"And here I thought you were clueless." Tracy came to his side, setting the lawn darts down on the grass with the rest of the outdoor toys.

"Why?"

"You didn't even know she was angry earlier. I had to tell you."

He just shrugged. "Maybe I'm paying better attention now."

"I guess I can stop asking whether you two should've moved in together so quickly. Seems like you know a lot about each other for such a short time."

Her words hit him like a skillet upside the head. They might know a lot about each other, but Juliana didn't know everything. "I haven't told her yet."

"You haven't?" Tracy put her fingers against her forehead, rubbing as though she was getting headache. "You mean you started a new firm with her, moved in with her, but didn't tell her? Are you stupid or insane?"

"Maybe a little of both. I only wish I knew what made her so upset."

"You don't think she figured it out, do you?"

That was exactly what he thought—Juliana had somehow learned his secret. "I don't know how...but..." He watched her, hoping to see that she'd calmed down.

She hadn't torn her gaze away from him, and he could feel the heat of her accusing stare burning straight through him.

Oh, she knows all right.

"I think someone told her," Connor said.

"But who?" Tracy asked. "Who in Cloverleaf knows? Did you tell anyone?"

He shook his head.

"Then how?"

"Beats the shit outta me."

"Look, Connor, I know you've got a lot on your plate already, but I need to tell you something."

As if things could get any worse. "Spit it out, Trace."

She glanced around before she spoke. "Your old partner called me right before you picked me up. I didn't want to tell you until you took me home—thought it would spoil the party if I did."

Great. Just great. "Jason called you? Why?"

"To tell me Max Schumm took a trip to Indianapolis. He went to Jason and asked about you. Jason said it was like playing Twenty Questions."

"Fuck."

"Yeah. At least Jason still cares enough about you to let you know, even if it was through me."

After all he'd inflicted on his old partner, Connor didn't agree. More likely Jason wanted to spare Tracy from taking a big fall by still associating with Connor.

Tracy's mouth bowed into a frown. "Max is gonna find out about everything. You know he will. What did you do to him anyway?"

"I got a lot of listings he thought should've gone to him."

"Beat him at his own game, huh? No wonder he's after your blood."

"If he finds out, that's exactly what he'll do. Draw blood. He'll ruin me in this town."

And with Juliana.

"You need to talk to Juliana, Connor. *Now.* If you're wrong and she hasn't figured it out, you want her to hear it from you and not from that snake in the grass."

Tracy was right. As usual.

Now he just needed to find the courage to bare his soul to Juliana. If he didn't, he'd lose far more than he'd lost back in Indianapolis. That had been a tragic nightmare.

Losing Juliana would be even worse.

Chapter Twenty-One

Can we talk now?" Connor sat down on the side of the bed next to Juliana.

They'd left not long after Ben served the meal. The Ladies Who Lunch went aside and huddled for a few minutes, and then Juliana announced the two of them were leaving. From the angry expressions her friends directed his way, the proverbial cat was definitely out of the bag.

Connor was pretty sure she'd shared his problem with her friends—at least that was what he thought happened. Until Juliana opened up, he couldn't know. If she had talked about it with them, he had a right to be troubled, but he understood how special and close the bond was between the women. Heaven knew he leaned on Tracy every bit as much. Juliana needed their support now.

He hoped she'd continue to need their support in the years to come because she'd stay with him, both as a partner and as the woman he loved. After what she'd learned, he could understand if she wanted to sprint the other direction. But they were good together in so many ways. How could she not see that? How could she not see how hard he was working to stay away from his addiction?

Marriage was his ultimate goal, and if Connor could get Juliana to agree, she'd have to adopt the important rules in his life— the twelve steps that kept him walking the straight and narrow.

The faraway and rather forlorn expression on her face made his heart beat faster as pure fear gripped him.

Would she leave him just because he had a problem that was now held in check?

He reached for her hand. "Talk to me, Red. Please."

She moved her hand to her lap, lacing her fingers in a tight clench. "I—I don't know. I just—"

"Juliana." This time he tried to wrap an arm around her shoulder.

She popped to her feet. "Not now. Not…yet. I—I can't do this yet."

With a weighty sigh, he raked his fingers through his hair. What if he'd guessed wrong and she didn't know his secret? Why couldn't she tell him exactly what had thrown her into such a sour mood? He needed to know for sure.

"You don't want to talk this out, but you're still pissed at me," he said. "Why can't you tell me what you're thinking? Then I can have a chance to explain."

Juliana gave her head a vigorous shake, grabbed her nightshirt, and retreated to the bathroom.

Tracy's warning echoed through his thoughts: *Tell her. Now. Before someone else does.*

But it was already too late. Juliana knew. She had to know. Nothing else would have caused this type of reaction.

Shit. He should've told her a long time ago. Things had been going so damn well, he'd thought the past could stay buried in the past.

He'd been wrong.

Connor jerked his shirt over his head and stripped off his pants, getting ready for bed even though he probably wouldn't sleep a wink. Since he'd moved in with Juliana, he often waited until she fell asleep, enjoying the peacefulness that settled on him to have her close. Then he'd sneak out to the office to get a little more of the never-ending paperwork completed.

But not tonight. Tonight he needed to hold her, to know she could accept him, no matter how flawed.

He went to the bathroom door. Knocking with the backs of his knuckles, he tried again. "Red? Come to bed? Please? I want to tell you something—something important."

Something you figured out but I was too much of a coward to confess.

The door opened, and she stared at him with an intensity that sent a shiver racing the length of his spine.

Oh yeah, she already knew every single embarrassing piece of the puzzle.

"I only want to know one thing, Connor." Her voice quavered. "Why didn't you tell me before? You should've told me!" She brushed past him to her side of the bed and plopped down. "You lied to me."

He wanted to deny the accusation, yet the words froze in his throat. He *had* lied to her—a lie of omission by keeping his silence. "You're right. I should've told you. I'm sorry." Watching for any indication she'd run, he eased down next to her. Their bare thighs brushed, but she made no move to pull away.

A good sign?

Now he was getting desperate.

"You're sorry?" Juliana gaped at him, her gaze full of fury. "That's *all* you have to say to me?"

"You found out. I get it. I'm sorry I didn't tell you sooner. There's no excuse for that. I—I was embarrassed. Humiliated. I wanted you to look at me without always seeing the condemnation in your eyes."

"I don't condemn you," she retorted. Then she shrugged. "It's not your fault. Not really."

"It was my fault. I should've controlled myself. I take full responsibility for my actions. And trust me, I always learn from my mistakes."

"It's a disease, Connor. Some people just deal with it better than others. Probably doesn't help that everyone is always throwing temptation your way. Including me. I'm sorry for that. If I'd have known..."

"It's not that bad," he replied. "Not really. I steer clear of anyplace that might be a problem. Staying busy helps, too. Good thing is we're really busy right now. It's not like I spend a lot of time with people who indulge. A disease, though?" He shook his head. "Nah. It's more of a personal weakness, and it's behind me. Forever."

"Forever? Isn't one of your steps admitting you have a problem and that it will always be a problem?"

"I suppose. I figured it's better to ignore it than dwell on it."

"I'll stop, too," she promised with a decisive nod. "That should make it easier on you."

"Didn't know you played."

"Played? Played what?"

"The lottery."

Her brows knit as her confused gaze searched his. "What in the hell are you talking about? I thought we were talking about you drinking too much."

Oh God.

Connor mentally kicked himself. He'd never come out and said what his problem was, so Juliana had obviously leapt to her own conclusion. A very wrong conclusion. "I'm not a drunk," he said.

"Connor," she took his hand. "I've dealt with this before. My ex had the same problem, although he'd never admit it. Not even after all this time. Denying it only makes it worse."

"I'm not a drunk, Juliana."

Her sigh hung in the air. "If you don't accept it—"

"I'm *not* a *drunk*."

* * *

Juliana wasn't sure whether to laugh or cry.

She'd finally come to terms with her discovery. Connor was an alcoholic. That was all there was to it. He would always be an alcoholic. The good thing was that he wasn't at all like Jimmy.

She could live with the revelation.

Connor had stopped drinking, reached out for help, and kept in close contact with his AA sponsor. He was a recovering alcoholic.

Of course, she hadn't seen him drunk yet. God willing, she never would. Besides, with her helping him—encouraging him, keeping him busy with their business—he'd have a strong ally in his fight for sobriety. "I accept it. I do. My ex was an alcoholic and—"

His growl was a lot more intimidating than Mallory's had been. "Yes, Red, I have a problem, but drinking isn't it."

"I'm confused."

"Obviously."

She blinked a few times, trying to solve the puzzle he'd tossed in her lap. "You're telling me you're not an alcoholic? You're not just in denial?"

Connor stood, walked to the wall, and rapped his forehead against it a few times.

Despite her anger and curiosity, Juliana hated seeing him so miserable. Her love for him hadn't changed. She went to him, rubbing her palms across his bare shoulders. "Tell me. Please. Trust me on this, whatever it is can't be as bad as the things I'm imagining right now. If you're not an alcoholic, what are you?"

He faced her, looking her right in the eye. "I'm a compulsive gambler."

"What?"

"A gambler, Juliana. If I start gambling, I can't stop."

Chapter Twenty-Two

Juliana couldn't seem to register his words.

A compulsive gambler?

Gamblers were people with no self-control. Connor couldn't possibly be a gambler. The man had anal retentive down to an art form. His whole life was an exercise in control.

A gambler?

No. No way.

But the words had spilled from his own mouth. He'd confessed with a clear, steady voice, the way any recovering addict should.

She shook her head, trying to clear away her confusion. "I—I don't understand. I thought…But you said…" She considered smacking her forehead against the wall the same way Connor had, maybe until she was unconscious and didn't have to deal with the revelation.

"Come sit with me. I'll try to explain." After he led her to the bed he pulled her down on his lap.

For the first time since she'd jumped to the wrong conclusion, Juliana allowed him to hold her. She leaned her head against his shoulder and surrendered. And it felt wonderful—wonderful enough she calmed down and could listen to his story.

Then she'd forgive and help him.

Because she could never live without him.

Why couldn't life ever be simple? What was it about her that turned everything in her life from normal to disaster in the blink of an eye?

"It started with the lottery." He slid up the hem of her night-shirt and stroked her thigh as he spoke, clearly needing the contact as much as she did. "A set of lucky numbers. Then another. Then I starting feeling like I had to cover every number I considered lucky. If I didn't…well…" He shrugged. "If I didn't, I couldn't stand it. All I could think was that if I didn't buy all those tickets I'd be losing out on a fortune. It became an obsession."

"What kind of lucky numbers?" she asked.

"Birthdays. Addresses. Phone numbers. You name it, I used it. I had a stack of cards to have some gas station clerk or grocery store worker run through a machine every day."

"Every day? I thought the lottery was once a week." Since she'd never played before, Juliana needed a quick education in her lover's addiction. The more she knew, the better she could help him.

"Nope. They have some kind of drawing every damn day. Twice some days. I couldn't make myself stop. I always won small amounts, just enough to convince me that I had a chance at the jackpot—at *all* the jackpots. The state lottery. A couple of national lotteries." He rubbed his chin against the top of her head. "You know what the stupidest thing was?"

She nodded, bumping his chin.

"I didn't need the money. I was closing five houses a week. Minimum. I had two assistants and was raking in the dough. It was like I'd suddenly caught some fever." He took a deep breath. "Then it got worse. A friend took me with him to the racetrack. Horse races can have some big payoffs, and I was positive I'd win a fortune there. I had a system, a surefire way to pick winners."

"But it didn't work?" she asked anyway, even though she already knew the answer. "Winning systems" never worked.

"No, it didn't," Connor continued, his voice quavering. "A few months later, they opened the slot machines at the track. So once the last race ended, I'd wander into the casino. I'd feed a slot machine for hours, like some mindless robot."

Juliana cupped his cheeks in her hands and rested her forehead against his, having no idea what to say. Someone had pulled the rug right out from under her feet, and she couldn't seem to get her balance back. Her heart ached for what he'd suffered even as her mind struggled to understand how a man that smart could be sucked into something so stupid.

But wasn't that the nature of addictions?

As she'd learned from her ex, smart had nothing to do with it.

"I'm sorry if I disappointed you." His voice choked with emotion.

"You didn't disappoint me."

"Bullshit."

She gave him a slow, heartfelt kiss. "You didn't disappoint me. You...surprised me."

"I'm sorry, Red."

"I know." Her heart was his.

But what about her career?

This man wasn't just her lover, he was her business partner. Would she have established that relationship if she'd known about his problems with gambling?

"Oh God!" Her hand flew to her mouth as the implications hit her. "Your firm...back in Indianapolis. You didn't..." She couldn't even say her worst fear—that Connor had embezzled to feed his habit.

"They found out. Since I was their most successful agent, they let things slide. For a while." He leaned back, held tight to her upper arms, and narrowed his eyes. "Wait, do you think I stole from them?"

"No." God help her, she wasn't sure.

The man she loved couldn't possibly be a thief.

Of course she hadn't known he was a gambler, either.

Maybe she didn't truly know him at all.

Although he didn't give her a hard shake, his eyes burned with the desire to. "I never took a dime from my old firm unless it was in the form of commission." His voice held a note of hurt among all the anger.

Not that she could blame him. "Connor, I'm sorry, I..."

What was she supposed to say? That she was terrified he'd start gambling again and destroy what they'd worked so hard to create?

Connor released a weighted sigh as he dropped his grip. "You were only thinking what everyone back in Indy thought. That was why I finally resigned and moved away." He nudged her chin until he stared into her eyes. "But I swear, Juliana, I swear the money I lost was all mine. My checking. My savings. My retirement nest egg. They're all gone. But I didn't touch money from my clients or my firm. Not once."

"What I don't get is why Tracy is your sponsor. She's an alcoholic. Shouldn't a recovering gambler be helping you instead?"

"Addiction is addiction. Besides, Tracy is the only constant in my life. She understands me in a way no other sponsor could."

"Why?"

"Shared history. We go back to middle school." He smiled, picturing different times he and Tracy had gotten themselves into a pickle only to bail each other out. "Once my parents died, she was all I had left. I didn't have brothers or sisters or cousins. I worked so much it wasn't conducive to making friends. Tracy was always there. So when I realized I had a problem, what better person to turn to? I'd helped her in her time of need, and she returned the favor."

Juliana nodded, finally releasing the gnawing jealousy that could have easily come between them. "How much did you lose, Connor?"

His gaze shifted to the wall. "A lot. An awful lot. Trust me, you don't want to know."

Bowing her head, she tried to make sense of the nuclear bomb he'd dropped and consider all the implications. Her heart felt shredded, and her body ached as though she'd been pulled in different directions until her muscles snapped.

Juliana loved Connor, that love driving her to hold him, to comfort him. To tell him she understood and forgave.

But what about Kelley-Wilson Realty?

Cloverleaf was a small town, and gossip ripped through the citizens with the intensity of a tornado. If anyone in this unforgiving burg found out why Connor left Indianapolis, no one would want to work with him—or her.

"I—I love you, Juliana."

"What?"

His eyes captured hers. "I love you."

* * *

Several emotions crossed Juliana's face. Some Connor expected after his confession. But one of them? One of them took him by surprise.

Fear.

Juliana's spine was made of steel, one of the reasons she was so damned good at sales. She could stand her ground, holding tight to her convictions and not showing an ounce of fear.

At that moment, she looked terrified, and she trembled in his arms.

But why? Because of his first confession?

Or his second?

Words crowded his throat, blocking a single one from spilling from his lips. While he desperately wanted her to return his declaration of love, she needed time. He'd thrown his addiction in her path with not a word to prepare her for the shock.

Then he'd told her he loved her.

No wonder the woman was catatonic.

He needed her to love him in return.

The silence stretched, growing awkward until she squirmed, trying to crawl off his lap.

Connor squeezed her tighter. "Talk to me, baby. Please."

"I—I don't know what to say."

"Just tell me what you're thinking."

She snorted. "*I* don't even know what I'm thinking."

"Touché." At least she'd stopped wiggling. "Look, I won't let you down. Not personally. Not professionally. I'm in control of this. I stay away from the temptation. I stay away from alcohol and—that's it! That's why you thought I was an alcoholic."

"You always have soda or tea."

"I've never been much of a drinker. It also dawned on me that if I drank while I played the slots, I kinda lost myself. Figured staying away from anything that reminded me of my problem was my best bet." This time, he snorted. "If you'll excuse the terrible pun."

At least Juliana chuckled.

He gave her a quick kiss. "I need to know, Red."

"Know? Know what?"

"That you understand." *That you love me, too.*

She burst to her feet and paced the length of the room and back, all the while wringing her hands. "Connor...I...I..." A low groan slipped out as she kept up her pacing. "I know you think it's behind you. But what if, what if it isn't?" Planting herself in front of him, she wrapped her arms around herself. "What then?"

"That's the same question I ask myself every single day. And I give myself the same answer I'm going to give you." He took a deep breath and blew it out. "I can only deal with my problem one day at a time."

Her eyes widened. "That's it? That's all you can say to me?"

"Afraid so." Standing, he tried to pry her arms away from hugging herself. He needed to feel her in his arms. "C'mere. Please."

After a moment of resistance, Juliana dropped her rigid posture and let Connor draw her into his embrace. She laid her cheek against his chest.

"I can't swear it'll never happen again," he said. "But I can swear I will do my very best to never disappoint you. I love you. I love working with you. I will try my damnedest to never mess up our relationship or our business."

She nodded, rubbing her cheek against his bare chest as he stroked her hair. Gently, he pulled the ponytail holder to let her locks loose, the way he liked them. Then he combed his fingers through the tresses.

Despite knowing patience was needed, he couldn't help himself. "Don't you have something to say to me?"

"Should I?"

"I told you I love you, Juliana."

"I know. Thanks."

" 'Thanks'? Who are you? Han Solo?"

Pushing back, she stared up into his eyes. "Connor, I never asked you to love me."

This conversation wasn't easy to follow. "Meaning?"

"Meaning that I consider your love a gift—one I return with all my heart." Her lips found his. After a gentle kiss, she eased back. "Meaning that I love you, too."

He hugged her hard, finding it difficult for him to lighten his hold. "You love me?"

"Not for long if you smother me."

But he didn't want to let her go.

"Connor, I can't breathe."

Reluctantly, he lessened his grip until she moved out of his arms. Then she kissed him again, throwing her arms around his neck and flattening her lightly clad breasts against his chest.

Desire flooded his senses, and the need to make love to her— to show her his love now that he'd confessed it—was overwhelming. Walking backward, he waited until the mattress hit the backs of his thighs before he collapsed onto the bed, dragging Juliana on top of him.

He ravaged her mouth, savoring her taste and the slide of her tongue over his. Bending his knee, he nestled her against his groin, letting each gentle movement of her hips stroke his already stiff cock.

The kisses continued, even as he dragged her nightshirt up, tearing his lips away only long enough to jerk it over her head. The first touch of her bare breasts against his pecs was heaven.

Rolling over, he pinned her to the bed. "I love you," he whispered before burying his lips against her neck.

She shivered and laced her fingers through his hair. "I love you, too."

He moved lower, taking a hardened nipple into his mouth as he also eased her panties down. One hard suck and she arched her back, making it easier to move the lacy barrier.

The scent of her arousal sent electricity racing straight to his groin. He kissed her stomach, stopping to press his lips to her lower belly. He glanced up to find her propped up on her elbows staring down at him.

"We haven't been very careful," she said.

His lips brushed her skin again. "Think you've got a baby hiding in there?"

"Time will tell."

He was only inches from kissing the most intimate part of her—not exactly the time for a serious conversation about having kids together. There had already been enough heavy discussions for one day. If Juliana was pregnant, that would be another issue to tackle at another time.

He eased one finger deep inside her as he licked between her folds.

* * *

Every thought Juliana had of babies and gambling and the future fled. The feel of his tongue and lips working on her sensitive nub took hold of her mind and her body.

Connor added a second finger, thrusting in a rhythm that had her hips rising from the bed to match him.

After the flurry of deep emotions they'd just shared, she wasn't at all surprised when her body strained for climax so quickly. She'd been tied in knots, and one by one, he was untying them.

Her core throbbed in need, and she tugged hard on his hair, wanting him deep inside her when she came.

And then he was there, his cock sliding into her as he groaned her name.

She was so close. Wrapping her legs around his hips, she bit him gently on his shoulder, lightly scoring his skin with her teeth.

His thrusts became hard and deep, the speed increasing until he was frantically pushing inside her. When he shouted his climax, she was only a heartbeat behind.

It wasn't until she was drowsy and snuggled up next to him that their baby crept into her thoughts. Sobering reality stole her state of lethargic satiety.

We're having a baby.

That was the last thing in the world they needed in their mess of a relationship. Connor was an addict, and stress fueled an addiction. She wasn't ready to tell him, not for a few more weeks when she was past the first trimester. Then together they could find a way to deal with the situation.

But would he resent her for not telling him sooner?

Chapter Twenty-Three

Good morning!"

Connor's head snapped up at Max Schumm's greeting. When Connor scowled, Max must have noticed, because his grin grew in response.

"So this is the fastest-growing real estate firm in five counties?" Max's gaze moved around the office, disdain plain in his words. "A garage." His eyes found Connor's. "You're really running your business from a garage."

Since it had been a statement rather than a question, Connor saw no need to confirm the obvious. Although he wanted to grab the back of Max's jacket and give him the bum's rush right out the door, he couldn't. He and Juliana sold a lot of Kelley-Wilson houses to Max's clients, and a few of their clients bought his homes. While they beat Max hands down in listing homes for sale, Max still held an edge on representing buyers.

For now.

"What can I do for you, Max?" Proud that he'd kept his tone civil, Connor waited to find out how quickly he could be rid of the pest.

Crossing his arms over his chest, Max leaned a hip against the half wall between the client area and the desks. "Why, Connor, I'd think you'd be happy to see me."

The last time Connor had a conversation with Max about anything except listings, the man had made him a job offer, then he'd been thoroughly offended when Connor passed. That had been months ago; surely Max wasn't here to repeat the proposition.

"If you're bringing me another offer," Connor said, "I'm thrilled to see you."

"Sorry. No offer this time. No, I came to let you know I had a rather enlightening conversation with a friend of yours from Indianapolis."

The hair on the back of Connor's neck stood on end. "Oh, really? And who exactly was that?"

"Belinda Stephens. She sends her best, by the way."

I'll just bet she does.

Belinda had been one of Connor's friends with benefits back when he'd been more than a little out of control. Since she seemed to enjoy blowing large sums of her rich daddy's cash at casinos, she'd been a great companion. Hours of gambling accompanied by far too many cocktails had usually ended back at her place with a drunken romp in bed. Although he normally didn't drink much, Belinda had a way of keeping the cocktails coming until he lost track.

Another of her numerous machinations.

In his typical fashion, he'd never spent the night. In fact, Juliana was the first lover he felt comfortable sleeping next to the whole night through. Sleeping made him...vulnerable. Better a cab ride home than to wake up next to Belinda or another just like her. Evidently his heart—and his body—had recognized Juliana as his soul mate.

When he'd finally gotten a grip on his life, Belinda hadn't been happy. She enjoyed her decadent lifestyle and couldn't understand why Connor wanted to clean up his act, probably because her well would never run dry.

His had. Bone dry.

"Ah, the lovely Belinda. Don't tell me she's thinking of moving to Cloverleaf. I'll never believe it."

"Actually, she wanted me to investigate a lake property in Paulson County—something she could put a nice houseboat on for weekends. The more we chatted, the more I realized just how...close the two of you are."

"Were."

"Pardon?"

"*Were* close, Max. I haven't seen Belinda in over a year."

His smile was downright reptilian. "It might have been a while since you two talked, but you obviously knew each other very well. I believe you even sold her father his estate in Carmel." Max gave a low whistle. "Bet the commission on that set up a nice IRA for you to spend when you're old and gray. Selling a mansion to Jeff Stephens? Quite a coup."

That commission was in the coffers of several casino corporations. And Jeff Stephens might be a bigwig in the pharmaceutical industry, but he was also a genuine asshole.

Since he had a good idea what was coming, Connor flipped his hand to get Max to spill his poison. Thank God he'd already confessed his problem to Juliana, because it was crystal clear Max was going to use it against him—against *them*—now.

"Let's just say I feel a fiduciary responsibility to my clients to inform them of some of the...um...less-than-savory aspects of how you conduct business."

"I've never conducted business with anything but honesty."

"Her father believes otherwise. When I called him, he told me a rather interesting story about inflated closing costs, most of which he believes you slipped into your own pocket."

Although that was total bullshit, he wasn't about to defend himself to Max. "He's a liar. So if you're done bashing my character, why don't you leave?"

"Is the gorgeous Ms. Kelley around?" Max asked. "I'd like to have a word with her."

"She's at a closing—one of three she's got scheduled today." Three of Max's former clients who'd jumped ship. No wonder Max was after blood. "You're probably not going to be able to reach her until after five."

Max pushed away from the wall. "Well, then I'll just have to see if I can catch her between meetings."

"Leave her a voice mail. I'm sure she'll call you right back." *When hell freezes over.*

The door had barely shut behind the annoying Mr. Schumm when Connor reached for his lifeline. She answered on the second ring. "Tracy! Thank God I got you!"

"Connor, what's wrong?"

"Everything."

* * *

Juliana didn't have to ask to know something wasn't right.

Connor and Tracy were huddled up at his desk, so wrapped up in their conversation that neither acknowledged her arrival.

The first thing Juliana feared was that he'd bought a lottery ticket...that he'd had some kind of relapse. When he finally looked up and his gaze captured hers, she feared he was about to tell her something much worse.

"Hi." Tracy popped up from her seat, took Connor's hand, and gave it a squeeze. "Call me if I can help."

"I will."

"I mean it. Day or night."

"I know, Trace. Thanks."

Brushing past Juliana, Tracy lightly touched her arm. "You, too, Jules. I'm here for both of you."

"Thanks" was all Juliana could say.

She had not a clue what disaster had happened while she'd been out closing three houses and picking up sizeable commission checks for the firm.

When the door closed, Juliana flipped their old-fashioned window sign to CLOSED, pulled the shade, and threw the lock. Then she turned and leaned back against the door. "What's wrong?"

His bitter laugh made her stomach pitch. "I don't even know where to start."

"At the beginning."

"Max Schumm has gone on the offensive."

Hearing that name always gave her a rash. "What are you talking about?"

"He knows."

Two words. Amazing how two simple words could strike such utter terror into her heart.

She had no doubt what it was that Max knew. What she wasn't so certain of was how he'd use Connor's past against him and against Kelley-Wilson Realty.

"How in the hell could he know?" she asked.

He patted the client chair next to his desk.

Juliana strode to the office area, dropped her tablet and briefcase on her desk, and settled onto the chair. "How did he find out, Connor?"

"He made some calls to some of my...connections in Indianapolis. Managed to dig up one of my old, um, girlfriends." He raked his fingers through his hair. "God, I hate that word. Makes me sound like I'm sixteen."

"Max Schumm is getting ugly and you want to talk about semantics?"

"Word choice is everything."

Her temper, already on a crumbling ledge, flared. "How about lovers? Fuck buddies? What the hell does it matter! Tell me what Max said!"

"Easy, Red."

She growled low in her throat, tired of him making an issue of her short temper. Ever since Connor had opened up to her a few weeks ago, Juliana felt as though the Sword of Damocles hung over her life. Her emotions were strung too damn tight, making her stomach a continuous flurry of queasiness and her head constantly ache.

Didn't help that Mallory, Dani, and Beth had all been back in the swing of school for weeks. Without her. Juliana seldom got to see them, and since she was often showing houses in the evening hours, she rarely even talked to them. Connor had Tracy as his support system. Juliana's had all but disappeared.

Did her students ask about her? Did the faculty toss her name around in their typical flurry of gossip? Did anyone at Douglas High School even miss her?

A wave of nausea wasn't a surprise, but she tried to hide her distress from Connor. She would have to tell him. Soon. But she had another issue to deal with for now.

"What did your old lovers say?" she asked when she was no longer afraid she'd upchuck on his lap.

"It was *one*, Juliana. One rich bitch who I let lead me around by my dick because she'd give me loads of money to waste at the casino. How's that for honesty?"

She winced. "Brutal."

"See why I was concerned about semantics?" He ran his hand over his face. "Her name's Belinda Stephens—as in Stephens Pharmaceuticals. Max evidently had a nice chat with her about my past. Her dad's a penny-pinching old miser. After I helped him close his mansion and—"

"Mansion? As in a real mansion or one of those houses we call mansions 'cause they have more than five bedrooms?"

"A *mansion*, mansion. Anyway, Jeff decided my three-percent commission was too high for his taste, even though I negotiated a sales price low enough to save him twice my commission. He also didn't understand some of those nickel-and-dime things that get thrown into closings and argued over paying for some things until the closing was threatened and he almost lost the place. Then he walked in on Belinda and me in a rather compromising situation and—"

She closed her eyes against the image of Connor with another woman. "And there went your reputation."

He sighed and leaned back in his chair. "I did enough on my own to ruin my reputation. Not too many people like to see their Realtor at a casino. Jeff Stephens badmouthing me only added to my downfall. Look, I'm sorry. This is *my* baggage, not *yours*. You shouldn't have to worry about Max Schumm or Belinda Stephens."

"It's *our* baggage now, Connor. That's all there is to it. We'll just have to handle any fire they spark and do our best to stomp it out."

She rose, but he grabbed her hand. "I really am sorry, sweetheart."

This time, she was the one to heave a resigned sigh. "I know you are."

He kissed her knuckles. "I love you."

Since her ex had probably told Juliana he loved her fewer than a dozen times, she should've savored each time Connor said those three words. Yet she didn't. Perhaps they'd mean more if he didn't toss them around only when he was trying to soothe her temper—as though *I love you* was a way to keep her from being irritated with him.

This time, they weren't the right salve for her wound. But she spit back a monotone response. "Love you, too."

Then she went back to her own desk and got down to work. Someone had to fix this mess.

Chapter Twenty-Four

Juliana smiled when a familiar ringtone, the theme from *Friends*, sounded from her cell. She touched the screen. "What's up, Mal?"

It was a nice surprise to get a call from Mallory, especially one in the middle of the day. It was next to impossible to talk with a teacher during school hours.

The last time they'd seen each other, Juliana had shared more of what she'd learned about Connor's addiction, something she still kept from the other Ladies Who Lunch. She needed her best friend's support and guidance, but telling Danielle and Bethany seemed out of bounds—as though she'd be betraying him.

Mallory helped ease some of Juliana's fears and concerns with logic and encouragement. That, and Connor had begun to talk about it openly whenever they were alone, acknowledging that he needed her support to keep his nose clean.

"Hi, Jules," Mallory said, her tone somber.

Then the repercussions rattled Juliana.

Midday calls from a teacher were *never* good news.

Her stomach dropped, leaving her close to heaving. "This isn't a friendly call, is it?"

"Afraid not," Mallory replied. "Ben just sent me a text about some sign he saw."

"A sign?"

"Actually, more like a billboard. He texted me a picture."

"Why not text it to me?"

"He doesn't have your number."

"What do you mean? He's texted me before."

Mallory chuckled. "Not since he dropped his old phone into a lake when he was fishing with Amber. He's still tracking down numbers to put into his new cell." She quickly sobered. "Look, Jules, this isn't good. I'm going to send it to you, okay?"

"Okay."

The line went dead.

A couple of moments later, her phone signaled a text message.

The photo was of a billboard not far from the "Welcome to Cloverleaf" sign on the north side of town, the one most people coming from Chicago passed as they traveled south. Max Schumm smiled down from on high, arms casually crossed over his chest as he leaned a hip against one of his yard signs. That image was enough to make Juliana nauseated.

But the words?

Don't gamble with your home and your future. Max Schumm—Cloverleaf's honest Realtor.

"Son of a bitch."

Her first instinct was to call a lawyer. Surely what he was doing amounted to slander.

Or did it?

He hadn't exactly named Connor or said he was a compulsive gambler. But the rumors were swirling in a fury throughout the town. She and Connor were still getting clients, including all the Barrett Foods employees, but their listings of homes for sale had dropped enough to make them both a bit alarmed.

Max's smear campaign was working.

Goddamn him.

The office phone rang.

"Kelley-Wilson Realty. Juliana Kelley speaking."

"Um...hi. Um...this is Sarah Whitaker."

"Oh yes. How are you today, Sarah? I was just about to call you. I've got those houses lined up for you to see tonight."

"Yeah, about that." The woman's voice quavered as her husband's muffled voice echoed in the background.

Juliana couldn't make out his words, but his angry tone came through loud and clear.

"We're gonna have to cancel," Sarah said.

"That's fine." Grabbing her calendar, Juliana looked through tomorrow's appointments. "How about same time tomorrow? I'm free Thursday, too. We could meet then."

"Yeah, um..." Sarah barely got the hesitant hum out before her husband's voice boomed in Juliana's ear.

"We're cutting you loose," Peter Whitaker bellowed, his voice loud enough Juliana had to ease the receiver farther away. "Not about to buy a house from a guy who's gonna take my earnest money and escrow to the closest casino."

She swallowed a gasp at the atrocious statement. "I can assure you, Peter, that Connor and I would *never* consider—"

Peter snorted. "I know all about Connor Wilson."

"What exactly do you think you know?"

"He's always gambling with other people's money."

"And who exactly told you that ridiculous story?"

"Heard it from Mona Clinton."

Figures.

Mona was one of the biggest gossips in Illinois. She wasn't happy unless she was setting some inferno raging. No one knew how or why she chose targets, she just did. Her cruelty had almost gotten a teacher at the high school fired because she'd passed around a rumor that she saw the man hugging a female student at a local park.

A two-week suspension was followed by the teachers, students, and parents rallying around him when it was discovered the girl had been considering suicide and the teacher had stopped her. He got his job back, but since his reputation was in tatters, he'd resigned the next year and moved away.

Now she'd set her sights on destroying Connor.

Why?

Who the hell knew? It was simply Mona being Mona.

That bitch.

What was Juliana supposed to say to the Whitakers and all their other clients? That Connor used to be a gambler? Would it be better to deny the accusations? To lie?

No. She'd never been a liar, and she wasn't about to start the bad habit now.

"Look, Peter, I don't know what Mona told you, but Connor and I are nothing but honest in our business dealings. We've closed close to a million dollars in sales just since—"

"You're telling me Mona's lying? Connor never gambled with his clients' money?"

She heaved a sigh. "My partner has never—I repeat *never*—risked a client's money. He—"

"But he gambles?"

She was getting sick and tired of being interrupted, especially by someone so intent on continuing his irrational rant. "As I said, my partner has *never*—"

"I knew it! We're done with you two."

"I'm very sorry to hear that. We had some nice houses to—"

"So does Schumm."

"Good day, Mr. Whitaker." She slammed the phone aside hard enough it bounced.

By the time she'd fielded three more phone calls from concerned clients, Juliana was ready to throw her coffee cup at the wall.

Then Connor came strolling in, whistling.

He lightly kicked the door shut behind him. "Hi, beautiful." The smile on his lips fell to a frown when his eyes caught hers. "Uh-oh. What happened?"

As a couple, and as partners, the two of them were totally in sync. For the first time, she wished that weren't true.

"Max is spreading his poison."

"What's that supposed to mean?"

She clicked to the image and tossed the phone to him, hoping the piece of technological wonder hit the floor and split into a bunch of useless parts.

He caught it midair, then fiddled with the touch screen. His eyes widened before narrowing to angry slits. "Son of a bitch."

If the world wasn't crumbling around her, she would've smiled at their identical reactions. "The Whitakers canceled."

"Did you reschedule?"

"They said they're going to Max's firm."

"Why?"

"They heard you had a gambling problem. After the Whitakers, three more customers called. I talked them all into staying with us by promising I'd personally handle any transactions involving their money."

The words felt like acid on her tongue. Connor hadn't done anything wrong. The only dipshit thing on his tally board was losing his own money. Clients shouldn't be thinking of him as if he were a crook.

Instead of getting mad, he hung his head. "It's just going to get worse, isn't it?"

The dejection in his voice made her heart hurt. He was so damned good at selling houses, and he stayed away from his addiction. Why should he be punished for mistakes of the past?

The unfairness of the whole situation made her want to scream.

Juliana got to her feet and hurried to him.

He held out his palm and turned away. "Don't."

She sidled around until she faced him. Then she squeezed his chin to get him to look at her. "We're in this together."

"You should bail on me, too. This isn't gonna get any better. Hell, it's bound to get a lot worse."

"Then we'll deal with it as it happens. One disaster at a time. Okay?" Her gaze searched his.

He tried to bow his head again.

It killed her to see him looking so defeated. There was more at stake than he knew, so she did what she'd always done with students who acted like they were ready to throw in the towel.

She pushed.

"I'm not letting you off the hook that easy, mister. This business is my life now." She swallowed hard before speaking what was in her heart. "*You're* my life now. Okay?"

"Juliana…"

"*Okay?*" she demanded.

Although his lips thinned into a sad line, he gave her a curt nod.

"I mean it. This is Kelley-Wilson Realty, not Connor Wilson Realty. There are two partners. *Two.* We're in this together."

"I love you."

Why did his tone remind her of a naughty child who didn't want his mom to be mad at him?

"Love you, too. Now, let's get down to work."

* * *

The afternoon went by in a blur. By the time Connor flicked the lock and flipped the sign to CLOSED, he wanted something he hadn't craved in a long time.

A drink.

Badly.

Juliana pushed her chair under her desk and turned off her monitor. "I'm beat." A yawn slipped out that she didn't bother to cover with her hand.

Connor yawned, too, probably in response to hers, because he wasn't physically tired.

But mentally?

Mentally he'd just gone ten rounds with Mike Tyson.

He needed to hold her, so he crossed to her desk and took her into his arms. "Lie to me. Tell me things will get better."

"Things will get better. And it's not a lie." She rubbed her cheek against his shoulder. "I'm exhausted."

"Want me to make you something to eat?"

"I'm not hungry."

"We missed dinner." His stomach was already growling in protest. "I could run out and grab some subs or some pizza."

"Ugh. No." Pushing back, she turned off the lights while he held open the door leading to the kitchen. "My stomach's a mess."

"That's happened a lot lately."

That very morning, she'd been chewing Tums instead of Cheerios. He wanted to burst right out and ask if she was pregnant, but a woman as blunt as Juliana would've told him if she so much as suspected she was. They were both so open about everything, about every aspect of their lives.

He'd thought about it—about a baby. The timing would be ridiculously inconvenient, but picturing a little girl with hair the same color as her mother's touched one of the soft places in his heart. Knowing Juliana, he could picture her showing houses with the baby sleeping in a sling, cradled against her breasts.

I'm an idiot.

Daydreams like that could never come true. Not now. Not when Max Schumm was on the attack.

Kelley-Wilson Realty wasn't going to survive this storm. And if their business partnership ended, he wasn't sure their personal relationship would survive.

So much of Juliana—money, heart, mind, and soul—was vested in the firm. If they went belly-up, she'd be devastated.

God, he wanted to drink himself stupid. He wanted to let his brain shut down and to mindlessly watch wheels spinning on a slot machine. Just spin. No thinking. No worrying.

Just numb.

The urge stole his breath. In all the time since he'd walked away from casinos, he'd never experienced such an overwhelming need to vanish into that world again. There was something comforting about plopping coins into a slot and punching a button. Over and over and over.

Until the world disappeared.

Connor instinctively reached for his cell, ready to call Tracy. She'd serve as a slap across the face and get his head back on straight.

Instead, he let his hand drop to his side. Tracy couldn't help him anymore. It wasn't fair. He should be leaning on Juliana instead. Poor Tracy had borne that burden long enough.

On the other hand, it wasn't fair to Juliana, either.

The time had come to man up.

He could handle this impulse—and their problems with Max—alone. They were, after all, his own making.

Juliana yawned again. "I'm going to bed."

"It's only nine. Figured we'd pop in a movie or head out for a bite to eat." Anything to keep him from giving in to the stress and the itch to head toward the closest casino.

"Not up to it." She glanced longingly down the hallway. "I'm only good for washing my face, brushing my teeth, and collapsing."

It took all his strength not to blurt out how much he needed her to keep him from thinking about gambling. Her eyes were shadowed by dark circles, and he could see how hard she was struggling to stay awake.

"Go," he said. He pulled her to him, gave her a gentle hug, and then turned her toward their room. "Go to bed. I'm going out to get a sandwich. Then I'll watch a little TV."

"You're sure?"

"I'm sure."

"Okay. Thanks, honey."

Honey. That was the first time she'd ever used an endearment. "Love you, Red."

He couldn't make out her reply as she yawned and tried to talk at the same time. With a weary smile, she headed down the hallway.

Connor grabbed his car keys and stood by the front door, waging a war in his mind. He should just drive to McDonald's, get a Big Mac, and come right home. There had to be something distracting to watch in all those satellite channels they paid for that neither of them ever had the time to watch. If things were going to slow down because of Max, that would be at the top of his list of things to cut to save money.

Max. The mere thought of the man made Connor's blood pressure skyrocket.

Sliding his wallet out of his pocket, he checked to see how much cash he had on him. Three twenties. That was all.

Surely a guy couldn't get in too much trouble gambling if he only had sixty bucks.

And the diversion would help him deal with all the stress without involving Juliana.

He made himself a promise as he left.

Sixty bucks.

Not a penny more.

Chapter Twenty-Five

I'm so sorry! It's just a mistake. Let me get things together, and I'll be there in fifteen minutes. Promise."

Juliana ended the call and started plowing through the documents piled on Connor's desk. He was supposed to be at a showing with a young couple who were both a little jumpy as they searched for their first house. Property virgins needed careful handling, and Connor had always done a great job with their type.

Where the hell is he?

She growled when she found their file. He'd left without it, which meant he'd forgotten the appointment. So unlike him. Ever since Max had started his insulting ad campaign, Connor had been acting…weird. While she wanted to continue to trust him, his disappearances weighed heavily against him.

Surely he wouldn't start gambling again. He wouldn't fuck up their lives like that.

Would he?

Shoving the file into her briefcase, she muttered a steady stream of profanities.

The door to the office opened, and she glanced up, ready to unload her temper on Connor. Thankfully, she bit back the words when Tracy was the one to enter.

"Shit." Juliana picked up the stack of sheets Tracy needed to pick her fixtures for the house Robert was building. "I'm going to have to meet you at the model, Trace. Sorry."

"No worries," Tracy replied. "I don't need a handhold. You look a little frazzled. Connor can always go with me if you've got other plans. Hell, I can just go myself. Picking out flooring and backsplash tiles isn't all that difficult." Her gaze combed the office. "Where is he?"

"Beats the crap outta me."

After Tracy took the papers, Juliana hefted her briefcase strap over her shoulder, ignoring the twinge in her gut.

Probably just another wave of nausea threatening.

"When you see him," Juliana said, "tell him I'd like to have a word with him."

"Would that word be 'asshole,' perchance?"

Since Tracy had become such an integral part of their lives, Juliana had warmed to her. They shared a sarcastic sense of humor and a love for strong coffee no matter the time of day, and both understood Connor better than he probably understood himself.

"I'll let you choose the appropriate insult," Juliana said with a wink. "You've known him longer."

"Where are you headin'?" Tracy asked.

Juliana heaved a sigh, thinking about all she'd have to do today if Connor was going to continue to be MIA. How could one person be in two places at the same time? "I have to help a couple of kids who are looking at the house they want for the third time. The selling agent told me if I ask for any more showings, I damn well better have an offer in hand. Not that I can blame her. I shouldn't be long, though. I can meet you at—" Tracy's horrified gasp stopped her short. "What's wrong?"

Hurrying to her, Tracy eased the strap from her shoulder and set the briefcase on the floor. "You need to change first."

"What?" If Tracy thought Juliana's outfit wasn't perfect, too bad. She didn't have time to play fashion queen now.

"I mean it, Jules. You've got a...problem." She nodded at the gray desk chair.

Juliana's eyes widened. A bloodstain on the seat cushion seemed as bright as a laser show.

"Go on. Go change," Tracy said. "We all get caught unaware when Aunt Flo pops in for an inopportune visit."

"No." The word was a quavering whisper. "Please, no."

The nightmare of her first miscarriage hit Juliana hard enough to make her head spin. The mere thought she was losing this baby told her that she hadn't been as nonchalant as she'd pretended. She wanted this baby. Desperately.

And now she was losing it.

"This isn't your period, is it?" Tracy asked.

Juliana's brain buzzed with fear. The first miscarriage had been devastating. Losing Connor's baby would be unbearable. "No," she whispered.

"That's it. We're going to the hospital."

"No!" Although she sounded like a broken record, she couldn't stop the shout. To her, the hospital meant all hope was lost. "I—I need to go to a—a doctor."

"Yeah, at the hospital."

"At an office."

"Fine. Call your OB," Tracy insisted. "I'll drive you there."

Juliana wandered into her house, mindlessly changing her

pants and underwear as she fixed a fresh pad onto a clean pair of panties.

There wasn't a lot of blood. Not like last time. This was just spotty enough to have left the stain on her pants and her chair.

But any bleeding was a bad sign.

"Please, God. Please, not again," she prayed as she tossed her soiled clothing into the washer. "Please."

Fishing her phone from her purse, Juliana dialed her gynecologist. She'd just assumed Dr. Fisher would be her OB. The doctor she'd seen when she'd miscarried had retired a few years back.

"Fisher and Zirkelbach O-B-G-Y-N. May I help you?" a friendly woman's asked.

"I'm a patient of Dr. Fisher's. I—I'm pregnant and I started bleeding."

"Name, please."

"Juliana Kelley. Can she see me?"

"Is the bleeding heavy?"

"Um, about like a period," Juliana replied.

"Give me a moment, please." Annoying music replaced the voice.

Tracy stuck her head into the kitchen just as Juliana was tying her shoes. "What's happening?"

Juliana was about to answer when the receptionist came back on the line.

"Dr. Fisher is at the clinic. She asked for you to get there as soon as possible so she can see you."

"I will." After the receptionist gave her directions, Juliana slid her phone into her pocket. "The doctor's not at her office. This is her clinic day. We're meeting her there."

"Then let's go!"

* * *

A quick glance to the clock made his heart jump.

"Idiot." Connor ran his hand over his face, slowly regaining control of his impulses.

The temptation was finally abating. He'd driven to the casino the night before, holding sixty dollars in his hand, ready to head inside.

But he hadn't.

Instead, he'd stared at the building, trying to figure out exactly what it was about gambling that drew him with such intensity. Without any answers, he'd headed home to lie next to Juliana as she slept. She'd snuggled up to him, murmuring his name. He combed his fingers through her soft hair, wishing he was a stronger man.

Wishing he was the man she deserved.

This morning, the urge to gamble was still there, gnawing at his insides until he could take it no longer. The sixty dollars sang to him, drawing him like a Siren's song.

Before Juliana woke, he'd driven straight back to the casino and spent so much time sitting in his car, staring at the people wandering in and out, he'd lost track of what he should've been doing. He'd forgotten the third showing with the McMillans.

Juliana was with them. He had no doubt she'd picked up the slack, but he was being an asshole to make her do so.

Time to man up, Connor.

You fucked up your own life, but there's no way you're gonna do that to her.

No. Fucking. Way.

There wasn't a slot machine in the world that could make the mess he'd made of things go away, even if only for a couple of hours, if he disappeared into that tempting numbness. Max Schumm wouldn't stop being a prick. Connor's past wouldn't fade into nothing. And houses weren't going to sell themselves.

As he fired up the engine, he picked up his cell and called Juliana. There was no answer, so he focused on hunting her down. They'd synced a GPS app between their cell phones, finding it a handy tool for when they were both so busy that they had to meet somewhere in the middle of showings or closings.

She didn't pop up at the office. Or at the house the McMillans wanted to see yet again. Or anyplace he recognized. Although he'd learned the grid of the town pretty quickly by showing so many homes, her phone was at a series of office complexes close to the county hospital.

Hospital?

He jammed the SUV into gear and sped out of the parking lot, convinced he wouldn't spend another minute of his life on gambling. Life was short. Too short. Meeting Juliana had finally taught him there were things worth fighting for.

Her, for example.

His heart slammed against his rib cage as his mind flooded with pictures of the horrible things that might have happened to the woman he loved. A car accident? His biggest worry. He'd lived that nightmare once before.

Please let her be okay.

He drove far too fast, trying to get to the address on the GPS before he went crazy with worry.

The office buildings in the complex made a maze that soon had him dizzy. Connor negotiated the twists and turns until he finally found the right building. The sign was small enough he almost missed it.

CLOVERLEAF WOMEN'S CLINIC

He checked his phone again, sure he'd made a mistake. He even reset the search for Juliana's phone and tried it again. The same address popped up.

What in the hell was she doing at a women's clinic?

From what he'd been told, only two types of patients were served by women's clinics. Teenage girls who wanted to get birth control without going through their family doctors and women who wanted to get an—

No. Juliana would never consider an abortion. Hell, she never even told him she was pregnant.

Was she?

They'd had unprotected sex a few times, so anything was possible.

No, she would've told him. They were lovers. They were partners. They shared everything. If they were going to have a baby together…

Oh God.

What if she knew where he'd been the last two days? What if she thought he'd started gambling again? Would her fears for the future make her choose an abortion?

Instead of making himself crazy with "what ifs," Connor was going to hunt her down. That was the only one way to figure things out. He had to get his ass inside that clinic and find out why she was there.

He gaped when he got to the parking lot and saw Tracy's car instead of Juliana's SUV. Tracy was there, too?

He'd never been so confused in his entire life.

Which woman needed the services of one of these doctors?

After parking, Connor started texting both women, asking what they were doing in the clinic even as he strode toward the entrance. When he got to the innocuous door, he tried to jerk it open only to discover it was locked. A quick glance revealed an intercom and a security sign that said all people needed to be buzzed in.

He hit the intercom button. "Hello?"

"Can I help you?" a woman's voice asked.

"I need to get inside."

"May I ask your business with our clinic?"

"I need to see a patient. Let me in."

"I'm sorry, sir. We don't allow anyone who isn't a patient inside."

His temper flared. "Look, my girlfriend's GPS says she's inside. I need to get to her before…"

Before what?

Before she has an abortion?

"I'm sorry, sir. We don't—"

"Just tell me if she's actually in there. Her name's Ju—"

The women interrupted him with an exceptionally loud sigh. "Laws don't allow us to reveal any information about our patients."

This was turning into one of the most frustrating experiences of his life. "I just wanna know if she's in there. Please. Her name is Juliana—"

"Sir, you're going to have to leave now, or I'll be forced to call security."

Great. That was exactly what he needed. The local compulsive-gambling real estate salesman gets arrested outside an abortion clinic.

Max Schumm would die of utter happiness.

Then he saw it through the receptionist's eyes. Here was a frantic man, demanding to know whether his girlfriend was inside. How often had the clinic employees faced people who could potentially hurt them? Angry spouses. Activists. No wonder they were locked tighter than Fort Knox.

"Fine. I get it." Connor turned and stalked away. He could

wait in his SUV and catch up on his calendar while he waited for Juliana and Tracy. No sooner had he plopped into the driver's seat than his phone signaled a text.

Tracy. Thank God. But her message was simply a curt reply.

busy right now

"I know that," he muttered to himself as he typed the same words.

r u and jul in the clinic? is jul ok? r u ok?

Instead of answering, she sent a cryptic message.

go to the office. will talk there later.

"Damn it."

What choice did he have but to obey?

Chapter Twenty-Six

Connor tossed his stuff at his desk, not caring if anything got damaged.

After he'd left the women's clinic, he'd been waylaid by the McMillans. He'd let their earlier calls go to voice mail, so he answered even though he wanted to be home before Juliana got there. They were both in a panic, waiting for him at the house they wanted to see one last time before taking the plunge and making an offer.

Since he couldn't do anything to help Juliana, he'd shown the house and written the offer as quickly as he could before hurrying home. If he hadn't spent that precious time with the McMillans, Kelley-Wilson could've lost them as clients, something that probably would've made Juliana angrier than if he got there after she was already back from the clinic. At least Tracy was with her, and she'd texted him just as soon as Juliana was allowed to go home.

He still had no clue what had sent her there, but he'd convinced himself she was pregnant. The subtle signs were there. Her moodiness. An appetite that wavered from nauseous to ravenous. And she hadn't had a period he could remember.

Oh yes. Juliana was definitely pregnant.

What he didn't know was whether she'd terminated that pregnancy.

His gut churned at the thought. When it came to the abortion debate, his mantra had always been "her body, her choice." But this was his baby. He wanted to make a family with Juliana. He wanted for them to share a couple of kids the way they shared the rest of their lives. He wanted this beautiful woman to be his happily ever after.

If she hadn't gone there to end the pregnancy, why in the hell was she at the women's clinic? A passing thought that perhaps she'd accompanied Tracy rather than vice versa was smashed when Tracy texted that Juliana was doing well and was heading home.

The kitchen was empty. "Red?" he called as he wound his way through the house to the bedroom.

"Back here." Juliana's voice was clear and calm.

A bad sign.

She'd developed a certain tone when dealing with emotional clients—a flat tenor with little or no feeling. Her easy control helped relax people despite her natural lack of tolerance. That out-of-patience tone was exactly how she sounded now.

Connor stopped at the threshold of the open bedroom door.

Juliana was dressed in gray yoga pants and a pink T-shirt. She leaned back against a stack of pillows behind her back exactly the way she did some of the nights they watched TV. Her fingers flew over her laptop keyboard.

"Did you get with the McMillans?" Her voice still held that same timbre that sent a shiver down Connor's spine.

"Yeah."

"And?"

"Can we forget them for a minute? How are you feel—"

"Forget them? Are you nuts? We need to get them to write an

offer. They've piddled around long enough. You know what first-timers are like. They need to work up some guts. Give them a call and ask them to come in tomorrow. I can push them a little."

He gaped at her, not sure how she could even think about the business at a time like this. Didn't she know how worried he was? Couldn't she see his fear for her and for what she might have just done? "Push them a little? Seriously, Red? That's all you've got to say to me?"

Her fingers stilled. "What exactly do you want me to say? They've seen the house three times. Of course I want to nudge them."

She was being deliberately obtuse, but before he could tell her so, her gaze caught his. For the first time since he'd met her, he couldn't read her emotions.

He'd always believed that first passionate, magical night they'd spent together happened because he'd not only recognized her desire, but that she'd been able to see how much he wanted her. Since then, they'd continued to share that connection.

Until now.

Something was wrong—something more than his concerns for what she might have done. Juliana had somehow thrown firewalls around her mind and her heart. He could no longer get in.

Worse, he wasn't sure he wanted to even try. She'd clearly lost faith in him. If she didn't trust him, what kind of relationship—or partnership—could survive that?

His own heart ached as he struggled for the courage to ask exactly what she'd done in that clinic.

The sound of a toilet flushing was followed by Tracy exiting the *en suite* bath. "Hey, Connor." Even her tone was a bit flat.

"Hey, Trace." He fixed his attention back on Juliana. "Are you…okay?"

"What about the McMillans?" she snapped.

The woman was a pit bull when it came to business. Unless he answered her, she'd never quit the topic and allow them to move on to more important matters. "I showed them the house. Again. They checked out the comparables I brought with me, and I wrote a purchase offer for them. They farted around so much, they might be competing with at least one other offer. I've got a call in to the listing agent but heard nothing back from her yet. *Now* will you tell me why you were at the women's clinic? I've been worried sick." He tunneled his fingers through his hair, hating the alarm bubbling to the surface.

Juliana arched an eyebrow. "Were you as worried as I was when I couldn't find you the last two days?"

Tracy moved to the side of the bed. "You two should have some privacy. You really need to talk." She threw a worried frown to Juliana. "Need anything before I leave?"

"No," Juliana replied. "Thanks for everything. You got me through this."

"Rest," Tracy ordered before she lightly touched Juliana's shoulder. She stopped at the door to stare up a Connor. "She's supposed to take it easy for a while. Don't let her do too much."

That order confirmed his worst suspicions.

"I won't," Juliana replied as though Tracy had spoken to her. "Thanks for being there."

"Call me later, Connor. We should talk, too." With a nod, she gave him a gentle push into the room and shut the door behind her.

Silence reigned.

Connor had so many questions flying through his thoughts he wasn't sure where he should even begin.

Juliana seemed lost in contemplation as well. She'd set her laptop aside and simply stared at him. She fiddled with the fringe on the afghan draped over her lower legs, pulling it up to her lap.

"Juliana, I'm sorry. I'm really sorry I disappeared on you the last couple of days."

Her hands dropped to the mattress. "Where were you, Connor? The truth. I need the truth."

He didn't need the stern warning in her voice. He wasn't about to skirt the issue. She deserved the brutal truth. "A casino."

* * *

Juliana closed her eyes, fighting the sting of tears.

She'd been right. He had been gambling again.

Her chest felt as though she'd taken a sharp blow, making breathing agony. But there was no way she'd let him know how much he'd hurt her.

Hurt?

She was devastated.

Everything in her life now rested like a smashed mirror at her feet. Broken shards were all that remained of her dreams, and each shard shredded a little more of her heart.

Didn't he understand that he'd shattered her trust in the same way? They were real estate agents. People depended on them to be the epitome of honesty in all they did. They handled their clients' money.

Shit, they handled their clients' *lives.*

And they were business partners. They should be able to trust each other implicitly. He'd betrayed her trust—destroyed any chance that she could allow him to remain her partner and not have her looking over his shoulder. She'd always have to worry whether he'd transferred money correctly or whether he'd delivered a check. How could she ever truly know if he'd done the right thing for the people who hired them?

Having been a teacher, she understood that even the appearance of impropriety was enough to ruin a career. A Realtor at a casino? Especially after Max Schumm's horrible smear campaign?

Kelley-Wilson Realty died the moment Connor pulled his car into the casino parking lot.

Even as she fought the urge to roll to her stomach and pummel the mattress until she cried herself to sleep, she thought about all the things she'd have to do to disband the firm and get her teaching job back. That was the only solution. She had to let the firm go and head back to Douglas High School—a failure with her tail tucked between her legs.

Max Schumm would break out in happy song the moment he heard they'd disbanded. Even that horrible thought wouldn't make her reconsider.

Besides, she had to think beyond herself now. There was more at stake. A lot more.

"Damn you," she whispered.

"I'm sorry. I really am. It was a slip, but I didn't gamble, not really. I sat in the—"

As if she'd let him come up with excuses. He was an addict. He should damn well admit his relapse.

She held up a hand to stop him. "Were you at a casino?"

"Yeah, but—"

"But nothing! You went to a casino. You risked everyone—customers, other Realtors, Max Asshat Schumm—seeing you there. That's all that matters." A small sob threatened to erupt, but she swallowed hard, forcing it back down. Because she'd given two precious things, her heart and her trust, to the wrong person, her life was unraveling and there wasn't a fucking thing she could do about it.

"I made a mistake going there. I see that. But you're keeping secrets, too. Why were you at that clinic?"

There was no way she would let him turn the blame for

this confrontation to her. "We're talking about you, not me."
She breathed a shuddering sigh. "I trusted you. Do you know how
hard that was for me? I trusted you! And how do you repay me? By
disappearing and keeping secrets. By destroying my life."

"What about *your* secrets, Juliana?"

Although she knew she was being hypocritical—holding tight
to her surprise while bashing him for his—she wouldn't let him
divert the topic. Not yet. He needed to know that she'd given
him something rare and dear and he'd spit on her gift. After
Jimmy, she'd sworn to never trust a man that way again.

But she'd trusted Connor with her heart and soul.

I'm a pathetic fool.

"What did you do at the clinic?" he demanded.

Tracy had told her addicts liked to deflect blame, and that if
he couldn't be honest and own up to what he'd done and the
implications of his behavior, he had no chance to stay clean.

One problem at a time.

"My 'secrets' aren't what we're discussing," Juliana insisted.
"Not yet."

That time would come soon. Then he'd see exactly how much
betraying her trust had cost him. He had no idea what he'd done
and what he'd lost by choosing gambling over her.

"I'm not an idiot, Red. I know what you were doing." Emotions played across his features, so many and so quickly she had
trouble reading anything except the one that finally settled.

Rage.

Juliana's own rage rose in response. What right did he have
to be angry with her? She hadn't messed everything up! He had!

When he opened his mouth, she beat him to the punch. "How
dare you! Do you have any idea what you've done to my life?" She
picked up the television remote and hurled it at him.

Connor ducked, and the remote hit the wall, shattering into a tangle of plastic and wires. He narrowed his eyes as he fisted his hands against his hips. "How dare *I*? How dare *you*!"

She was so taken aback by the forcefulness of his shout all she could do was gape at him.

"You didn't even tell me you were pregnant!" he roared. "Then you go off and have an abortion! What the fuck's wrong with you? Sure, I screwed up. I went to the casino. *Twice*. But I didn't get out of my car. And you know why?"

Stupefied by his atrocious accusation, she could only shake her head.

An abortion? He thought she'd had an abortion? What did that say about his true feelings for her?

Sure, she'd waited to tell him she was pregnant. Holding tight to the news was nothing but a matter of sparing his feelings for those first scary weeks. She would've told him. Soon.

She wasn't the bad guy here, and he had no right shifting the spotlight to her to get it off him.

He waited before answering his own question, breathing hard enough his nostrils flared. "I didn't get out of my car because of you. Because I didn't want to let you down by having Kelley-Wilson—a name I allowed to please *you*, by the way—get destroyed by that sanctimonious, underhanded bastard. I decided I'd fight back and bring Max Schumm down. I've even arranged a press conference where I would humiliate myself and admit to being a compulsive gambler in hopes of clearing the air and getting some of our clients back."

By saying nothing, Juliana was learning a lot about Connor. Some good things. Some *very* good things—like how much he wanted their firm to succeed.

Unfortunately, there was one thing, one very bad thing, she couldn't ignore.

He doesn't love me. He probably never did.

There was no other explanation for his indictment of her character. How could a man who loved a woman accuse her of doing something as deceitful as having an abortion without his knowledge or approval?

She swallowed hard. "I—I want you out of my house. Now. Get the hell out."

"Juliana...*please*. We need to talk." He took a few steps toward the bed.

"About what? My abortion?" Her laugh sounded hysterical. "Get out, Connor. I want you out of my house and out of my life. We'll settle up business matters when I'm well enough to deal with you."

"Jules?" Mallory's raised voice came from the kitchen.

"In the bedroom," Juliana shouted back.

"I'm not leaving," he insisted. "Not until we talk."

A tear spilled over her lashes despite her best efforts. She wiped it away with the back of her trembling hand. "There's nothing to talk about. Go. Just...go."

"Jules? I came as fast as I—" Mallory stopped short the moment she opened the door and stepped through. "Oh. Sorry. I'll let you two have some privacy and—"

"Stay," Juliana insisted. "Connor was just leaving."

He ran his hand over his face, a gesture she knew well. It was his signal that he was exasperated. "Juliana..."

Mallory's gaze shifted between the two before settling on Juliana. "I should go."

"Don't you dare." Connor stomped to the door. "She needs you to take care of her. Besides," he hissed, "we're done here. For good."

Chapter Twenty-Seven

The front door slammed, making Juliana flinch. Not because she hadn't expected it, but because it sounded so final.

Problem was it was anything but final. This was only the beginning of what could be a long and drawn-out battle. Connor Wilson was going to be a part of her life, regardless of what she wanted.

Is that really what I want? To have him gone forever?

She was an idiot. Instead of opening up and sharing her news with him and making plans, she'd done what she thought she'd grown out of—she'd had a temper tantrum. Everything inside her hurt, from not only his accusation but from her broken trust. But those weren't fatal wounds. She could heal, and she thought she could help him heal as well.

Way to go, Jules. Fucked that one up, didn't ya?

"Jules?" Mallory knit her brows. "What just happened?"

"I'd think it was obvious." Tugging the afghan higher up, Juliana fought a chill that seeped all the way to her bones. She pulled her legs up and hugged them, resting her forehead against her knees.

Connor had accused her of having an abortion. The notion had jarred her so much, she hadn't even defended herself. After the months they'd spent together, working side by side, sleeping side by side, the man didn't know her at all.

Sniffing hard, she refused to cry, hoping numbness would settle in. The doctor had given her stern orders to rest and to avoid stress. Yet here she was in the middle of an emotional tornado.

"So you just sat there and let him walk out?"

Juliana looked up at Mallory's question to find her friend's arms crossed over her chest. She glared at Juliana with her teacher-is-pissed face, one Juliana knew well.

Mallory gave her head a shake. "What exactly is going on in that brain of yours?"

"Juliana?" Bethany called, her voice echoing down the hallway.

"We're here!" Danielle added. "Got the frozen custard!"

A reunion of the Ladies Who Lunch. What better way to end the most humiliating and demoralizing experience of her life?

"In the bedroom," Mallory replied. She still leveled that stare at Juliana. "Out with it. What's going on?"

"He went to the casino. He chose gambling over me." It was so much easier to focus on his sin than hers.

"I hadn't realized they were mutually exclusive," Mallory drawled. "He gambled again?"

"Actually...he said he didn't," Juliana whispered. In fact, he'd said he walked away because of her.

Everything she'd read about addictions claimed the addict had to recover for himself or he'd never stick to his path. Connor had to stay away from gambling for himself, but his words were finally sinking in now that she'd stopped talking and started thinking.

When he'd been throwing his anger at her, she'd believed

he didn't truly love her. Yet if he was able to fight his desire to gamble because he didn't want to hurt her, he had to hold strong feelings for her.

Her life was so confusing, she wanted to yank the covers over her head and hide forever.

Quit being a baby.

Bethany and Danielle spilled into the room. Beth stopped at the foot of the bed and tilted her head while Dani set her sack on the nightstand.

"We missed the drama, didn't we?" Dani asked. She shed her jacket before tossing it over the chair. "Bring us up to speed."

"Yeah," Beth chimed in. "Talk."

Mallory inclined her head at Juliana. "She just told Connor to get out, and he obeyed."

"What the hell?" Danielle narrowed her eyes. "Why? He's your partner. You love the guy. Why would you do that, Jules?"

"Seriously?" Bethany's frown was no less fierce than the other Ladies. "For God's sake. What could he have done that's bad enough for you to kick him out?"

Juliana gave in to her urge and pulled the afghan over her head.

These were *her* friends, not Connor's. Why were they sticking up for him?

While she wallowed under her protective cover, Mallory gave them a quick summary of Connor's gambling troubles. The last thing she told them was that Juliana had kicked him out when he accused her of having an abortion.

"Doesn't he know about your miscarriage?" Dani asked, her eyes wide.

Juliana nodded.

"And he still thought you'd had an abortion?"

"But you didn't," Beth said. "I know you didn't."

"You're right," Juliana confirmed, "I didn't."

"Then what happened?" Mallory asked.

After taking a bracing deep breath, Juliana told her tale. "It started when Tracy came over this morning..."

* * *

Connor couldn't make himself leave. Despite Juliana's angry demands, he wasn't going anywhere. What he shared with her was far too special to let die, personally *and* professionally. Her anger, however, would fade in time.

But how much time?

And how much damage would be done before they found their way back to each other?

Tracy came out of the office door, her gaze catching Connor's. "I was right!"

He cocked a brow. "About?"

"I didn't think you'd leave."

He folded his arms over his chest and leaned back against his SUV. "I don't have anywhere else to go. My house is still gutted to the walls because I haven't had time to pick out fixtures."

She turned and mimicked his actions as she snorted. "Yeah, sure that's why you didn't leave."

As if she'd ever let him get away with a fib. "Is she okay?" he asked.

"Why didn't you ask her?"

"You heard everything. You know damn well she wouldn't answer my questions about what happened today."

Tracy turned to face him. "Let me ask you something... What if she did have an abortion? Would that be a deal breaker?"

Since he'd thought of nothing else from the moment he walked away, his answer came quickly. "No. It definitely wouldn't be a deal breaker. Even if she did, I would understand."

"Then you need to tell her that instead of accusing her as though she committed some crime."

"I would tell her, but she kicked me out."

She narrowed her eyes. "Don't make me slap you. You were both acting like idiots in there. Shit, I've seen teenagers fight with more maturity. What the two of you need to do is talk, *really* talk. You were honest with her about going to the casino—something we'll have to discuss at length soon—but you didn't tell her why."

"There is no 'why.'"

"Okay, one more stupid thing, Connor." She held up her index finger to emphasize her point. "Say one more stupid thing and I will smack you. You and I both know there's always a why. What's yours?"

His arms dropped to his side as he finally began to relax. He needed to open up, and Tracy was the one person who wouldn't judge him.

Juliana? She'd already tried and convicted him. How could he ever explain it all to her? How could he make her understand the insidious nature of addiction? If she couldn't find a way to see his point of view, she'd never change her mind.

Perhaps what he needed to do was get a better understanding of himself. Maybe then he could explain things to the woman he loved. "Can I ask you something, Trace?"

"Sure."

"Do you still want to drink?"

"Every. Damn. Day."

His gaze found hers, searching for the sincerity he'd heard in her voice, needing to see it in her eyes.

And it was there.

"Thank God." Connor breathed a weighty sigh. "I—I…" He shrugged. "I don't know, I guess I thought I was weak. I thought there was something wrong with me."

Tracy laid a comforting hand on his arm. "Connor, you know better than that. You have an addiction. So do I. It's no different from any other chronic problem. Arthritis. Diabetes. Lupus. It won't disappear. Some days will be fine, and some are going to be difficult. It's the nature of the beast. Accept it. Embrace it. Then she will, too."

"She won't. I killed her faith in me," he said in a ragged whisper. "There's no way she'll ever be able to trust me again."

The same hand that had just soothed him rose to clip his chin hard enough to make his teeth clack together.

"Self-pity? Seriously?" She shook her head. "Juliana's a smart woman. Explain things to her."

"What are you talking about?"

"Tell her what you were thinking, how your fears are what made you drive to that casino. I know guys are kinda dense where feelings are concerned, but you need to make her see yours. That's the only way you can earn her trust back."

Fear. Tracy had nailed it on the head. Fear had sent him running. Sure, he wanted to put all the blame on Max Schumm's shoulders. Connor knew better. His own worries were to blame.

He was going to have to be a stronger man. Although Max was fighting dirty, that didn't mean the war was over. Not by a long shot. Gambling wasn't going to make Max disappear, and the problems that would result if Connor opened Pandora's box and actually gambled would make that bastard look about as serious as a fly buzzing around a room.

This was all about Connor fighting his own demons. For Juliana—and for himself.

"Still wanna do the press conference?" he asked. "Still wanna tell the world you're not deserting me?"

"Oh, hell yeah," Tracy replied. "You know how much I love putting sniveling little rodents in their place. I swear, if that Schumm guy sends me one more e-mail or leaves one more voice mail, I'll hire a hit man to deal with the problem." She cocked her head. "But what about you? Are you ready to confess your sins?"

A slow smile spread over his lips. "You know, I think I finally am."

Chapter Twenty-Eight

If Bethany asked about Connor leaving one more time, Juliana vowed to throw her pillow right at her face.

"Beth," Dani said, "enough. She kicked him out. Period." She sent a glare at Juliana. "Yes, she's going to apologize and try to make it right."

Mallory plopped on Connor's side of the bed, moving close to Juliana. She wrapped an arm around her shoulder. "Of course she is. This is only a stupid misunderstanding. They'll work it out."

There were very few people Juliana let inside her personal space. She wasn't a hugger, except maybe with her students. And the Ladies. And Ben, if he'd helped fix something.

And Connor.

She laid her head on Mallory's shoulder as Danielle and Bethany sat on the foot of the bed so the four friends faced one another.

Beth's eyes widened. "He should know better than to think you'd have an abortion. Not someone as nice as you."

With a shake of her head, Dani said, "Nice has nothing to do with an abortion."

Since Beth had always been adamantly against abortion and Mallory and Dani were strongly pro-choice, Juliana tried to ward off an approaching political debate. She had a hell of a lot more to worry about.

"He was supermad, so I think he just reacted without thinking." A sigh slipped out. "I should've set him straight, but I didn't."

Mallory pulled her arm away. "What?" Her voice was loud enough for Juliana to lean away. "For God's sake, Jules, you let that poor guy leave—"

"*Demanded* that he leave," Dani corrected.

"—without telling him you're still pregnant?"

Her silence then had been pretty damned thoughtless, but Juliana would sooner have her fingers broken than admit it. Her current silence had to confirm Mallory's suspicions.

"You have to tell him," Bethany insisted. "Now."

"You're right. I know you're right." Juliana's shoulders dropped. "But what if he only sticks around because he's gonna be a father? How will I ever know if he really loves me and isn't just doing the 'right thing'?" She punctuated the words with air quotes.

That thought stung. A lot. Added to his accusation and her loss of trust, she wondered if they would ever be able to mend their broken relationship.

They'd become a couple too quickly, falling into being partners and then a twosome before they had time to get to know each other well. In some ways, that was a blessing. Every day was a revelation, and their chemistry drove them forward. Yet they hadn't laid a strong foundation to weather these kinds of storms.

Was it too late to try?

"I think there's a bigger concern." Mallory crossed her legs, affecting a perfect lotus position. "If he does come back, will you be able to trust him again?"

"Exactly." Danielle frowned. "Didn't you say he hadn't gambled, that he'd only sat in his car?"

"Yeah. But—"

"No 'but,' Jules," Bethany said. "He didn't betray your trust. You owe him the benefit of the doubt."

Good ole Beth. Always forgiving. Always looking on the bright side.

"It's not that simple," Juliana said. "I believe him, that he didn't gamble, but the damage was already done. A client could've seen him there, and you know damn well anyone who saw Connor would assume he'd gambled."

"How likely is that?" Mallory asked. "I mean, really, how likely? The closest casino is almost an hour's drive. Most people in Cloverleaf are ultraconservative, almost antigambling. Do you think the odds are—"

"Pun intended?" Danielle interrupted with a smirk.

Mallory let out a chuckle. "No, but I'll still take credit for it." She sobered. "Look, Jules, you have to let this go. You have to forgive and forget. He slipped up. He's human. We all are."

"Exactly," Bethany added. "You also have to be honest—as honest as he was by telling you he went to that casino. Tell him about the baby!"

There was a whole lot more to tell Connor about than a baby.

Her friends were right. Before Jules could assure her friends she would, there was a soft knock.

Connor stood in the doorway, hands in his front pockets and head bowed. "Can we talk, Red? Please?"

"That's our exit cue." Mallory untangled her legs and bounced off the bed.

Jostled, Beth and Dani crawled off the mattress as well.

Each of her friends gave her an entreating glance, their way of demanding Juliana be reasonable and not her normal ticking time bomb.

Ah, but they knew her so well.

"Thanks," she said, nodding at each of her friends.

Mallory gave Connor a gentle nudge into the bedroom and closed the door behind her after she stepped through.

"You doing okay?" he asked.

That question was becoming tedious. "I'm fine."

Juliana got out of bed, hating feeling like some invalid. She calmly folded the afghan as she struggled for the right thing to say.

Her friends were right. As usual. She needed to be honest with Connor, and now was the time, before his wrong assumption festered into a wound that might never heal.

When she turned to face him, she ran into a wall of hard muscle. How had he moved so close without her realizing?

"I'm sorry," he said, hands still in his pockets.

His unease was odd. The man had exuded confidence from the first moment they met. Had he not, she wouldn't have followed through with her attraction and that first night never would've happened.

What she wanted was for him to wrap his arms around her and give her a rough squeeze. "About what?"

"About assuming. I should know better." His eyes found hers. "I should've waited to ask you what happened at the clinic."

"I guess you're right." Juliana swallowed hard, not sure where to begin. She sat on the edge of the mattress and patted the spot next to her. "Sit down. Please."

Connor obeyed, his gaze still glued to her.

"I wasn't at the clinic to have an abortion. I was there to see my doctor—my gynecologist. She works there a couple of days a week."

"Oh, I didn't know that." At least he had the common sense to sound contrite. "I just figured…never mind. I was being stupid."

"Not stupid. Not really. I should've told you sooner."

"That you were pregnant? I'd suspected for a while. I just wish…" He gave his head a shake. "Never mind. What's done is done. I understand. I'd lost your trust. I get that."

Instead of correcting him, she opened the top drawer of the end table and picked up the precious envelope. "This is why I went to see my doctor." Picking up his hand, she laid the envelope on his palm.

With the same intensity a child attacks a Christmas gift, Connor opened the envelope and plucked out the black-and-white picture of the ultrasound Juliana had been given at the clinic. He stared at it, turning it this way and that.

Smiling, she took the image and made sure he was looking at it right-side up. "I have trouble seeing what I'm supposed to in ultrasounds, too. Look hard for a face."

"So—so you're still pregnant."

"Oh yeah." She pointed at a baby's face and traced the outline. "See the eyes? The nose?"

He squinted. "I think so." His finger brushed over the left side of the image. "What's that? Looks the same as what you said was a face."

"It is. That's the *second* set of eyes and another nose." She held her breath, waiting for his reaction.

"Second set of—" Eyes wide, he gaped at her, glanced back to the ultrasound, then gaped at her again. "You mean there are…*two*?"

The way his voice cracked made her smile. She'd been close to catatonic when the technician had pointed out that second little face on the screen. "Yep. Two. Two healthy babies. Due in April. Probably conceived the night the condom broke."

He hadn't moved his finger away from the picture, and he stared with an intensity that raised her concern.

"Connor? Are you...okay with this? I want these babies."

He glared at her, mouth agape. "Okay? Are you serious?"

"Yeah, I'm serious. Dead serious. I'm having twins and—"

"*We're* having twins."

That said everything she needed to know. Connor wasn't going to run from this challenge.

She laid her head on his shoulder. "Yeah, honey. We're having twins."

* * *

Connor wondered if his heart would ever settle into a normal rhythm again.

Two babies?

Two babies.

All of his anger and suspicion evaporated. Juliana wanted these children every bit as much as he did. He was wrong to have jumped to conclusions, and made a mental note to remember that she was chock-full of surprises. Predicting what she was going to do would never be truly possible.

That was one of the things he loved best about her.

"I went to the clinic because I had some bleeding," she explained. "The doctor said everything's fine, and the bleeding had already stopped. I'm supposed to take it easy and get my feet up when I can."

"I'll make damn sure you do."

Silence reigned as Connor continued to trace the images on the ultrasound. He vowed to the two children he could barely make out on the paper that he'd be the best father in the whole world.

And he'd never gamble again. Not a lottery ticket. Not a slot machine. Not a horse race.

Ever.

"So…?" she nudged, her voice a whisper.

His Juliana was an extrovert, and his quiet was probably killing her.

"So…" He set the ultrasound aside and took her hand in his. Raising it to his lips, he brushed a kiss on her knuckles. "We raise a couple of twins, most likely redheads with their mother's temper, and live happily ever after."

Not that he believed that. Their road wasn't going to be smooth. His addiction would always be throwing potholes in their paths, but it was his job to steer around each and every one.

"I won't gamble again, Juliana. I swear to you. I won't." He meant every word.

"I know you'll try."

At least there was no bite to her words. "I *won't.*"

She heaved a sigh.

He gripped her chin and made her look at him. "I won't. I'd sooner cut off my hands than touch a slot machine again. Got it?"

Green eyes searched his face. "It won't be easy."

"Never said it would be. Good thing I'm a guy who likes a challenge." He kissed her forehead. "Like you, Red."

"Twins, Connor," she said, her words a raw whisper. "How are we going to handle twins?"

"The same way we handle everything. With style." Connor rose. "Are you up to going out?"

"Yeah. Why?"

"I've got something to show you. Rest for a little bit. I'll be back in an hour."

Chapter Twenty-Nine

Juliana hadn't expected Connor to stop at the red brick building in the middle of Old Town, the center of Cloverleaf.

The Lamb-Brooks Law Offices had been empty for a good number of years despite rumors from time to time that someone was going to restore the place to its glory days.

She kept glancing from him to the building. It was a solid structure almost as old as the town. The lawyers, who used to call it an office as well as a home, had passed away, and when the economy went south, people stopped showing any interest.

A shame.

With some restoration, the place would make great offices again. She'd even entertained the idea of one day trying to buy it for a song. A fleeting memory of mentioning that to Connor came floating back.

"You didn't buy this place." She gaped at him. "Did you?"

His face lit with a grin. "Actually, I did. Got it for next to nothing, too. You know me—I always get the best price."

"But—"

"Nope, Red. You don't get to argue this time. I bought it

for us, and that's that." He pulled a set of keys from his pocket. "There's no turning back." Grabbing her hand, he dragged her toward the front door. "C'mon in and let me show you what I see. Put on your 'potential glasses,' lady. Prepare to be dazzled."

That was an unnecessary suggestion—one the two of them used whenever they were showing a place that needed some TLC. *Always look at the* possible. *Put on those "potential glasses."*

She already knew what he saw because she'd had the same vision, albeit before she knew they were going to be parents to twins. They'd turn the bottom floor into Kelley-Wilson Realty's new home. The second floor was a rather large apartment—close to two thousand square feet—the old lawyers had shared. Everyone in town referred to them as "best friends." In reality, the two were a committed couple who used the upstairs as their home for more than thirty years.

Connor opened the front door and let her pass inside first.

Sunlight spilled through the dirty windows, highlighting the dust in the air and the cobwebs in every corner. But the place had character to spare. The woodwork might be covered in a layer of white paint, but she could see it restored to the original finish, from the crown molding to the twisted spires of the lavish staircase rails.

"It's so big," she whispered.

Still holding her hand, he led her to the stairs and headed to the apartment on the second floor. "I figure once Ben gets his hands on this place, it'll be a masterpiece." He plucked another key from the ring and opened the ornate oaken door. "Welcome home."

It was like stepping into the 1960s. The men had been living in a virtual time capsule.

The great room and kitchen were one big, open space. While she loved that configuration, a combination of piss-green tile backsplash against a faded yellow countertop was enough to cause a wave of morning sickness. Even the cabinets were dated, their hardware a tarnished gold. The white enamel sink was chipped, and the faucet was lime-covered.

The carpet in the great room was forest-green shag, and the furniture came straight from an episode of *Mad Men*. While a vintage shop owner might be drooling, all Juliana could think was how much work Ben would have to do and how many workers he'd have to hire to make the place livable and drag it into the twenty-first century.

What had Connor been thinking?

Their business was hanging by a thread, and Max wasn't easing his attack. Every new Schumm advertisement referenced "taking chances" or "honesty." If they couldn't find a way to launch an offensive and restore the public's confidence in Kelley-Wilson Realty, the firm might not have a future to plan for.

He gave her hand a squeeze. "Well? What do you think? I mean, we could stay at your place until the upstairs is done. Then we can live up here until Ben finishes the offices. After that, we sell both our places and this will be home base—for work *and* play. One of our customers told me this belonged to a couple of old guys who were gay before it was acceptable. She said they were together forever, so I figured…" He let go of her hand and fumbled through his pocket.

"You figured what?"

He held a red velvet box on the palm of his hand as he dropped to one knee. "I figured we could get married."

Her trembling hands flew to her mouth, covering a gasp.

While her heart wanted to sing at his plans for their future and the romantic gesture, the realist in her fought back. "Connor, we can't—"

"Hear me out first. Okay?"

"But—"

"*Please*, Juliana. Let me explain."

She nodded, blinking back the blur of tears in her eyes.

His smile stole her breath. "I figured this would be a great place for us to have a new beginning—to start our married life. The last couple was together almost forty years from what I've heard. This building needs some work, but it's got a great track record." He winked.

Juliana could barely process anything after the word "married."

But why now?

Because he wanted them to be a couple?

Or because of her pregnancy?

That notion made her sad. She wanted him to want her, not marry her because she was pregnant. At least she knew where'd he'd been the hour he was gone. He'd hit a jewelry store.

"Think about it," he continued, his voice full of confidence. "Can't you see us here? Picture our furniture, a great granite countertop, new cabinets, hardwood floors—the works. Ben will turn this into a showplace. The upstairs will be comfortable and homey. Did you know this place has three bedrooms and two full baths?"

"No. I—I didn't realize it was that big."

"The downstairs will be a great place to bring our clients. And what better location? Smack-dab in the middle of town."

She reached out for the velvet box—her curiosity screaming to open it—before she pulled back her trembling fingers.

Her heart shouted for her to say, "Yes!" To grab for happiness with both hands.

She loved this man. He was a part of her and would always be a part of her. She carried his children, a miracle she'd never expected. They were suited for each other, from the office to the bedroom.

Everything inside her wanted to accept his proposal—except one worry that refused to move aside.

"Connor…we might…what if…" She closed her eyes and hugged herself. "The firm might not survive, not if Max keeps up his onslaught."

"It'll survive. I guaran-damn-tee you it'll survive."

While she loved the conviction in his tone, she had to deal with the reality of their situation. "How? How can you be so sure the firm won't go under?"

"Faith, Red. I have faith—in you and in me and how damn good we are together."

Faith.

The one thing that had always seemed to elude her.

How absurd that she, Danielle, and Bethany had told Mallory to have faith in Ben when the couple had hit a rough patch. Mallory believed he'd left her when he'd feared her breast cancer had returned. But the Ladies told her to listen to her heart and have faith that all would work out in the end.

And it had. Ben and Mallory got their happy ending.

Why was advice always so easy to give and so damned difficult to take?

Connor plopped to the floor and patted his lap. "Sit down, Juliana. Let's talk."

His patience must have been at an end, because when she didn't obey, he dragged her down and wrapped his arms around her.

"Why not take a shot at happiness?" he asked. "What do we have to lose?"

My heart.

My soul.

Everything.

She simply shrugged.

"Do you love me?" he prodded.

"You know I do."

"Then marry me."

"What if you gamble again? Will you trust me enough to let me help if things get rough? Tracy isn't the only person in your life anymore. I'm here, too." *So like me to ruin an utterly romantic moment.*

His grip tightened for a split second. Then he relaxed. "I won't gamble."

"You don't trust me to—"

He shook his head. "I trust you, Red. I do. Think about it. I'm sharing a company with you. If that doesn't take trust, I don't know what does!"

"Addictions don't disappear. Keeping our firm going with all of Max's bullshit is going to be stressful. *Very* stressful."

"I agree, but when I was sitting in that car, I had the worst craving I've ever had to hit the slot machines. I was in agony, but I didn't go inside." He sighed. "I wish I could explain it, but I know I've got this licked. Like I've already told you, I'd cut off my hand before I'd pull another lever or scratch another ticket. Just to be sure, I'll keep going to meetings, and I'll keep Tracy close." Leaning back, he looked her in the eye. "You're not worried about how close I am to her, are you?"

"No," Juliana replied firmly. "Not one bit. But I want you to trust me, too. Lean on *both* of us when you need to." She was actually grateful that Connor had someone else, another strong person, helping him. Adding that to his faith in staying away from temptation, and she could almost believe he would keep his word.

He gave her quick kiss. "Good. 'Cause she came up with a great idea on how to topple Max from his high horse."

"Really?"

"Yep. But I don't want to talk about him now. I want to talk about us." He rested his hand against her abdomen. "All four of us." A chuckle slipped out. "Twins. I think my heart stopped for a second when I saw that ultrasound."

"So did mine." Things were still far too serious, so she couldn't smile at his teasing. "Is that why you're proposing? Because of the babies?" How she found the courage to ask was beyond her, but she needed to know.

"That's what you think?" he asked, his tone dubious.

"I don't know what to think."

"How about you love me and we should make a family together?"

She glanced away. "Then why didn't you ask me before you knew I was pregnant?" Her protective walls had really fallen or else she'd never have allowed herself to show her vulnerability so plainly.

Connor's fingers on her cheek urged her to turn back to face him. "Hold out your hand."

She obeyed.

He set the box on her palm. "How long have we known each other?"

Dropping her hand, she laid the box on her lap. Holding it made a happy ending seem real—a luxury she couldn't afford. "This is October, so five months, almost six."

"I thought it was too soon to ask." His eyes searched hers. "Should've known better, though."

Everything he said made sense, and yet she couldn't see how they were all related. "Should've know better about what?"

"About you." He jostled her on his lap as he wiggled around to get something out of his pocket.

When she picked up the velvet box and tried to rise, he held her firmly in place and dangled a white paper in front of her.

"Here," he said. "Check the date on this."

Juliana grabbed it with her free hand, trying to figure out what the paper had to do with proposals, the time they'd been together, and her.

She quickly realized it was the receipt for her ring. Her eyes widened at the price. "Please tell me you didn't pay that much for this ring!"

He rolled his eyes. "Not the *price*, Red, the *date*."

With a disgruntled snort, she found the date. "August sixteenth. So what?"

August sixteenth.

Holy shit.

"You bought this in August? Seriously?" Her incredulous tone echoed through the cavernous room.

"Seriously. I knew. Even back then, I knew."

His cryptic comments were fraying her already shaky nerves. "Knew what?"

"That you were the only woman in the world for me."

Cradling the little box against her chest, she fought tears as things added up. "I would've said yes. If you'd have asked me in August, I still would've said yes—even if it was probably too soon."

"I know that now. Like I said, I should've known better. You and I clicked from that very first moment. We dove into this partnership headfirst that very first night."

"We dove into the sex that very first night," she couldn't help but point out. "The partnership came later."

"Did it really?" His smile warmed her from the inside out. "Would you have ever bluffed the Ryans that we were partners if we hadn't made love when we met?"

He had her there. "No. It wouldn't even have crossed my mind."

"Then the partnership began the moment the relationship did."

"It was just sex then."

"You're wrong. It was so much more." Rooting around in his pocket, he slowly pulled out a sheer black stocking as though he were a magician. "Would I have saved this if it were just sex?"

"M-my stocking?" The one she couldn't find the morning after they'd made love the first time.

He nodded. "I saved it because I knew. That night was the spark of what we have now—a relationship. And the relationship and the partnership are inseparable—*we're* inseparable." He took the box and tapped her on the nose with it. "This only seals the deal."

* * *

Connor wasn't sure exactly what he'd expected when he brought Juliana here. Although his fantasy involved her letting a few tears of joy fall before accepting his proposal, he knew better. Juliana never let herself be ruled by her sentiments.

She might be a woman with great depth of feeling, but she kept her strong emotions under lock and key, always leading with her brain instead of her heart.

He knew her well enough to anticipate her questioning the timing of his marriage proposal, bringing along the receipt to show her how long he'd planned to ask her to be his wife.

That, in and of itself, was a bit of a miracle since he'd sworn he would never marry. For years, he'd watched far too many of his friends grow bitter after their marriages turned sour. He'd sold their big houses and helped get them into trendy condos, where they brought their kids for visitations. He'd never wanted to find himself in such ridiculous circumstances. Once he had even scheduled a vasectomy before he chickened out. Condoms were better than having his balls worked on.

All of his plans on being a committed lifelong bachelor with no children sailed out the window with one look at Juliana. Never much of a romantic, he suddenly found himself thinking of things he could do to please her. Then he'd been driving by the mall after a house showing that middle of August. The jewelry store's sign had twinkled in the sunlight, and something inside him told him it was an omen—that she was "the one" and that he couldn't lose her.

Now he needed to convince her.

What they shared was so new to him he'd forgotten that she wouldn't be nearly as giddy about love. She'd been burned once already. While it seemed patently unfair that he should have to pay for another man's sins, he would.

Perhaps that would serve as penance for his own sins.

He shoved the stocking back into his pocket.

"I was going to ask soon," he insisted. "Learning about the twins only made me stop hesitating."

A tear spilled from the corner of her eye as she ran her fingertips over the ring box. "You bought this in August."

"Yeah, baby. I bought the ring in August."

She threw her arms around his neck. "I love you."

Her lips found his before he could answer her in kind.

There was a desperation to her kiss, which Connor found

both endearing and exciting. Juliana had let the last of her guards down, and it couldn't have happened at a better time.

She slipped her tongue into his mouth, probing and retreating in a way that had him hard in a matter of moments. He shifted in discomfort and tried to get a little more breathing room for his poor, bent cock.

Thankfully, she moved, rolling off his lap and dragging him on top of her.

Her enthusiasm and passion almost made him forget she'd just pressed her back against filthy, ancient shag carpet. He tried to ease up, but she clutched at his shoulders and deepened the already incredible kiss.

A few more moments passed before he could find the self-control to break away. Crouching, he helped her into a sitting position. Then he sat down and picked up the box that had fallen aside.

Holding it out to her, he asked again, "Juliana Kelley, will you please marry me?"

Her smile hit him like a punch to the gut. "Yes. I'll marry you."

Chapter Thirty

Connor slid the ring on her finger. It was a surprise when Juliana stretched out her arm to admire it like any new fiancée. As she turned her hand this way and that, he smiled. "What do you think?"

"It's beautiful." Her voice was a breathless whisper, making the marquis diamond worth every penny. "I just wish you hadn't spent so much on it." Her gaze swept the room. "We could use that money for fixing up this place. It's gonna cost a fortune."

"But think of how many deductions we can take for the renovations since half of the building will be our offices."

"If we still have a firm after Max is done assassinating your character all over town."

"Wilson Realty will survive."

She arched an eyebrow. "*Wilson* Realty? What happened to Kelley-Wilson?"

"You're going to be a Wilson now. Remember?"

Her impish grin meant she was coming out of her earlier dark mood. "Maybe I'll just keep my maiden name. Or hyphenate it. Then everyone will think Kelley-Wilson is just *my* name." She tossed him a wink.

Connor chuckled. "We have bigger problems right now. We can discuss names later—when we're in bed." A thought sobered him. "We can't have sex now."

"Like hell we can't."

"What about your…trouble—whatever sent you to the clinic."

Her smile sparkled as brightly as her diamond. "The doctor says sex is okay."

"Thank God." He drew her into his arms and kissed her, letting his tongue lazily mate with hers until he was close to losing control.

Fitting her hand between them, she gently eased away. "We do have to wait a couple of days, though."

"But everything's okay?" His palm covered her lower belly.

"Everything's great." She took a seat on the old couch, creating an eruption of dust. Waving her hand to clear the air, she coughed twice. "You said you had a plan to take down Max?"

He nodded as he sat on the coffee table, facing her. "It's more Tracy's idea than mine, but I'm gonna run with it. We'll need her help to make it work."

"Explain."

"How much do you remember from history class?"

A scoff slipped out. "If you have questions about autism, I'm your girl. But history?" She shook her head. "What does history have to do with Max?"

"I'm going to turn him into Thomas Dewey."

She rolled her eyes. "And then…you lost me."

"Remember Harry Truman?"

"*Him*, I know. Became president after Roosevelt died. Didn't the press predict he'd tank his reelection run?"

"Smart lady!" He gave her a quick kiss. "The reporters were

unmerciful to the poor guy. They dragged his name through the mud—even stopped polling weeks before the election because they all thought Thomas Dewey was gonna win. They were even cocky enough bastards to print early editions of newspapers."

"Oh, now I remember! There was a picture of Truman holding up a newspaper. Said something like 'Dewey defeats Truman.'"

"Exactly. Well, Schumm is Dewey. He thinks he's won, but he hasn't. Not yet. Not ever. We're gonna do what Truman did," he announced.

"Which is?"

"Take the fight to the people and let them decide for themselves who should be the victor."

* * *

Juliana looked around, taking in the large number of people who had come to the first Barrett Community Day. She wasn't sure exactly what she'd expected, but the turnout was beyond her wildest dreams. "I cannot believe this crowd."

"You know how Illini love their chowders," Mallory said. "Add the barbeque-sauce contest, and it's no wonder everyone in Cloverleaf is here."

Connor strode over, dressed in one of the aprons printed with the Barrett Foods and Kelley-Wilson logos that had been given to the people working the event. "Great crowd."

"That's what Jules was saying," Mallory said.

"Helps that it's so warm," he added. "Who'd believe it would still be short-sleeve weather the end of October?"

"Yeah, well…" Mallory grinned. "It's Illinois. Whatever the weather is, just wait five minutes. It'll change." She held up her sacks. "My contribution to the chowder."

"Chowder?" He chuckled. "I still can't believe that's what you people call this."

"What else could we call it?" Juliana asked. "It's always been a chowder."

"Chowder is something with clams in it. This is more of a, um"—a snap of his fingers—"I know. It's a Community Contribution Soup-a-Thon?"

"Who has time to say all that?" Mallory handed him her bags. "It's a chowder, Connor. Get with the program."

"Yes, ma'am." He winked at her. "What'cha got there?"

"Those are the last of our tomatoes, at least the ones Ben didn't already turn into salsa and marinara."

He took a quick peek. "I still don't understand how people throw whatever they bring into the mix and it still ends up tasting good."

"Just wait," Juliana said. "You'll see. It tastes a little different but it's always good."

Bethany and Danielle came walking across the grass, heading for the park shelter. Both held bottles of sauce.

Juliana smiled at Mallory. "Better tell Ben the competition's here."

"Fierce competition," Beth said.

"Better believe it," Dani added. "I'm gonna kick some barbeque sauce ass."

"On that note," Connor said, nodding at the bags he held, "I need to get these to the cookers."

As he headed toward another park shelter in the distance, Juliana watched him go. Of all his physical assets, his ass was the finest, and she never missed a chance to watch him walking away. She hummed her approval.

"Nice buns," Bethany said.

"Damn right." Juliana switched her stare to her friend. "And they belong to *me*."

"Just window-shopping." Beth set her bottle of homemade sauce on the table. "Definitely not in the mood to buy."

"Oh?" Danielle put her bottle next to Beth's. "I heard you and Robert were an item."

A gasp spilled from Beth's lips. "Who told you that?"

"I did," Juliana replied. "I figured with all the time you two were spending at the model house—"

"He likes my taste in décor," Bethany insisted. "I help his clients, and he pays me enough to make it worth my time. He might build a fantastic house, but he's colorblind. Literally."

"He is?" Juliana asked. "After all the houses we've sold for him, I never knew that."

Danielle opted for the ninth-grade approach to teasing. "Beth and Robert sittin' in a tree..."

"K-I-L-L-I-N-G her best friend," Bethany said, leveling a hard stare at Dani. "For God's sake. How old are you anyway?"

"That's what you get when your BFF teaches freshmen," Mallory said. "The immaturity is contagious."

"Grab your bottles, Ladies," Juliana said. "Time to head to the competition tent." She pointed to the big tent bearing the Barrett Foods logo and the enormous Kelley-Wilson cloverleaf. "Last I checked there were twenty-six people entered. Think you can take them all?"

"Oh yeah!" Beth said with a nod.

"That blue ribbon is mine." Dani pumped her fist in the air.

"Then go get 'em."

Juliana waited until they were out of earshot before she fished her engagement ring out of her sweater's bodice. Although she wanted to wave her hand under the nose of every woman in town to show them that Connor was hers, it stayed anchored to her with her grandmother's gold chain.

"What's that?" Mallory asked when Juliana whipped the gold chain over her head and dangled it in front of her. "Oh my God. Is that a ring? An *engagement* ring?"

"Yeah, it is."

The squeal Mallory let out was loud enough to draw a lot of stares to their shelter.

"Shh." Juliana closed her fist over the ring. "Thanks a lot, Mal. Half the town's looking this way."

Mallory held out her hand. "Well?"

"Well, what?"

"Hand it over. I wanna see the size of the rock Connor gave you." When Juliana didn't jump to her command, Mallory snapped her fingers. "I mean it, Jules. Hand it over."

"Fine." She dropped the jewelry on Mallory's outstretched palm.

Holding the ring between her thumb and index finger, Mallory let the chain dangle. "Wow. That's gotta be at least a carat."

Juliana shrugged. "It's showy, that's for sure. Should make a few ladies drool with jealousy."

"You forget how well I know you. There's nothing precipitous about you. That ring could be nothing but a diamond chip or cubic zirconia, and you'd still love it. All you care about is that it's from Connor, and you're worried about anyone knowing that." Mallory handed her back the ring and chain. "Why in the world aren't you wearing it?"

"I *am* wearing it."

A scoff slipped out. "You're hiding it. Why? It's not like everyone doesn't know you're a couple."

"We're talking marriage, Mal. Marriage. It's not dating someone. It's not living together. It's marriage." Juliana slipped the chain over her neck and shoved the ring back between her breasts, jerking the sweater up to cover any sign of the gold.

"Ah, *now* I get it."

Her friend's knowing smirk was almost Juliana's undoing. Tears stung her eyes, but she wasn't about to cry. Not even in front of Mallory. "Get what?"

"You're scared."

"I'm never scared."

"It's me. Mallory. Your best friend. You're scared to death that it won't work—that you'll get divorced again—so you're gonna make sure that never happens by not marrying Connor."

Juliana shook her head.

"Then there's the firm," Mallory continued despite Juliana's occasional derisive snorts. "After you and Jimmy broke up, you still had to see him at school. At least there you could stay in your part of the building while he stayed in his. Only an occasional awkward greeting in the mailroom or at graduation."

It was like listening to her own thoughts. "Enough, Mal. Okay? *Enough.*"

As if a stern warning would be enough to deter Mallory Carpenter when she was on a roll. "Remember when I got in my own way with Ben?"

A heavy sigh slipped out. "Look, I know you're only trying to help. But Connor and I are different."

"You were the one who told me to open my eyes and see everything instead of using my emotions."

"Lotta good that did," Juliana retorted. "Ben had to shave his head and propose in front of the whole school to get you to talk to him."

"But you were the reason I let him back in. If you hadn't talked some sense into me, we might not have worked things out."

"Silly me, I thought it was his gorgeous chrome dome and the diamond that did the trick."

Why couldn't Mallory understand?

Juliana had been miserable working with Jimmy after the divorce.

Working with Connor after he left her would be unbearable.

Mallory shot her a scowl. "Listen to me, Jules. For once, take advice from someone who loves you."

Juliana bowed her head. "Sorry, Mal. I'll listen."

"You're getting in your own way, exactly like I was. Connor isn't Jimmy. You've got to stop making him pay for your ex's crimes."

"I'm not—"

The truth hit her hard.

She *was* treating Connor as if he'd do exactly what Jimmy had done—walk out when the going got tough.

For shit's sake! How much tougher can it get?

Connor was being painted as an irresponsible gambling addict.

Their firm was in danger of failing.

Juliana was pregnant—with twins.

If he hadn't already run for the hills, he wasn't going to.

Ever.

"I need to go." Juliana waved at Mallory as she ran from the shelter.

Chapter Thirty-One

Juliana stopped in the middle of the tent, scanning the crowd for Connor.

To the right were the vats of soup being stirred by a couple of guys holding homemade wooden paddles they used like enormous spoons. Between tending the chowder and the bottles of Budweiser in their other hands, the men were well-occupied.

Next to the vats were three tables full of baked goods donated by people from the town. The cakewalk—another Illinois tradition. People donated money for a chance to win homemade cakes, cookies, and brownies in a raffle.

Tons of people milled about.

But no Connor.

To the left were the people serving beverages, everything from soda and iced tea to beer and wine. There were more donations to the chowder being prepared to go into the vats. Those who didn't want the potpourri chowder for their meal could have the hamburgers and hot dogs that were laid out on grills. A large display of antiques and handmade quilts to be auctioned later in the day was somehow stuffed into the tent as well.

When the event was over, all the money raised would go to The Pantry—a charity Tracy and Connor set up to help people who needed help getting their families fed.

The Pantry had been Tracy's brilliant idea. She said to get Kelley-Wilson Realty back in Cloverleaf's good graces the firm would need to make a goodwill gesture that showed how committed Juliana and Connor were to the community. It was only step one of what she called her "master plan."

Step two would happen when he served as auctioneer, his chance to let his wonderful personality shine. Juliana had let him practice with her, having him describe all the vintage items they donated from their new home. The money would go to the food pantry—and to "step three"—but she considered it well spent for the publicity and to help restore Cloverleaf's faith in Kelley-Wilson Realty.

Step three was still a secret that Tracy impishly refused to reveal to either Juliana or Connor. She was scheduled to make a speech before everyone commenced eating, when the crowd would be at its largest.

"Hey, Red."

Juliana jumped and put her hand over her racing heart. "You love doing that, don't you?"

Connor gave her a quick, no-nonsense kiss. "Absolutely. Were you looking for me?"

"Yeah." She had a wave of a foreign emotion. Contentment. "I—I want to tell you something."

He arched a dark eyebrow.

She whipped the chain from her shirt and removed the ring. Then she slid it onto her finger. "I love you, Connor Wilson."

"Ah, I wondered where that was. Figured you wanted to keep from gunking it up while you cooked."

Since he obviously knew better than that, she punched him lightly on the upper arm.

"I love you, too, future Mrs. Wilson." He tugged her into his arms.

For the first time, she didn't care what people saw or what they thought. She returned Connor's kiss, even grinning against his mouth at some of the men's ribald comments and the women's longing stares and sighs.

"Making a spectacle, I see."

"Max." Connor tried to ease away.

She wrapped her arms around his waist and refused to let him go. "Guess I didn't think a newly engaged couple sharing a kiss made us a 'spectacle.'"

Max's cocky smirk made her ache to punch him in the nose. "I suppose in and of itself, it doesn't. But added to some of Connor's less-than-appropriate activities and—"

The high-pitched microphone feedback couldn't have come at a better time, almost as though it had been planned as an interruption.

"Folks, if I could have your attention." Tracy had taken her place on the small stage that had been erected for the auction.

Conversations dwindled as people packed the tent to listen to the woman most people called the "savior" of Cloverleaf. Barrett Foods moving to the town had renewed it—restored it to a place full of life and promise for the future.

Tracy smiled down at Juliana when she dragged Connor to a prime spot to the right of the stage. If this was going to be Tracy's unveiling of the third part of her plan, Juliana wasn't about to miss a single word.

"What a great crowd!" Tracy nodded at a few of the people. "Glad to see so many of you here today to help Barrett Foods and

Kelley-Wilson Realty kick off The Pantry. There will never be a reason for anyone in and around Cloverleaf to do without. The Pantry is there in your time of need, and I hope all of you will spread the word that we're here to help. Food. Clothes. Household goods. And one thing more...which is what I'm here to tell you about." Her hand swept out toward Connor. "Let me introduce my best friend and the man who convinced me to bring Barrett Foods to Cloverleaf—Connor Wilson." She gave a chuckle. "Of course, if any of you were lucky enough to have him sell you a house, you already know him."

His brow knit as he turned to Juliana. "Red?"

"You know exactly as much as I do," she said, squeezing him tightly then turning him loose. "I imagine this is where you have to be totally honest."

"I don't know—"

"It'll be fine. She's got your back. So do I. Go on."

He stepped up to Tracy's side as the crowd applauded.

"The Pantry," Tracy continued, "will also offer an important service to the community. But let me start by telling you something key to why we're making this change." She took a deep breath and blew it out. "I'm an alcoholic."

The murmurs started immediately, and Juliana's heart leapt to her throat. Tracy's honesty was refreshing, but if she intended to focus on Connor's gambling addiction, it could be the death knell for Kelley-Wilson Realty. The rumors were damaging enough. Could these small-town people accept the truth?

Barrett Foods was an international firm. If the CEO wanted to tell the world she'd struggled with a drinking problem, it wouldn't faze too many people. She'd probably earn a lot of admirers, especially among people who were also battling alcoholism or other addictions.

But announcing that Connor was a gambler in a judgmental town?

"God help us," Juliana whispered.

Tracy waited until the crowd quieted. "Why am I telling you this? Because I'm not the only one who fights addiction. Alcohol. Pills. Gambling. There are so many problems plaguing people. Addictions have the power to ruin lives, especially when those addictions are used by competitors to hurt them." Her gaze settled on Max Schumm. "I can't imagine anything more reprehensible than spreading unsubstantiated rumors about someone simply because of an addiction, especially when that person is doing everything in his power to keep his life balanced."

Many of the people in the crowd turned to glare at Max as a flush spread up his neck. He hooked a finger in his collar and tugged, his discomfort as plain as a neon sign on a starless night.

Juliana wanted to dance a little jig, loving the sight of the man feeling the sting of public scorn that he'd directed at Connor. All the ads. All the gossip. All the implications.

Good. Getting a dose of your own medicine, Maxy Boy?

Tracy pressed on. "If I didn't have the help I needed to find my sobriety, I'd never have been able to expand Barrett Foods to this wonderful town. So now, I want to thank the friend who's always there, keeping me on the straight and narrow and encouraging me every step of the way." She turned and hugged Connor while the crowd went wild with applause, hoots, and hollers.

With a dramatic sigh and a quick swipe of the well-timed tear that had hit her cheek, she returned to the microphone. "Now, I'm paying it forward. As a part of The Pantry, we're adding an addiction center. There will be counselors available free of charge, and support groups will be run through local churches and supported by Barrett Foods grants and community fund-raisers like this—the first annual Pantry Chowder. Don't be afraid to admit you need help. We're here to give it to you, no matter your addiction." She turned to Connor, an expectant grin on her lips.

In one fell swoop, she'd turned her addiction into an asset, revealing her inner strength—one she was trying to share with him. If he confessed, there might still be a few people who would condemn him. But others, *many* others, judging from the crowd's reaction to Tracy, would see him as human. Just a real person trying to make his way in a scary world.

His head bowed for a moment before he glanced to Juliana.

She knew what he was asking, and she wondered if Tracy knew that she was downright brilliant. The crowd was in the palm of her hand, and she would use their love for her to help them accept Connor.

Who can resist a reformed hero?

With tears in her eyes, Juliana nodded.

He took the microphone Tracy passed to him.

Connor took Juliana's breath away.

He'd changed since Max had launched his smear campaign. His cocky attitude had muted. Yet the moment he faced those people, the ones who now cheered him, the old Connor was back.

He loudly cleared his throat. "For those of you who don't know me, I'm Connor Wilson." He inclined his head at Juliana. "This beautiful lady is Juliana Kelley. We're the pair who make up Kelley-Wilson Realty. First, let me offer our heartfelt appreciation for welcoming me into your community. Many of you already know Juliana as a former teacher at Douglas High School and—"

"Go Warriors!" a young male voice boomed, setting off laughter and cheers.

Connor smiled and tossed her a wink. "And I have the pleasure of sharing with all of you some fantastic news. Ms. Kelley has agreed to marry me."

The women went nuts, applauding as a few elbowed or poked the reticent men standing next to them.

"But that's not what I'm up here to talk about," he continued. "After Ms. Barrett's brave confession, I have one of my own. Like her, I also have an addiction. While most people understand what she goes through every day, fewer look at my problem as an addiction. They consider it a character flaw. You see, I'm addicted to gambling."

Tracy put her arms around his waist and leaned her cheek against his upper arm.

At that moment, Juliana entirely understood what the two of them shared. As she'd told Connor, there was no jealousy. Only gratitude, not only for the public backing but for all she did to help Connor be the man he was today.

"I assure you," he said, "that it *is* an addiction, one I will try to control every day for the rest of my life. Despite what you might have heard, I never—not once—misused any of my clients' funds. My work as a real estate agent requires your trust."

Tracy put her hand on the microphone and pulled it closer. "Trust that I give him with every home he helps buy and sell for Barrett employees."

"I would never betray that trust. With Juliana and Tracy's help, I will keep adding to my year and a half of being addiction free."

* * *

By the time Juliana kicked off her shoes, she was sure if she closed her eyes she'd sleep for a week.

Flopping into the easy chair, she popped the footrest up to elevate her aching feet.

Connor dropped his organizer on the coffee table and crouched next to her. With gentle strokes, he rubbed her feet, forcing groans and then sighs from her lips.

"You need to take better care of yourself, Red. You ran around like a demon all day."

"And I've got the puffy feet to prove it," she teased.

"Don't push yourself too hard. Can't be easy carrying twins."

"I won't," she promised. "This was a busier than normal day because of the chowder."

"I'm going to have to rein you in and keep you from overdoing."

"I won't, honey. These babies are everything to me. I'm going to do everything I can to keep them safe, even if it means cooling my jets and"—she shuddered for effect—"relaxing."

The pain of the miscarriage was there, just below the surface. She tried not to let that infect her happiness. She wouldn't lose these babies.

She *couldn't* lose these babies.

He rose and cupped her face. "You're worried. I can tell. Repeat what the doctor said about our kids."

How like him to be able to remind her of the good and drive away the bad. "She said they're both healthy with strong hearts and that everything's perfect right now."

"Perfect. Keep your mind on that and stay positive." He brushed a kiss over her mouth.

"Tell me this—are we going to get married before or after the twins come?"

He scoffed. "Before, of course!"

"Then it better be quick. A couple more months, and I'll be as big as a water buffalo."

His smile was enigmatic—a smile she'd learned well over their time together.

"Spill," she demanded.

"You know me far too well." He sat on the arm of the chair. "How about two weeks from Saturday?"

"Two weeks? That's all I get to plan a wedding? Two weeks?"

"Don't even pretend you want a Cinderella wedding."

"I don't. But that's not the point."

"The point is if I give you too much time to chew on this, you'll analyze it to death." Connor wrapped his arms around her, pulling her until her cheek rested against his side. "I'm not giving you a chance to get away."

"I don't want to get away. But I do want to know what plans you've already made."

"Let this be a surprise, Red."

Juliana's trust in Connor was absolute. "Since I have four closings this week and two the next—on top of being a pregnant woman who needs her rest—I'll leave it all in your hands."

Chapter Thirty-Two

I now pronounce you husband and wife." The minister closed her Bible and smiled. A gust of wind ruffled her tropical-print shirt and long brown hair. She simply swiped the wavy tresses out of her eyes and said, "You may kiss the bride."

Juliana smiled against Connor's lips when he kissed her, trying hard not to laugh at the cheer that rose from their friends. Fast on the heels of her laughter came a wave of emotion, a happiness impossible to contain—something she'd learned to expect with the hormones churning through her system.

Tears in her eyes, she kissed her new husband again and turned to Mallory, Bethany, and Danielle. They were lined up, all in flowery, flowing sundresses, holding small bouquets of fresh orchids and wearing colorful leis. The ruffled canopy protected the bridal party from the tropical sun, although it wasn't an absolute necessity since the heat of the day had abated with dusk approaching. A cool breeze blew in from the west, bringing the fresh smell of the ocean with it. The sound of murmured congratulations competed with the whoosh of the waves as they hit the shore.

Connor accepted hugs as Juliana did the same. To have the Ladies, Ben, Amber, and Tracy there made the day magical. Everyone she loved was there—even her parents, who'd never ventured to Hawaii before.

He'd arranged the wedding around the high school's two-week winter break, with their wedding day being the day after Christmas. Sure, it was a little longer than the two weeks he'd wanted, but it was worth every minute of the wait.

Although Tracy would be leaving in a few hours to attend an international conference in Hong Kong on battling world hunger, she'd graciously postponed her trip to be at the wedding. After all, she was Connor's best woman.

Juliana had to chuckle at how her growing abdomen would soon make hugging anyone next to impossible. She'd gone from a flat stomach to a "babies bump" practically overnight. The twins seemed to know how their movements would warm her heart and ease her worries, so they kept up their calisthenics nearly twenty-four/seven. The only complaint about their constant activity came from Connor. He claimed that when she snuggled up against his back at night, he was so enthralled by their twisting and turning that he couldn't sleep.

Tracy gave her a hug that Juliana returned with all her heart.

"I'll always owe you," she whispered to Connor's friend and sponsor. "You saved things for us."

"Nah," Tracy replied. "We're friends, and friends never owe each other."

After the cake was cut, Juliana walked to where the ocean met the shore. Since she was barefoot—as was the entire bridal party, including the minister—she wiggled her toes in the warm, wet sand. The breeze made her gauzy ivory dress cling to her body, making her wonder how she looked carrying twins.

Mallory swore the weight was all up front and that if someone saw Juliana from behind, they wouldn't even know she was pregnant.

Ah, so sweet to have a friend who loved her enough to lie.

Settling her palm against her belly, she smiled. The weight gain didn't bother her a bit, not if it meant she was carrying two healthy, active babies. That, and the day was as close to perfect as she'd ever experienced.

For the first time in her life, she wanted nothing more than what she had.

"Your dad made an honest woman of me, kids," she said, stroking her stomach.

"Damn right he did." Connor's arms wrapped around her as he pressed his chest to her back. He rested his hands over hers. "So was this the kind of wedding you dreamed of?"

"I'm standing on a gorgeous beach with my parents and my friends and marrying a guy too handsome for words. What do *you* think?"

"Depends," he teased. "Do you love the guy who's too handsome for words?"

"I love him stupid—more than I could ever explain with mere words."

"He loves you, too, you know." His lips touched her neck.

Juliana leaned back against him and breathed a sigh full of contentment. "I know."

He kissed her cheek. "Ready to tell everyone about our sons? The Ladies, Tracy, and your mom have been hounding me ever since the ultrasound."

"I know, but it's kinda fun with only us knowing." She gave a rather fake exaggerated sigh. "I guess we can go tell them the happy news."

"Think you can handle two boys? The way they move around now, imagine them as two-year-olds."

"Two boys? I'll have three," she reminded him.

"Three? I was at the ultrasound, Red. Don't go telling me it's triplets. Two babies are plenty." He held up two fingers in front of her face.

"You forgot about *you*."

"I'm not your kid, my darling Juliana. I'm your partner."

"And now my husband."

"And you're my wife." Connor grew pensive. "I'll be good to you, you know. I promise."

"I know, honey. I'll be good to you, too. Didn't I just vow to love, honor, and cherish you?"

"I could swear an 'obey' was thrown in there somewhere."

Juliana turned in his arms, the babies putting enough distance between them to make her chuckle. "I can guaran-damn-tee you I never said 'obey.'"

He arched an eyebrow. "Turning my words against me?"

"Never." Rising on tiptoes, she kissed him—a long, lazy kiss. "I love you, Connor Wilson."

"In that case...let's discuss the firm's name..."

Turn the page for a preview of the next book
in the Ladies Who Lunch series,

Sealing the Deal

Chapter One

One more person.

If one more person told Bethany Rogers how sorry he was that her sister was dead, she might just punch him right in the nose.

She swallowed her anger. It wasn't her normal response to stress anyway. Of course, she'd never been through this kind of stress before. Perhaps this was normal for grief.

It wasn't often a girl lost her only sister.

I never said good-bye.

That would haunt Beth for a good, long while—if not the rest of her life. Even though she kept reminding herself that not talking to Tiffany wasn't her fault, she couldn't push the guilt aside.

Her sister had been in a war zone. Communicating with someone overseas wasn't easy. The time difference alone made it a chore. While the army allowed Skyping, Tiffany had only reached out to her big sister a few times. Their last video chat had been over a month ago when Tiffany had just arrived in Afghanistan.

And now Tiffany was dead.

Beth went to the chapel early, wanting a private moment alone with her sister. Now she'd be denied a private farewell. An army officer stood guard over the flag-draped coffin. While the family had been offered a chance to view the remains, the officer who'd escorted Tiffany to Princeville had cautioned them against doing so. The suicide bomber had done his job well, savagely destroying the three people at the guard post that fateful morning.

Sick at heart, she turned to head back up the aisle and nearly collided with Danielle Bradshaw. Her best friend was dressed in a perfect little black dress, had pulled her long blonde hair into a tight bun, and wore very little makeup.

Mourning chic.

"Hey." Beth swallowed hard to keep the threatening tears, the ones she wanted to shed in private, at bay.

"Hey," Dani replied, her tone wary. She studied Beth with her crystal blue eyes before understanding dawned. Then she opened her arms wide.

Without a moment of hesitation, Beth threw herself into Dani's embrace. As short as Dani was tall, Beth found her cheek pressed against her friend's shoulder. "Thanks for coming."

"Shit, Beth. Where else did you think I'd be?" came Dani's characteristically acerbic reply.

Having narrowed her vision to focus on her best friend, Beth hadn't realized the rest of the Ladies Who Lunch had arrived as well. Mallory Carpenter and Juliana Wilson came forward to sandwich Beth and Dani between them—a group embrace of four women who needed each other's friendship in a way most people might never understand.

That bond had been formed years ago as the four of them shared their lunch period when they'd all been teaching at Stephen Douglas High School. As time passed, they'd learned to lean on one another through thick and thin. Mallory's breast cancer. Juliana's choice to leave teaching and start a new career.

And now Beth facing the loss of her little sister.

They simply held on to one another for a few precious moments, crying softly. Then one by one they eased back.

Mallory sniffed and wiped the tears from her cheeks with a tissue she'd wadded in her palm. Her light brown hair had recently been cut into a short, sassy style. After she'd lost her hair to chemotherapy, it had taken her a long time to allow anyone to put a pair of scissors to it. Now that her breast cancer was four years in the past, she'd finally decided to cut it the way she wanted instead of focusing on growing it out. Her dark brown dress matched her eyes. Although those eyes were red-rimmed, they still reflected Mallory's boundless kindness.

Juliana was stoic. Dressed in a navy suit, her long red hair loose around her shoulders, she looked the part of the successful Realtor she'd become. But beneath that rough exterior beat a heart full of compassion.

"Thank you all for coming." Beth gratefully accepted a new tissue from Danielle.

"Where else would we be when you need us?" Mallory asked with a sympathetic smile.

Beth shrugged. "It's about the only thing I can say without getting choked up. I sound like a broken record."

Mallory spared a quick glance over her shoulder. "The guys came, too."

Hanging back a few feet were Ben Carpenter and Connor Wilson. Since Connor wasn't holding two toddlers, Beth assumed the Wilsons had left their twin boys back in Cloverleaf with their nanny. She tossed each man a grateful smile. They nodded in return.

Dani took her hand and gave it a quick squeeze. "How are you holding up, Beth?"

"I'm okay. Still a little catatonic. I just can't believe Tiffany's gone." Beth's gaze drifted to the double doors, and she caught her parents walking in. Carol Rogers held Emma—Tiffany's nine-month-old daughter—against her hip.

"They brought the baby?" Dani whispered.

"They're in Florida now, remember?" Beth replied.

"Oh yeah. The retirement community."

Crossing her arms around her middle, Beth tried to ward off the chill that seemed to have settled in her bones. "They don't know anyone here. Neither do I, for that matter. We didn't want a stranger to babysit."

"Then why's the service here and not Cloverleaf?" Juliana asked.

"Tiffany's friends are all here. Princeville was home to her."

Dani frowned as she stared at Beth's parents. "Carol looks pissed."

"Emma was really fussy last night. I finally took her from Mom and slept in the recliner with Emma lying on my chest."

"You're a good aunt."

"Mom's good with her, too. You know, they'll have Emma down there until Tiffany's tour of duty ends and—" Beth had to stop and close her eyes. Tiffany's deployment had ended the day she died.

Will I ever stop thinking of her in present tense?

"Will they keep Emma now?" Dani asked.

That was the same question Beth had been asking herself, especially in the wee hours of the morning as she'd cradled her niece against her. Her parents' Florida condo was smack-dab in the middle of a community of fifty-five-and-overs. It was one thing to keep their granddaughter for a tour of duty. Even then, Beth was going to have the baby for two months in the summer.

But forever?

Before Beth could ponder that again, her mother came over. "Can you take Emma for the service? My back's killing me."

Emma reached for Beth before she could even answer.

Settling Emma on her hip, Beth kissed her cheek.

With an enormous yawn, Emma put her thumb in her mouth and rested her head against Beth's shoulder. As if none of the dozens of people were in the church, Emma fell asleep moments later.

There was no worry about the baby fussing through the service. Emma was her mother's opposite. While Tiffany always craved being the center of attention, Emma was calm and oddly quiet for her age. Tiffany had been a reed-thin blonde with blue eyes, while Emma shared Bethany's curly brown hair, brown eyes, and chubby cheeks.

The more she thought about it, the more she realized Emma favored her aunt rather than her mother. Of course, Tiffany and Beth looked—and acted—nothing like sisters. A short, plump brunette and a lithe blonde. Tiffany's wildness came in direct contrast to the tight rein Beth kept on her life. Perhaps their different temperaments were from being older versus younger sibling.

Beth's pondering was interrupted as the minister stepped into the chapel through the side door. She nodded at her friends as they took their seats in the second row. Then she moved to where her parents waited in the front pew. Before she could sit, her gaze was drawn to the back of the chapel.

A tall man with short-cropped dark hair came inside, his gaze darting around as though he felt completely out of place and sought a friendly face.

Her heart began to pound. Robert Ashford had arrived. She gave him a small wave, wanting, *needing*, him to come to her.

About the time she feared he'd given up finding her in the crowd, his brown eyes caught hers. With an insistent flip of her wrist, she begged him to join her. Even though the Ladies and their spouses were only a row behind, she wanted Robert at her side.

The overwhelming desire to lean on him took her by surprise. Robert was her friend, her former colleague—technically her boss as well. But none of those roles explained the keen yearning to have him near.

Beth was emotionally overwrought at losing her baby sister and couldn't examine that feeling too closely. Not now.

He strode up the aisle, not even stopping to acknowledge their friends.

"Hi, B. I'm s-sorry about your sister." The way he shifted on his feet spoke of his discomfort. That, and he kept tugging at his tie as though it was too tight.

Come to think of it, she'd never even seen him in a suit.

"Thanks for coming," she said.

"I was, you know, worried about you." His gaze drifted to the full second pew. "Should've known you wouldn't need me."

"But I do!" She didn't realize she'd shouted until Emma stirred and several people gaped at her. Beth lowered her voice. "Can you sit by me? Please?" Why did she suddenly feel as awkward as a girl talking to her first crush?

"Um, sure. If that's what you want."

"I do."

Since the minister was clearing his throat, she took a seat, settling Emma on her lap and letting her rest against her shoulder again. Thankfully, the baby went right back to sleep.

Robert took his place next to Beth, and as if it were the most natural thing in the world, he draped his arm behind her, resting it on the back of the pew. A few minutes later, after the minister started talking about how Tiffany had given her life in service to her country, Robert's arm moved to rest on Beth's shoulders.

It wasn't until his touch stilled her movements that she realized she'd been trembling.

* * *

Bethany kept a wary eye on Emma throughout the dinner in the church social hall.

All of Tiffany's friends were pretty much ignoring Emma, which wasn't a shock. From the time she'd turned fifteen, Tiffany had been wild—living for the moment and spending her time with people who shunned responsibility. She'd used alcohol, taken drugs, and slept with pretty much anyone. The only reason she had a high school diploma was because Beth had tutored her through her toughest classes.

Although she'd spent time in the local juvenile prison and the county jail, Tiffany's first felony arrest sobered her. Up until the judge told her she might be in prison for up to five years, she'd done no more than thirty days in custody. Prison scared the shit out of her. So her lawyer had worked out a deal. If she straightened herself out and joined the army, she'd only be charged with a misdemeanor.

She'd sobered up and enlisted, hoping to go to college one day. Emma was conceived on her mother's first leave after basic training. Emma's father—a man Tiffany refused to identify—wanted nothing to do with being a parent. Since she'd been quite content to be a single mother, Tiffany didn't even ask for child support.

The problem was that although she'd wanted to be with Emma, she still owed the army time. And that time saw her deployed to Afghanistan.

Beth accepted a soda from Robert. "Thanks. I'm so grateful you're here."

He gave her a shrug. "The Ladies had your back. I just thought…" Another shrug.

"It meant a lot to me." She saw her three friends drawing near.

"Ah, speak of the devils," he quipped.

"Who are you calling a devil?" Dani asked, giving Robert a jostle with her shoulder.

"If the high heel fits." His wink and the bantering helped Beth relax.

With a grin, Mallory said, "Actually, I think we're more witches than devils."

"Yeah," Juliana agreed with a nod. "But I left my broom back in Cloverleaf."

"Thank you all for coming." Fighting strong emotions, she tried to give her friends a smile. Judging from the unsettling quiet, she didn't succeed. "I mean it. Thank you all for—" A shuddering breath slipped out as tears spilled over her lashes.

"Robert," Mallory said, "my husband wants to ask you something."

He frowned, staring at Beth. "In other words, you womenfolk wanna be alone?"

"Bingo."

His hand settled on Beth's arm. "You okay, B?"

"I'm fine."

He wiped a tear from her cheek with callused fingertips.

Funny, but his touch helped her regain some control over her emotions. "I'm fine. Really. Thanks."

"Then if the beautiful Ladies Who Lunch will excuse me…" With a flourish of his hand and a half bow, he walked away.

"What a flirt," Dani said.

Beth couldn't let that misconception stand. "Far from it. He's really very shy."

"Robert?" Juliana furrowed her brow. "Shy?" She let out a snort. "I've never seen that side of him."

"It's all bravado," Beth insisted. "He stuttered when he was little. Took him a long time to be able to talk to people."

Dani's quizzical stare made Beth uncomfortable. Her best friend knew her far too well—sometimes better than Beth knew herself.

A hot flush spread over Beth's cheeks. "He told me about it when we were working on one of the houses."

"Beth?" Dani asked. "After all these years, are you falling for our Robert?"

It *had* been years—nine, to be exact—since Beth had walked into Douglas High as a new teacher. At the time, all of the Ladies and Robert had also taught there. The women became fast friends while sharing their lives every day at lunch, often pulling strings and calling in favors to be sure they shared the same lunch period. Those precious moments had built a friendship strong enough to weather any changes, even Juliana leaving teaching to become a Realtor.

The name came from one of the women's Chicago excursions to shop and see plays. After watching *Company*, they'd adopted one of the song titles. From that time on, everyone called them the Ladies Who Lunch.

Robert had taught industrial technology. Beth had gotten to know him through time spent on school committees, chaperoning dances, and chatting in the corridor almost every passing period. Then his side business of building custom homes had taken off and, like Juliana, he'd sought greener pastures.

Beth had missed seeing him, even stopping by one of his open houses just to talk to him. The place was nice but poorly staged. After she made a few friendly suggestions, he'd insisted she become his decorator. Since HGTV was her favorite network, she'd loved the new challenge. She'd also quickly discovered they made a good pair.

At least when working together.

He'd never once hinted that he wanted anything from her beyond friendship. The women he dated explained his lack of interest. They were all tall, blonde, and thin.

Beth would always be a size fourteen, probably a good four sizes above anything he'd ever find attractive.

"He's my boss," she reminded Dani. "Besides"—she quickly found Emma in the dwindling crowd—"I've got other things to worry about now."

"Like your niece," Dani said. "Have you and your parents talked about what's gonna happen to Emma now?"

"Aren't they keeping her?" Juliana asked. "I mean, they had her while Tiffany was in Afghanistan, right?"

Beth nodded. "But having her there was already getting to be a problem. They were going to send her to me for the summer." Something she'd been looking forward to.

"You said their condo's in a fifty-five-and-over community," Juliana commented. "If they want Emma to live with them, they'll have to move." A frown bowed her lips. "A retirement community isn't a good place for a kid, even for a short time."

"Yeah," Mallory added. "Definitely not kid-friendly. No playgrounds. No libraries. No other children."

"I know, I know." Beth heaved a sigh. The choice was obvious to her if not to her friends—just as obvious as it had been when she'd made up her mind last night. "I'm taking Emma."

"For how long?" Dani asked.

"Forever."

About the Author

Sandy lives in a quiet suburb of Indianapolis with her husband of thirty years and is a high school social studies teacher. She and her husband own a small stable of harness racehorses and enjoy spending time at the two Indiana racetracks. She has been an Amazon Best Seller and has won numerous writing awards, including two HOLT Medallions.

Please visit her website at sandyjames.com for more information or find her on Twitter or Facebook at sandyjamesbooks.

www.ingramcontent.com/pod-product-compliance
Ingram Content Group UK Ltd.
Pitfield, Milton Keynes, MK11 3LW, UK
UKHW022258280225

455674UK00001B/87